The Real
Allie Newman

Janice Carter

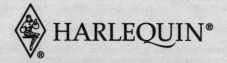

HARLEQUIN®

TORONTO • NEW YORK • LONDON
AMSTERDAM • PARIS • SYDNEY • HAMBURG
STOCKHOLM • ATHENS • TOKYO • MILAN • MADRID
PRAGUE • WARSAW • BUDAPEST • AUCKLAND

ISBN 0-373-71079-8

THE REAL ALLIE NEWMAN

Copyright © 2002 by Janice Hess.

This edition published by arrangement with Harlequin Books S.A.

® and TM are trademarks of the publisher. Trademarks indicated with ® are registered in the United States Patent and Trademark Office, the Canadian Trade Marks Office and in other countries.

Visit us at www.eHarlequin.com

Printed in U.S.A.

Dedication:

For family and friends

Acknowledgment

A big thank-you to Linda Christensen,
Pat and Linn Hynds of Grosse Point Farms, Michigan

CHAPTER ONE

ALLIE LOWERED her head, tucking her chin in until the strap of her helmet bit into her skin. The wind still carried with it the nip of winter, even though April had just arrived and summer was more than a promise away. She figured she was crazy to go cycling on such a misty morning— the streets were slick and the ground was saturated with a week's worth of torrential rains—but she hadn't trained once that week and the triathlon was drawing closer.

Her feet eased on the pedals as the cycle whizzed around the bend of the paved bike and footpath that bordered the east side of the Cataraqui River. Allie raised her head just enough to view the stretch of path ahead and swore. The dim outline of a man walking his dog appeared out of the swirling mist scarcely a hundred yards ahead. To make things worse, the man was on the outer edge of the path nearest the riverbank. She'd have to slow down or risk nudging him off the bank. It meant losing time and writing off her goal for the cycling part of her session that morning.

She began to apply the brakes, slowing down as gently as possible to avoid skidding on the wet asphalt, keeping her eyes on the man's back as he plodded into the plumes of vapor wafting up from the river below. Allie rang her bell, but the sound seemed muted in the damp, heavy air.

The distance between her and the figures shortened. She was just thinking that any second she'd call out a warning and skim past the pair when a rumbling vibration beneath her caused her to brake hard. A section of the riverbank and footpath ahead suddenly broke loose. Allie stared in shocked horror as the man and his dog slid silently down the embankment and disappeared into the shroud of fog blanketing the river.

The bike skidded to a stop inches from the jagged tear of mud, tree roots and broken asphalt. Allie leaped off. She couldn't hear any shouts for help above the roar of the brown, frothy river, but in the first panicked seconds of the disaster, she shouted for help herself before plunging down the mucky slope into the freezing water. When she surfaced, Allie fought to catch her breath. The man was thrashing in the water just feet away and she kicked hard, propelling herself toward him.

The current had pushed him into the crook of a partially submerged tree and was pummeling him. Allie shouted for him to hang on, but from the way his head kept bobbing back and forth, she doubted he'd heard. She managed to grab on to the collar of his overcoat just as the branch he was caught on broke loose and was carried downstream.

His arms shot out at her touch, clutching at her, pushing her down. Allie swallowed a mouthful of water. The Styrofoam lining of her helmet kept her head up, but the dead weight of his body threatened to send them both careening along with the current. Using all her strength, she pushed his hands up and off her shoulders, grabbing onto his coat again before he could be swept away. She pulled herself closer to him, shouting into his ear to relax, that she was going to try to get him ashore.

He understood then and stopped struggling as she pulled him slowly to the riverbank. Then Allie stretched out her free arm, digging her fingers into the muck where land met water, and pulled. And pulled again for what seemed an eternity of slipping, gouging again and again into the thick, claylike mud until at last she heaved herself and the man onto the narrow strip of shore at the base of the embankment.

He collapsed face forward, gasping for air. Allie rolled onto her back beside him, registering for the first time that he was elderly, his white hair slicked with mud and bits of leaves and other debris. He raised his head and turned filmy eyes in her direction.

The pounding in Allie's head intensified. The man was blind.

"Jeb?" he asked, his hoarse voice pitched with fear. "Jeb?"

The dog. A Seeing Eye dog. Allie sat up. Less than fifty feet downriver she could see the animal's small dark head.

"Where's Jeb?" the man cried.

"It's okay," Allie said, "I see him." She jogged along the shore, slipping and sliding all the way. The closer she got to the dog, the more she could hear its frantic yowling. It seemed to be caught on something, too, which had saved it from speeding down the river and out of sight. Fortunately, the dog was only a few feet from the shore and Allie was able to reach it by wading into the river up to her waist. The leather inverted U handle attached to the dog's harness had snagged onto the forked tip of a deadhead, and the dog, struggling to keep its head above water, was treading water in a futile effort to reach shore.

It was a young chocolate-brown Lab, and Allie almost wept at its grateful whimpers as she struggled to release the handle. Her fingers were stiff and numb with cold, but after three attempts, she managed to disengage the handle from the end of the deadhead.

The dog barked twice and began paddling toward shore. Allie held on to the handle and was half-pulled along as she and the dog finally crawled up out of the river. Jeb leaped against her as if to thank her, shook himself briskly and then bounded along the strip of shore to his master.

By the time Allie reached them, she could hear the distant whoop of a fire-department rescue unit. Someone, she thought, must have spotted the commotion, probably from the condominium complex on the other side of the river. Exhausted, she fell back onto the muddy slope, half-aware of the dog's excited yelps and licks as it leaped from master to rescuer, expressing an uninhibited gratitude that Allie sensed she'd likely never experience again.

She unclasped her helmet and let it fall to her side, sucking in deep, calming breaths as she wondered distractedly if she could count this unexpected incident as her workout for the day.

ALLIE PUSHED OPEN the screen door of Evergreen Natural Foods and paused, scanning the store for her stepmother, Susan. When she saw her bent over one of the flour bins, Allie headed straight for her.

"That fifteen-minutes-of-fame thing is highly overrated," Allie said, waving the rolled-up *People* magazine she held. "No sane person would want more than five." Then she realized that Susan was struggling with a ten-pound sack of flour. "Want some help with that?"

The sack thudded onto the hardwood floor. Susan tried to straighten, groaning audibly. Allie dropped the magazine to help. Susan clutched at Allie's extended forearm, pulling herself to a vertical position, and let Allie lead her to the stool behind the cash counter.

"You really should go to the doctor and talk about that back surgery again," Allie murmured. A twinge of guilt that she hadn't really been noticing Susan's difficulty colored her face. She should have been more observant, instead of going on about the *People* magazine.

What was there about seeing yourself in print in an international magazine, anyway? she wondered. And how could she justify her own self-indulgence after bad-mouthing the phenomenon of instant celebrity ever since she'd pulled Harry Maguire and his dog Jeb from the Cataraqui River? The shameful truth was that she'd been irresistibly drawn to the magazine blurb about her rescue of the blind man and his Seeing Eye dog. Even if it had only been one paragraph in the sidebar of a larger article on heroic acts.

"Susan, why don't you take some time off and stay at home to nurse your back?" Allie asked. "As soon as I've finished marking the last of my exam papers, I'll be a free agent. Beth and I can run the store."

Susan Matthews grimaced. "I hate to put you out, Allie. You've got that triathlon and all the training. And you deserve a break, too. You've been working hard this year, especially since your dad..."

Susan's voice dropped off. A lump rose in Allie's throat. She and Susan had seldom mentioned Rob Newman since his death ten months ago. It was too painful a subject for either of them, Allie supposed, though there'd been many times when she'd wanted to talk about him with the woman who'd been his constant companion for the past twenty years. Allie may have referred to Susan as her stepmother, but she was, in fact, the only mother Allie had really known.

Allie dropped to her knees in front of her. "Look, the papers will be finished by the end of the week. Beth can manage on her own with the high-school kids when I'm training. Take two weeks."

Susan smiled. "One week will be all I need, trust me.

I'd go crazy sitting around any longer than that. And yes,'' she put in as Allie began to interrupt, ''I promise not to do any more lifting or bending.''

Allie sighed, knowing the compromise was all she'd get from her. ''Right—there're plenty of young bodies around here to do the heavy labor for you.''

''Don't rub it in,'' Susan half laughed, half moaned. ''I'm only fifty.''

''Well, I just want you to get fit so we can go dancing at AJ's.''

That brought a real smile. ''Yeah, right.''

It was an ongoing family joke. Whenever Allie had been late coming home, she offered the excuse that she and Beth had been dancing at AJ's, a local Kingston nightspot. The line had become a catchphrase for Susan, Rob and Allie, and was always used for any lateness or absence.

''I'll drive you home and come back here to close up. I could pick up a pizza or something and bring it over for dinner. Okay?''

Susan looked fondly at her. ''That would be nice, Allie. We haven't done that in ages.''

Another shaft of guilt struck. Allie had moved back home for a few weeks after her father's fatal heart attack, but at Susan's insistence, eventually returned to her own apartment. Now she wondered if she'd been wrong to assume that her stepmother was managing fine on her own. ''It's a deal, then. Why don't you get your things while I finish this? Beth should be back from her dentist appointment any moment and she can take over.''

''All right.'' Susan rose slowly from the stool, using the counter to brace herself.

Allie watched her walk gingerly toward the rear of the store. A rush of love for the woman who had meant so much to her, especially since her teen years, overwhelmed her. While Allie was just beginning to reclaim her life after the unexpected loss of her father, it was obvious that Susan was having more difficulty. And why not? Allie asked herself. She'd been his wife in every way but on paper. In fact, Allie had often wondered why the two had never made the relationship official.

"Excuse me." A voice broke into Allie's thoughts.

Swinging her head sharply to the right, Allie saw a man standing on the other side of the counter, holding up the *People* magazine.

"Is this yours?"

Allie blinked. She hadn't even seen him come into the store, unless he'd come in earlier and had been behind the higher shelving units at the front. She flushed at the thought of someone overhearing her conversation with Susan.

"Yes," she said, extending her hand for the magazine.

But he didn't pass it over right away. Instead, he uncurled it, exposing the page she'd been looking at before she'd entered the store.

"Is that you?" he asked, pointing to the photo accompanying the paragraph about her rescue of Harry Maguire.

Still unaccustomed to the questions people had been asking since the local newspaper had featured her on its front page a month ago, Allie shrugged. "Uh, yeah," she answered, making herself sound nonchalant as she again extended her hand.

He didn't seem to get the message that he ought to give back the magazine. His dark-brown eyes continued to scan her face like a bar code. Allie mentally shook herself. She'd been putting in too many long hours at the cash register. And he'd definitely been staring too long.

"My magazine?" she prompted.

"Oh, sorry," he said, blinking as if he'd been caught in

a daydream. "I was imagining what it must have been like—diving into a river to save a blind man."

Allie smiled and came up with the answer she'd framed weeks ago. "Cold."

Unlike the many people who'd posed that same question in the past four weeks, he seemed satisfied with her response. For that, Allie warmed to him.

"Can I help you with anything?"

"Actually, I was just looking around." As if to prove his point, he craned his head to look behind him. "This is a beautiful place. Reminds me of those Western movies with general stores. The wooden bins and barrels. Especially the old brick walls."

"Well, it *is* an old building. That part is authentic at least."

"Is it yours?" he asked.

"No, my...my parents'," she replied, unwilling to get into a long explanation of relationships. Her father had left his half to Susan, along with the house they'd shared for two decades. "Shall I leave you to browse, then?"

He frowned, looking indecisive. "Uh, well..."

The door at the front of the store swung open, and Beth, Allie's longtime friend and Susan's assistant, breezed in. "That's that for another six months," she announced, bustling toward the counter. "Everything okay here?" she asked, her eyes flicking from the customer to Allie and back again.

"Thanks," he said, nodding at Allie, and moved past Beth to the door.

As it closed behind him, Beth winked at Allie. "Never seen him in here before, and I'd remember a face like that! Is he new in town or what?" She headed behind the counter and plopped her handbag and sweater on a chair.

"No idea," Allie mumbled.

"You two looked like you were in deep conversation when I walked in," Beth teased.

For some reason, Allie was annoyed by the remark. She'd barely noticed how good-looking the man was. But that was Beth, always trying to matchmake.

"He saw the magazine article."

"Oh," was all Beth said, knowing how Allie felt about the fanfare.

Susan returned, carrying her purse and all-weather coat. "Beth, thank goodness you're here. Allie's driving me home, then she'll come back to close up with you. My back," she explained at Beth's look of concern.

"Sue's going to take a week off and I'll fill in for her," Allie said.

"Want me to call in some extra help in the morning?" Beth asked.

"That would be great. When will the full-time summer help be starting, do you recall?"

"We asked the two university students to start on Monday. The high-school kids are taking the weekends and Friday night."

Susan nodded. "We should be okay for help, then."

"We'll be just fine," Allie said quickly, afraid Susan might change her mind about taking time off. "It's been pretty quiet, so by the time I get back, we'll probably be ready to close." She grasped Susan's elbow and accompanied her to the door.

JOEL DUCKED his head as soon as he saw the two women round the corner of the health-food store and enter the tiny paved parking lot next to it. Fortunately he'd found a place for his car in the far corner, guessing that owners of the stores adjacent to the lot would use the four reserved spaces.

He watched as the Newman girl solicitously helped the older woman into the hunter-green van, its paneled sides emblazoned in bright yellow with "Evergreen Natural Foods," and then climbed into the driver side.

Of course he'd recognized her as soon as he'd stepped into the store, although she was leaning over the other woman at the time and hadn't noticed his arrival. He'd wondered what had been on her mind those few seconds she'd watched the other woman limp toward the back of the store. Concern and worry, he'd figured, for when she'd swung around, her forehead was furrowed.

The magazine photo hadn't done her justice at all. It hadn't caught the glossy sheen of her dark-brown hair or the tiny dots of amber in her hazel eyes. It hadn't even picked up the pale, crescent-shaped scar at the corner of one eye. Allie Newman was definitely more interesting in real life, he thought, as were most things.

The van roared to life and started to back out. He waited until it was angled onto the one-way main street—what was it called again? Princess?—waiting for a break in the rush-hour traffic. At least what counted for rush hour in a city the size of Kingston, Ontario. Then, he turned the key in the ignition and followed the van out of the lot, leaving at least three car lengths between them.

Not that he expected her to notice him following her. Few people did, unless the cars were alone on a country road or something—unlike the movies, where actors were always peering into their rearview mirrors and spotting a tail. Of course, he didn't even need to be following her, because he already knew where she lived, having passed by the house on Wellington Street on his way to the store. But he didn't know about the other woman then—Susan, he thought she'd called her—and decided to check her out.

The van took a left at the waterfront and headed toward

the army base on the outskirts of town. Joel frowned. He hadn't expected to be leaving the city, but then, he had no one to answer to and no time commitments. Not yet, anyway. The van drove over the metal lift bridge spanning the Cataraqui. Joel looked upriver to his left, wondering where exactly Newman had jumped in after the old guy.

She had nerve, that was all he could say. The days were still brisk in early May; he couldn't imagine how frigid the water must have been a month earlier. Cold, as she'd so curtly informed him. He'd smiled to himself at that, figuring she was fed up with answering the same questions over and over. And for some damn inexplicable reason he'd felt himself admiring her for not succumbing to the preening affectation of celebrityhood.

The van chugged up the hill past the Canadian Forces base and stopped at the traffic light that marked the intersecting road to Fort Henry. He'd been there last night, acting the tourist for once and almost enjoying it. When the light changed, the van made a sudden left. Caught unawares, Joel was glad he was far enough behind to make the turn, too. Was this an impulse turn, he wondered, or had she forgotten to signal?

The sign at the corner had indicated she was heading toward Barriefield. Joel liked the sound of that. In his mind, he imagined a different spelling—Berryfield—and pictured the fields planted with strawberries that people would come to pick in late June. Except the land was currently under development, and the fields that might have once produced crops were now harvesting partially built houses.

The van swung right onto a gravel road, jolting him from his brief philosophical interlude. Joel swore, reminding himself to stay alert. He'd found himself drifting off into these dreamlike states too often over the past year, ever since Trish had walked out on him for the last time, taking Ben with her. This time they hadn't even gone through the pretense of a marriage counselor. Joel had signed the papers without any protest, especially when Trish had agreed to let him have six-year-old Ben for one weekend a month and three weeks in the summer.

Access to his son had been the only dispute in their divorce, and Joel knew, given the uncertainties of his job, that he couldn't and shouldn't ask for more. As it was, he'd had to constantly juggle his schedule. But for once, Trish was willing to be flexible, letting him shift weekends when necessary.

The van was less than a quarter of a mile ahead of him on the gravel road now, so Joel slowed down. There was no more traffic to hide behind. This section was undeveloped, and the fields were sprouting with crops that had a whole growing season ahead of them. What few houses there were, were hundreds of yards apart, well back from the road, and accompanied by small barns and sheds. No big farming operations here, Joel noted. Maybe the people who lived here were what people called gentlemen farmers.

Joel spotted the van turning into a narrow lane, and he pulled onto the shoulder next to a stand of fir trees. He had a good line of vision through the trees as he watched the van stop in front of a two-story limestone farmhouse with a couple of sheds out back. A big golden retriever bounded out the front door as soon as it was opened; good to know about the dog, Joel thought, in case he had to return here at night, which was unlikely.

The Newman girl—Allie, short for Alyse, his notes had stated—got out to help the woman called Susan into the house. Joel remembered her saying she'd go back to the store to close up and decided to give her fifteen minutes.

If she didn't reappear by then, he'd have to do it here and he didn't really want to, not with the other woman present. He checked his watch and leaned against the soft leather of the seat's headrest.

The Cadillac was a great car and he loved driving it. The monotony of his journey all the way from Michigan had been greatly diminished by the luxury of the car and its terrific sound system. Too bad it wasn't his, he thought, sighing at the realization that he would never own a car like this one as long as he was making child-support payments. *Hey, buddy, are you saying you'd rather have a car than your kid? No? So quit complaining.*

He didn't have to wait fifteen minutes. She was out the door in less than ten, revving up the van like a Harley-Davidson and reversing down the drive with scarcely a backward glance. Maybe a tad too accustomed to lack of traffic in the area, Joel figured, making a mental note of that last fact. He had just gotten the Caddie back onto the road when she passed him. He drove another fifty feet before making a sharp U-turn and followed her dust into town.

She didn't bother parking in the lot this time, finding a spot on the west side of Princess across from the store. Luckily he noticed a car pulling out just ahead of him, also on the west side, and was angling into the space when she jumped from the van to dash across the street.

Joel switched off the engine and waited. The sign on the door of the health-food store had posted a closing time of six, and it was about forty-five minutes to that now. If his lucky streak continued, the other woman would leave first. Then he'd have the Newman girl to himself. He got out of the car and leaned against it, ready to dodge the traffic when the moment was right.

Unexpectedly he felt a twinge of guilt about what he

was about to do. Chastising himself, he was reminded that Allie Newman wasn't the first pretty girl whose dreams he'd shattered. Or whose life he'd changed irrevocably. And likely she wouldn't be the last. Joel couldn't figure out why he felt so down about the whole thing all of a sudden. Perhaps he was getting too old for this business. Certainly he'd lost his taste for the thrill of the hunt.

On the dot of six the front door opened and closed again behind the woman who had come into the store when Joel was talking to Allie, waving a goodbye as she left. Joel was across the street and inside the store, flipping the Open sign over to read Closed before Allie had a chance to lock up.

She was standing behind the counter totaling what looked like the day's receipts, and her head shot up at the sound of the door. Her big hazel eyes widened in recognition. And something else, he thought. Puzzlement? *Or fear?*

"Uh, we're closed," she said. "Sorry. Can you come back in the morning?"

Joel didn't say anything, just turned to bolt the door behind him.

"I said we're closed," she repeated, her voice a bit higher now.

Definitely fear. But well-contained, Joel thought, noticing the way she kept her hand poised above the cash register while her other hand fumbled under the counter for something. Not a gun, he decided, considering this was Canada. But maybe a police-alert button or something.

"Please, don't worry. I'm not here to hurt you." *Liar,* his conscience reprimanded. "I meant to ask you something before and didn't get a chance to because that other woman came in. It's personal. My name is Joel Kennedy and I'm a private investigator."

That stayed the other hand. She was more relaxed, though still wary. "I wonder if I could talk to Mr. Newman—would that be your father?"

"My father's dead."

She announced this without a flinch. Joel sensed the part she didn't verbalize was, *So buzz off.*

"Oh, I'm sorry. When, uh…?"

"Almost a year ago. Heart attack," she said, looking down at the magazine on the counter.

"And your mother?" Joel asked, knowing the answer.

She took a deep breath before raising her head. Her eyes were darker than ever, her cheeks bright red. "Look, I think you should leave. As I've said, my father's dead and Susan isn't here to answer any questions."

"Is Susan your mother?"

"My stepmother. Since you seem so keen to find out, my real mother left my father and ran away with another man when I was three. Now, was there something else I can help you with?"

Joel could tell from her tone that she just wanted to get rid of him. He ignored the sarcasm in her voice, keeping his eyes on hers for a long moment before saying the words he'd come all the way from Michigan to say. "Actually, it wasn't your mother who ran away. It was your father." He paused. "And he took you with him."

CHAPTER TWO

For a moment Allie was swept back into the Cataraqui River, the roaring in her ears just as it had been that day. The man's lips were moving, but whatever he was saying was obliterated by a thunderous noise. Her mind flashed to Harry Maguire shouting at her over the boom of rushing water. But now, all she could do was stand absolutely still, frozen by the implication of what she'd just heard.

"I don't understand," she said, her voice foreign to her ears.

"It's a long story," he began. "Perhaps we could go somewhere?"

Allie thought of Susan, waiting at the farmhouse, anticipating a cozy evening together. That would be impossible now, Allie realized.

"I've got to call Susan and let her know I won't be coming tonight. She's expecting me."

"Fair enough. I can wait."

Allie looked from his face to the receipts now squeezed into a ball in her hand. She tossed them onto the counter. "I'll be right back," she said, and marched to the office at the back of the store.

Fortunately Susan wasn't the prying type. She accepted Allie's explanation that something had come up with her usual grace. Allie promised to call her first thing in the morning, grabbed her backpack and returned to the front of the store. She'd had a crazy hope while she was on the phone that the guy might have taken his wild story and disappeared. No such luck.

He was standing in front of the naturopathic medicines. "You take any of this stuff?" he asked.

"Not really. But you didn't come here to learn about holistic medicine, did you?"

He stifled a grin. "Where would you like to talk?"

"There's a coffee shop down the street," she said, and led the way out of the store, stopping to lock it behind them.

"I was thinking of someplace more private," he said as they started down the street.

Allie cocked her head, looking up at him. "Such as?"

"The park by the water. Or my hotel room. I'm staying at the Ramada down by the marina."

Your hotel. Yeah, right. "The park," Allie said. "But first I want to pick up a coffee, if that's okay."

He nodded. "I could use one, too."

They reached the coffee shop and went in to order. When the coffee came, he swiftly handed the clerk a large bill to pay for both, and Allie muttered a grudging thank-you as she headed for the door. He seemed to get the message she wasn't interested in small talk and remained silent for the rest of the walk down Princess to Confederation Park on the waterfront. Allie headed for a bench in the sun, facing the water, and sat down without a backward glance.

"Is that Lake Ontario out there?" he asked, setting his backpack on the grass at his feet as he sat down beside her.

"The St. Lawrence River. The lake starts farther down that way," she said, swinging her arm across his line of vision to the west. "See the outline of those islands? The biggest one is Amherst and the lake officially starts there."

"So where are the famous Thousand Islands then?"

She squinted at him. "You're not from around here, are you?"

"Nope. First time in these parts, though I've been to Northern Ontario."

Allie frowned. "Are you American?"

"Is it that obvious?"

"No. Usually I can pick out Americans right away because of their accent. But you don't have one."

"Maybe not, but you do."

The grin took at least five years off him, Allie thought, which would put him in his midthirties. It also made him, as Beth might say, unforgettable in the looks department.

"Something wrong?" he asked.

She shook her head. "No, just…uh…wondering why an American has something to tell me about my mother."

He liked that she got straight to the point, dismissing any attempt at niceties. "Right. Let's get to it, then." He flipped the plastic tab on his coffee cup and took a long swallow before turning to look at her.

"As I said before, I'm a private investigator. Here," he said, pulling a slim leather billfold from the inside pocket of his jacket. He flipped it open and withdrew a business card, which he handed to Allie.

"Not long after that article about you in *People* magazine came out, I was contacted by a man in Grosse Pointe, Michigan. His name was George Kostakis and he was acting on behalf of his great-uncle, Spiro Kostakis." He paused, watching her face for any hint of recognition and, when none came, went on. "He told me that you looked just like his second cousin, Katrina Kostakis." Joel took another sip of coffee and studied Allie's face in profile.

She was listening attentively, frowning slightly in concentration but giving no suggestion that the names meant anything at all to her. But Joel noticed her tapping his business card against her other hand until she tucked it into the pocket of the windbreaker she was wearing. Anxiety level increasing? he wondered.

"Katrina was the only child of Spiro Kostakis, George's great-uncle and patriarch of the Kostakis clan in Grosse Pointe. George said that there'd been a granddaughter—Elena—who'd disappeared from the family home when she was only three. Spirited away, apparently," Joel added, wanting to give some benefit of doubt for Allie's sake, "by her father, one Eddie Hughes—Katrina's husband and Elena's father."

At that, Allie's head turned his way, her expression almost challenging him. "So far I get no connection to me, other than the fact that I coincidentally resemble this woman—what was her name again?"

"Katrina Kostakis. Or Trina, as she was sometimes called."

"Was?"

"She's dead. Killed in a car crash twenty-six years ago."

"And she is—*was*—supposed to be…"

"Your mother," Joel said softly, keeping his gaze on her face.

Allie broke eye contact first, turning her gaze toward the water. But not before Joel caught the devastation in her face. He stared bleakly at the water, too, hating himself for what he'd said. What he still had to say.

"My father's name was Rob Newman," she said, her voice low and hoarse. *"Rob Newman."*

Joel sighed. He rose from the bench, strode over to a garbage can and chucked his empty coffee cup into it. She watched him as he leaned over, picked up his pack from the grass and unzipped an outer pocket. He pulled out an envelope and paused, noticing the slight trembling of her chin. But when she tilted her head, defiantly raising her face to his, Joel flicked open the envelope and withdrew the photograph, handing it to her in a swift movement that caught her unawares. She fumbled, letting it float to the ground.

He started to bend down for it, but she beat him to it, sweeping up the picture and bringing it to the tip of her nose as if inspecting it through a magnifying glass. Then she leaped to her feet and, clutching the photo in her right hand, began to jog across the grassy park lawn to the sidewalk beyond.

"Hey!" Joel shouted, but she didn't turn around. It seemed as if she increased her stride at the sound of his voice. She was running now, dodging the busy traffic to cross the road, and heading down a side street. Joel swore. He swung his small pack over a shoulder, grabbed the one she'd left behind and took off after her. Though judging by her pace, he doubted he'd catch up to her.

He was about half a block behind and starting to sweat with the extra load of packs, while she seemed to be just getting into a rhythm, loping ahead of him as effortlessly and gracefully as an antelope. He swore, realizing how all of those postponed sessions at the fitness center were working against him. When she turned right at Wellington, he slowed down, knowing where she was headed. Her apartment.

Allie, once inside her apartment, knew exactly where to look. Whisking the photograph from the journal in her desk drawer, she charged back down the stairs and onto the front porch. Her heart was pounding against her ribs, but she knew it wasn't from the run. That had scarcely raised a sweat.

The private investigator hadn't fared as well, she noted.

His breath sounded ragged, as though he were barely holding himself together. Although he didn't appear to be on the verge of total collapse, his eyes were beginning to get that wild look that unfit people sometimes get when their bodies are screaming at them to stop. She waited on the top step while he got his breathing under control.

"I guess you recognized the photo," he finally said.

At least he had *some* sense of humor. "I have the same one," she said, extending her right arm. "At least, part of it."

He took the fragment of photo from her. "You must be—what? About two when that was taken?" he asked.

"I think so."

"And the other half? Do you know—"

"Who snipped my mother out?" Allie shrugged. "Dad, I guess. I found that in his papers after he died. At the time, it was just another reminder that he wanted to forget my mother. Maybe he did it out of love for me—wanting to protect me from questions he couldn't answer," she added.

The P.I. was heading up the steps now, standing so close she could feel the heat from his run still evaporating off him. Allie instinctively backed away.

"Or maybe he just didn't want you asking any questions, in case you stumbled on it one day. You have to admit, the resemblance is—"

"Striking," Allie put in.

"Which is why your grandfather was certain you were Katrina's daughter."

Allie waited a moment, letting that register. "So now what?" she asked, striving for calm.

"There's more," Joel said. "My client—your grandfather—has a proposal for you, so to speak. We'll need somewhere quiet to talk."

The roaring in her ears came back and with it, a surge in blood pressure. Allie covered her face with her hands. She didn't want to hear or discover anything more. *Enough was enough.* She breathed deeply, using her tented hands to ease the hyperventilation. That is, until they were gently lifted up and away, and folded into Joel's as he pulled her closer.

"I know," he murmured, his breath whispering across the top of her head. "It's all too much to take in. You just want me to go away so you can get back to your life."

He was so close to her any passerby would have thought they were about to kiss. For a second he seemed almost like an old friend—there to give comfort and refuge. Then she remembered why he was really there and eased her hands out of his clasp, stepping back at the same time.

"Yes," Allie said. "I do, so why *don't* you go and let me get back to my life?"

"Too late, isn't it?" He shook his head. "I'm sorry, but you're *never* going to be able to go back."

"Of course I am. I'm a very determined person when I want to be."

"I know," Joel conceded. "Otherwise you wouldn't have rescued that man and his dog."

That made her pause. Most people gushed about her bravery when all along, Allie had known the force that drove her into the icy Cataraqui twice had been something different. Instinctively she'd known that there was no way she was going to let Harry Maguire and Jeb die.

"And that very determination," she said, her voice rising, "will see me through this…this situation."

"If you were the kind of person who didn't care about others, you might pull it off. But I suspect that even if I leave without telling you the rest of the story, you'll always wonder. That unavoidably huge question of why your father ran away from his wife and family—and abducted you—will hang over you the rest of your life. You know it and I know it.'' He turned to descend the porch steps.

''Wait!''

He paused.

Allie was back in the icy Cataraqui again. Only this time, she herself was being swept downstream with no hope of rescue in sight. ''You'd better come upstairs,'' she murmured, turning away from him so he couldn't see her face.

SHE WAS EITHER a minimalist or unsentimental, Joel instantly decided, surveying her second-floor apartment. Throw in neat freak, too, he mused. No knickknacks to collect dust, not that a speck of it would be allowed to linger. The clean, crisp style of the decor matched her physical self—unadorned, tidy and in spectacular condition.

Joel repressed a smile. He sounded as if he was composing ad copy. But really, he was relieved that she seemed to be a no-nonsense kind of woman. More than likely, he'd be spending quite a few hours with her in the days ahead, and he dreaded the possibility that she might be overly emotional about everything she was about to learn. It was hard enough juggling the various roles he'd assumed without having to worry about Allie Newman's state of mind.

''More coffee?'' she asked, closing the apartment door behind her.

''Uh, sure,'' he said, not really wanting another coffee so soon but anxious to postpone the inevitable. She headed into the hall—toward the kitchen, he guessed—and he took the opportunity to check out the small living room that overlooked the street. A faded plump sofa in front of the bay window had a worn but comfy air. He almost felt like sinking into it, putting up his feet and having a snooze.

Joel scanned the pine bookshelves lining the wall opposite the window. If he hadn't already known she was some kind of college professor, he'd have concluded so after one glance at the titles. Many were familiar—classics that he'd once stacked on his own shelf years ago as a college undergrad.

"You take it black, right?" she called out.

She must have noticed his preference at the coffee shop earlier. Following her voice along a dark, wood-paneled hall, he appeared in the doorway of a medium-size, old-fashioned kitchen.

"Yes, thanks," he said.

Her head shot up from pouring coffee into two mugs. "I didn't hear you coming down the hall."

He took the mug she held out and shrugged. "Professional habit, I guess."

One corner of her mouth seemed to twist under as she muttered, "Yeah," and after splashing some milk into her own coffee, led the way back to the front of the house.

Joel glanced left and right along the hallway. There were two closed doors and an open one leading into a sunlit bathroom. "You live alone?" he asked.

"Yes." She sank into the sofa and propped her feet on a coffee table stacked with magazines, books and what appeared to be exam papers.

Joel settled into a black leather armchair adjacent to the sofa. No roommate. That was good. No complications.

"Nice place," he remarked. Then, nodding to the pile of papers, he asked, "Are those exam papers?"

"Yes."

He went on, unfazed by her terseness. "You a teacher or something?"

Her sigh echoed in the room. "I'm sure you know all about me, Mr. Kennedy. Shall we get to why you're here?"

"Joel," he murmured, flashing what he hoped was a placating smile. "High school?" he ventured, pushing her just a tad more.

"I teach math at Queen's—it's a local university."

"Ah! Professor?"

"Hardly. But someday perhaps. I haven't done my doctoral thesis yet." She stretched forward to set her mug on the coffee table, brought her feet back to the floor and sat up straight. "Now, about my mother..."

"Right." Joel leaned over and set his half-empty mug on the floor. "As I said, your father's real name was Eddie Hughes. Thirty-two years ago he married Katrina Kostakis, the only child of Spiro and Vangelia Kostakis. Apparently Katrina had always been fragile, and shortly after your birth, she spiraled into a serious postnatal depression. From what I've been told by the family, she kept this a secret for quite some time, but when you were just a year old or so, it was evident that Katrina had problems. She was put on antidepressants and they seemed to help for a bit. Then—" he paused, noting how Allie's eyes seemed to disappear into her face at each new sentence "—she began to drink. You can imagine how things became much worse very quickly."

Allie's face paled.

Joel hesitated. "Do you want me to get you something? A glass of cold water?"

She waved a limp hand. "No, just continue. But thanks, anyway."

He was beginning to wish he had a cold drink right then

himself, though water wasn't what he had in mind. "Adding to the equation was the fact that Eddie—your father—worked for Spiro in a fairly high managerial position."

"Managerial? *My father?* He was, like, the ultimate hippie," Allie said. She shook her head. "This is all too much. What kind of business does this Spiro operate?"

"Your grandfather has a number of enterprises. I did some checking on him after he first consulted me. He has a chain of Greek restaurants in Michigan, along with a few importing-exporting companies. Some corporate real estate."

"So what part did my father supposedly manage?"

There was more than a hint of disbelief in the question. Joel knew enough to make his answer vague. "I'm not really sure, to be honest. Just before he took off, he was being touted as Spiro's new right-hand man."

Allie frowned. "Then why would he take off?"

Joel leaned forward in the chair, sensing he'd hooked her at last. She was starting to ask important questions. "I was told there was an argument between Spiro and Eddie about handling some business deal. Spiro made some comment about Eddie not being any more adept at managing his own marriage. Eddie blew up and implied that the marriage wasn't going to last the year, anyway. Then Spiro reminded him that he had enough connections—politically and legally—to ensure that Eddie would walk away from the marriage with nothing, not even visitation rights to his daughter."

Joel waited for a reaction, though none came. Instead, he saw that she'd been drawn completely into the story as if it was a tale about some strangers, not her own family. He went on. "Eddie replied that Katrina would never get custody of you, given her depression and alcoholism."

"That's true, I'm sure," Allie put in.

"Perhaps, but Spiro made it clear that he and your grandmother would sue for custody and would have no problem getting it."

"So he ran off with me," she whispered.

"Apparently."

Allie sat staring into space, imagining a tableau of how it might have been, trying to put faces on the people whose names she was hearing for the first time. Then her eyes must have focused, for she realized she was looking directly at Joel Kennedy. If only her mind would focus, as well, so she could decide which of the thousand questions clamoring inside to pose first.

"How did you get this information?" she asked. Not a great question, she knew at once, but a start. And it seemed to take him aback, because he blinked a few times before replying.

"From Spiro at our first meeting. I also interviewed a few people who worked with Eddie at the time. Also, your aunt—Ephtimea, or Effie—provided some background."

"My *aunt?*"

"Well, I guess cousin, or second cousin is more like it. She was married to Spiro's nephew, Tony. Their two sons—George and Christopher, or Christo—work for Spiro."

"A real family enterprise," she mused.

"A wealthy and powerful family enterprise," Joel added.

He must have picked up the bitterness in my voice, Allie thought. All those years when the only blood relative she had was her father. "How can you be sure this Spiro's account is true? My father isn't here to defend himself."

"I don't think you should take this as an indictment against your father. You lived with him all these years—you know what kind of man he was."

Allie felt the sting of tears in her eyes. She *did* know. He would never have run away unless he was desperate or feared for her well-being. In that case, she reasoned, Spiro Kostakis must be a man to be wary of. But she wasn't about to reveal that thought to the investigator who'd been hired by Kostakis to find her.

"Precisely," she said. "Which leads me to the next point—why did he hire you to find out if I was his granddaughter *now?* It's been twenty-seven years."

"Until that magazine article appeared, your grandparents and mother believed that you and Eddie were dead."

Allie stared at Joel, unable to speak, trying to absorb what he'd said.

"The night Eddie disappeared with you, the police set roadblocks and searched for hours. In the early hours of the morning, Eddie's car was discovered partly submerged in the Detroit River. Divers went in and found suitcases of clothing, including clothes belonging to a child, toys, Eddie's wallet and personal papers. Even money. He'd cleaned out his joint bank account before leaving. Days later the search was called off, though Spiro had private investigators continue for a few months. By then Katrina's condition had deteriorated so much that Spiro devoted his efforts to getting her well."

Joel's account of their flight was so vivid that for a moment, Allie forgot the larger implication of the whole disappearing act. That it had all been a lie—a deliberate hoax. She felt light-headed and disconnected. While she was attempting to keep herself from being carried away in this wave of new information, she had not noticed that Joel had vanished and returned, and was now handing her a glass of ice water.

She drank slowly, letting the cool liquid soothe the drumming in her head and the heat in her face. When she finished, she set the glass down and looked at Joel. There was concern in his face, and for the first time since she'd met him, she liked him. Not his story, she quickly added to herself, but him.

"My father must have been very afraid to pull off something like that," she finally said.

"He obviously felt he had no choice," Joel said.

She thought for a long moment before asking what she knew she had to learn. "And my mother?"

"Grew more despondent. Stopped taking her medication. Drank more. The police report of her car crash a year later was inconclusive about the cause."

"So it might have been an accident or...or not," Allie murmured.

"Yes."

She knew then she needed to be alone. "If you don't mind..." she said, standing up.

Joel got up, too. "There's something more. I might as well tell you all of it right now."

Allie didn't have the energy to protest. She simply stared at him, wishing he'd disappear himself.

"After your aunt showed the *People* magazine article to him, Spiro was determined to find you. Also, there were circumstances that prompted him to rush more than he might have."

"Circumstances?"

"A few years ago Spiro was diagnosed with leukemia. None of the traditional treatments have worked. His only chance of surviving another few years is a bone marrow transplant." He waited a moment. "George and Christo aren't a match," he prompted. Then, "You're his only living blood relative."

Allie sat back down.

Joel sat down on the sofa next to her. Allie flinched at

his closeness, though she knew he meant to be sympathetic. Still, the one person in the world she wanted at her side right now was buried in a cemetery on the outskirts of town. It had been months since she'd felt such a pain of longing for her father.

Joel Kennedy's revelations magnified not only her loss but the futility of ever knowing the truth. No matter how much more information came her way in the days ahead— and she knew now she wasn't going to shake off this whole thing anytime soon—she'd never be able to hear her father's own account.

Unless Susan knows something. The thought of her stepmother distracted her from Kennedy's announcement. "You haven't approached Susan, have you? About any of this?"

"Susan?"

"My stepmother!"

He grabbed her hands, which she was waving in front of his face. "No, Allie. I wouldn't do that. This is your—"

"Problem."

He pursed his lips as she pulled her hands free. "I'm only the messenger, Allie. None of this is my doing, either."

Again Allie got to her feet. She needed to get the whole rotten business over with. "Tell me what this…this Spiro Kostakis wants of me." She stood on the far side of the coffee table opposite him, her arms folded across her chest.

"He wants you to come to Grosse Pointe, to meet the rest of the family and to undergo a test to see if you're a bone marrow match."

"Hah! Not a lot to ask, is it, from someone I've never met? From someone who threatened to take me away from my father?'' Allie heard her voice border on hysteria, but she felt powerless to stop herself.

Joel was on his feet at once, inches from her face and clutching her upper arms as if to keep her grounded. ''You need to be alone, to take all of this in and to decide what you plan to do. You have complete control over this, Allie. Whatever happens is up to you. If your answer is no, then I'll be driving out of Kingston ten minutes later.'' He paused, lowering his voice. ''Talk it over with Susan if you want to. If you decide yes, then I'm hoping you'll be willing to drive back to Michigan with me. Or come on your own. Whatever. Just remember that none of this has to diminish your memory or feelings for your father in any way. And it shouldn't. It seems to me he did an admirable job of raising his daughter.'' With that, Joel brushed past her.

Allie heard the door close behind him. She felt herself sinking slowly back to earth, relief at Joel's departure snapping every taut nerve in her body. And yet, she thought, sagging into the sofa cushions, his hands had been warm and comforting. If he'd held on a millisecond longer, she knew she'd have gratefully leaned into his arms, too.

She lay back into the indentation he'd just left and stared at the ceiling. Gradually her mind regained control of her body as she decided her first move had to be to talk with Susan, but that would have to wait until morning.

CHAPTER THREE

SUSAN GOT UP to make a pot of tea. She was amazing, Allie thought, watching her go through the steps without uttering a word. In fact, it had been Susan who'd reached for the box of tissues as Allie recited the whole story in a robotlike trance, until she got to the end where she'd unexpectedly burst into tears.

Allie had stopped the story just short of Joel's last words to her, about Rob Newman's admirable job of raising his daughter.

Susan brought the tea to the table and, echoing Allie's thoughts, said, "Your father can't be here to advocate for himself, so we shall have to do it for him. He was a good, decent and honest man. We know that and so does everyone who knew him. That's not to say some of this Kennedy's story isn't true." She stirred a spoonful of honey into her cup and blew on the tea gently before sipping.

"I guessed about six months after we'd started dating that your father had a former life he wanted to forget."

Allie glanced up from spooning honey out of the jar. Susan had never spoken about her personal relationship with her father, not even after his death. She had never once uttered an irritated or perplexed word about the man who shared her life for twenty years. Allie, who often prided herself on her intuition, felt a pang of guilt that she'd so blindly assumed Susan's calm nature had signified unconditional acceptance of Rob and his daughter. What doubts and questions ran through her mind all these years? Allie wondered.

"He was always so vague about his origins. Said his parents had both died, and he had no siblings or family nearby. Of course, I gathered immediately that he'd grown up in the States." She looked across the table at Allie and smiled. "His accent."

"How come I never noticed it?"

"You grew up with it. Besides, he never used the colloquial expressions that Canadians use. Although he told me he was from Northern Ontario, he never spoke like anyone from there."

"Did you ever ask him?"

"No. Somehow I never had the courage to confront him directly." She gave a small, deprecating laugh. "Maybe I was afraid of frightening him off, even losing him. And you."

"Dad wasn't like that," Allie blurted out, reaching out her hand to stroke Susan's. "He loved you. You know that."

"I know, but this was early in our relationship. Suddenly this big bear of a man with a tiny waif of a daughter was attracted to *me*—the stereotypical librarian—and I didn't want the fairy tale to end." She laughed again.

"And it didn't," Allie said. "You were the love of his life."

Susan smiled fondly at her stepdaughter. "I know that. As you were. He'd have done anything for you." She took another sip of tea, then said, "That's why I can believe this private investigator's story."

Blood rushed into Allie's head. "But—"

Susan raised a hand. "Hear me out, sweetie. When I realized your father was probably an American, I thought he might have been a draft dodger. The war in Vietnam was winding down then, but American soldiers were still being sent over. My suspicion was reinforced by his almost paranoid fear of authority. He drove very carefully, so as never to be stopped by any traffic police. He kept to himself out here on the farm. Some people in town thought he was reclusive, but I knew he was too social to be a real hermit. It was just that he avoided big public functions or occasions.''

"Lots of people are like that," Allie protested.

"Yes, but he was very protective of you. Don't you remember all those sleepover parties you had here, rather than going to someone else's house?" She nodded at the glimmer of recollection in Allie's face.

"He came with me to every swim meet. And I always had to check in with him if I went out of town for any reason. I used to think that's why he got Casey for me. She was meant to be a friend, as well as a protector.''

"Of course she was. You were fifteen the Christmas you got that dog. Just starting to be interested in boys." Susan chuckled. "That was no coincidence, my dear.''

"I guess not. I'm happy that you raised one of Casey's pups. Tiggy looks just like her." Allie smiled at Susan, warming to the reminiscences they were sharing at last.

"Remember the argument you had with him when you told him you were moving into town?" Susan asked gently.

Allie sobered at the memory. It had been the one serious quarrel she'd had with her father. "I was twenty-four years old and still living at home. I was a freak," she whispered. "God, that was an awful fight." Allie laid her head on her forearms. Susan stroked her hair back from her face, the way she'd done whenever Allie had been sick or upset. *If only I could turn back the clock,* Allie thought. *And make everything right again. Make Dad come back.*

"I guess we'll never really know the whole story now," Susan said with an audible sigh. "That's why we must never doubt our faith in Rob. We must always believe that whatever he did, he acted out of love and concern for you."

"I *do* believe that!" Allie cried. "I just wish Joel Kennedy would leave Kingston and let us go on with our lives."

Susan gave a quiet laugh. "You know *that's* never going to happen, Allie. It's too late. Whatever choice you make will stay with you the rest of your life."

Allie shivered at this playback of Joel Kennedy's words. "But I don't want to have to make a choice. That's the problem. I just want things to go on—unchanged." She sat up to look at Susan.

Her stepmother smiled. "There's that ten-year-old face I remember so well! You've always resisted change, Allie. And always had difficulties making decisions. Remember when we'd go for ice cream?"

"That's because there were too many flavors. If there'd been only a few, I could've managed a quicker decision."

"So you shouldn't have difficulty with this. Aren't there only two choices?"

"But a man's life may depend on *me!*" That fact struck Allie for the first time. The horror that such a decision was up to her brought her hands to her face.

Susan waited a few seconds before murmuring, "Then maybe there's no choice at all."

Allie locked eyes with her stepmother, knowing then what she had to do.

JOEL HUNG UP the phone and shifted back onto the pillows plumped up against the headboard of his bed. He felt a tinge of satisfaction that his judgment of Allie Newman had been spot on, but at the same time, a tiny part of whatever conscience was still operating inside him held back his usual grin of satisfaction at a job well done.

She was coming with him to Grosse Pointe. He knew from the moment he walked out her door that she would. Mainly because she hadn't shouted after him or angrily protested his parting comment. Walking down the stairs, he'd thought that he might have overdone it, but his parting line had just popped out. Such spontaneous remarks were rare for him, and that worried him. For some reason Allie Newman's very presence seemed to prompt stirrings he hadn't felt since he was a gangly teenager. She had a way of making him feel, well—he hated to admit it—*out of control.* As if the game could go any way and it made no difference how he played his hand.

Joel rubbed his face. He'd taken an afternoon nap, unusual for him, while he waited for her phone call. It was now almost four o'clock and probably a good time to call Grosse Pointe with the news. He should be exulting, but instead, he felt flat inside. Probably because he knew the game was just starting. There were so many more cards to deal and he hoped Allie Newman could stay in the play. Then he thought, she's a grown woman, she can handle things. *Save your concern for yourself, chum.*

JOEL SAUNTERED UP to the front of the car ferry. It was a bright morning, warmer than the day before. Puffy cotton-ball clouds drifted across an achingly blue sky. The ferry was almost empty. There were only two other cars, a Canada Post truck, a small transport and an RV with an American license plate. People on holiday, he guessed.

He couldn't remember the last time he'd had a real holiday. Probably before his divorce. Wolfe Island loomed ahead. He'd spotted it from his hotel and, needing to kill a few hours, had impulsively joined the line of cars waiting at the ferry dock in Kingston.

It was either that or take one of the Thousand Island cruises, but he was afraid of being stuck on a boat for three hours with nothing to do but look at scenery. He returned to the Caddie and sat patiently waiting for the boat to finish docking. Heaven only knew what he'd do when he disembarked, but he figured the round trip would take up most of the morning. Then, he was assuming there would be another day and a half before he'd be heading back to Michigan with Allie.

She'd said she'd come only if she could have a day or so to get some things in order. Apparently there were still a few exams to finish marking, and she had to arrange for extra help at the store—something about Susan's back. He'd noticed that the woman had been walking a bit gingerly when he'd followed them the other day.

God, was it only two days ago? He felt as though he'd been in Kingston for ages. Must be the boredom, he decided. Or restlessness to get on with the job. More likely a combination. Maybe even a bit of anxiety about what lay ahead. He wondered what Allie would make of her newfound family.

Perhaps he ought to prepare her a bit more for what was coming. Certainly he'd told her as much as he needed to, and it had all been true, more or less. If things went well, she might never fill in the gaps, though he somehow doubted that. She was too sharp. And when those gaping holes were exposed, would she turn on him? Probably. And he wouldn't blame her.

Joel sighed, then shifted into Drive as the truck ahead of him rolled off the ferry. Allie wouldn't be the first woman to view him as a betrayer. Yet, for some damn reason, he hoped she might be an exception.

He drove a few yards to an intersection and stopped. A sign read Marysville, and Joel made a quick right just to get the Cadillac out of the way of the vehicles behind. He pulled up in front of a general store called Fargo's and climbed out of the car. Marysville seemed little more than a handful of buildings. A paved road stretched east and west as far as he could see. There was a line of cars across the street waiting to board the return ferry, and Joel considered joining it. It was at least another forty-five minutes before the ferry back to Kingston left, and he doubted the two or three stores he saw here would fill the time. Of course there was a diner across the road that might offer a good cup of coffee, and he could always tour the island itself. That might use up twenty minutes.

Joel swung through the sagging screen door into Fargo's in search of a newspaper. He wandered about, admiring the weathered hardwood floors and the sturdy wooden cabinets and shelving units. There was an old-fashioned butcher's counter complete with weigh scales, a roll of paper and twine. An aproned man stood behind the counter waiting on a woman, while her children prowled about sucking lollipops.

The whole scene was so gosh-darn wholesome that Joel felt as if he'd walked onto the set of some 1970s family-values sitcom. He handed the teenage girl at the cash register fifty cents for the newspaper and headed for the door. He had his hand on the handle just as a gang of people appeared on the other side of the screen, about to enter. Joel stepped back inside to let the group pass.

Several young women and men, all attired in sleek cycling outfits, clomped in with Allie Newman bringing up the rear. She did a double take when she saw Joel. He found her smile ambivalent, not quite as if he was the last person on earth she wanted to see at that moment, but almost.

"What are *you* doing here?" she asked without preamble.

"Checking out the local sites," he said, aware of several helmeted heads turning his way.

"That shouldn't take more than five minutes," she quipped. She unstrapped her headgear and shook loose her hair. It bounced softly against her neck and settled in a feathery web around her face, sticking to parts of her cheek where perspiration lingered.

Joel was tempted to brush those wisps away but knew the gesture would seem too familiar. Still, he couldn't keep his eyes from skimming across the skin-tight spandex suit she was wearing. No doubt because of the excellence of her physical condition, he decided.

"Nothing better to do?" she asked, grinning.

He felt his face heat up. Was she talking about sightseeing on Wolfe Island or his perusal of her cycling suit? "And you?" he couldn't help asking. "Putting things in order?"

"Yes, as a matter of fact I am. I'm supposed to participate in a triathlon at the end of June, and I missed my training session yesterday." She shot him a look as if he were to blame.

Was there no end of wonders about this woman? He muttered something vaguely congratulatory and started to squeeze past her for the door.

"Are you really driving around the island?" she asked, stopping him before he had his hand on the door.

"Uh, guess so, since I've almost an hour before the next ferry. Why? Tired?"

A patient smile crossed her face. "Not yet, but one of my friends has a serious leg cramp and she's waiting about two miles down the road. We were going to see if anyone here could go for her.''

"Two miles," he repeated. "She could probably manage on her own when the cramp subsides.''

"She's just getting over a hamstring injury and has to be careful, but don't worry about it.'' Allie turned away, seemingly intent on joining the group clustered around the ice-cream freezer.

"Sorry," Joel said quickly, touching her shoulder. "That was petty. Of course I'll go for her. Maybe you could direct me?''

She nodded and pushed through the screen door. Joel followed meekly, wishing he could replay the past few minutes. He was reminding himself that Allie Newman had an uncanny talent for bringing out weird responses in him when he noticed she was already seated in the Cadillac.

"Good guess," he said, sliding behind the wheel.

"The only one with an American plate. Make a left here and go east as far as you can. The road will curve inland toward the south side of the island. She'll be waiting on that stretch.''

In less than a minute Marysville was merely a snapshot in his rearview mirror. "Not a lot to do hereabouts," he commented.

"Not if you're a tourist," she said. "Though if you live here, I imagine working a farm keeps you busy.''

He decided to keep quiet the rest of the way, which took scarcely five minutes along a paved road that stretched across flat acres of farmland.

"There she is!" Allie pointed.

A young woman was sitting under a tree beside the shoulder just ahead. Joel slowed and pulled well over, in spite of the lack of traffic. He helped Allie load the bike into the trunk and then tie the lid down with a bungee cord he just happened to find in the trunk. Allie sat in the back seat with the other woman and began to massage her calf muscles.

Before he climbed into the car himself, Joel noticed how expertly Allie's long slim fingers moved up and down the injured leg. Finally he forced his gaze away and got in behind the wheel, wishing he could trade places with the injured woman.

See? he chastised himself. *There you go again.* It was almost as if he was bewitched. *Get a grip, fella.* There were long days ahead—turbulent ones—and his part in them was just beginning.

They pulled up in front of Fargo's and Allie helped her friend out of the car while Joel retrieved the bike from the trunk. The friend thanked them and hobbled away to join the rest of the group, standing around the outdoor pop cooler. Allie hovered near the car.

"Guess I'd better get in line," Joel said, jerking his head at the cars waiting for the return trip.

He hoped she'd suggest they wait together, but she only nodded and said, "See you on the boat," as he climbed back into the Caddie.

As he reversed the car, he saw her wheel her bicycle toward the group. During the wait to get aboard, Joel had a long talk with himself about letting his guard slip every time Allie Newman was in his presence.

When the boat returned, he took his time parking the Caddie on board and heading for the upper deck. There, he saw the gang of cyclists lounging on the benches on the far side of the ferry. Joel leaned over the railing to view the Kingston skyline.

It was a pretty town, he thought. Or small city. There were lots of old limestone buildings and a waterfront that had so far managed to escape major development. This was a place where tourists flocked during the summer months, and to accommodate them, outdoor restaurants and sport bars stood in abundance. Having grown up in Philadelphia, Joel couldn't imagine a childhood in such a small place. That reflection led him to wonder what kind of childhood Allie had with a parent on the run, ever vigilant about the past catching up to him.

A burst of laughter from the other side of the deck caught his attention. Allie stood in the midst of the cyclists, regaling them with some story that had them in stitches. Joel watched her hands gesturing to elaborate her tale, throwing her head back to laugh with them. He envied that ability to hold a group in thrall. He'd once had a partner who could do that. Joel contented himself with observing, taking in the nuances of expression and body language of the group. That was what he did best. Watch and observe. Draw conclusions. Then act.

Feeling hadn't been a part of the routine for years, it seemed. He sighed and looked away, back to the city skyline. Back to the job ahead.

ALLIE WHEELED her bike along the pedestrian path of the ferry dock, occasionally glancing around for Joel's car. She'd noticed him standing alone at the front of the deck on the return trip. For a moment she'd considered calling him over, but dismissed the idea almost immediately. She doubted he'd have wanted to join them, and more, she was reluctant to have to make some explanation about who he was or how she knew him. Not that any of the gang would have asked; they were basically cycling pals. But her friend Linda might well have picked up on the vibes between her and the private investigator.

And what vibes there were! Allie was shocked at the way she'd behaved around the man, why she let him get to her as he so obviously did. Perhaps it was simply a matter of that old cliché—about killing the messenger. She certainly had good reason to wish Joel Kennedy's message had never been delivered. As for the messenger, well, he'd be gone from her life as soon as they arrived in Grosse Pointe. Which suited Allie just fine.

The cycle group split up at the end of the dock, after agreeing to meet the following week. Linda raised a brow at Allie's comment that she'd be out of town but said nothing. Allie figured her friend would be calling her later that day, and what would she tell her? She'd have to come up with some explanation for Beth and the staff at the store, as well. She was about to strap on her helmet when a car horn beeped lightly behind her.

Joel Kennedy smiled at her from the open driver's window. "Want a lift?"

Allie reminded herself to relax and take the offer at face value. "Thanks, anyway, but by the time we get this into the trunk, I could already be home."

The smile froze on his face. Allie saw that he was regretting the invite. Plus, she suddenly felt her words had sounded ungracious. "Look," she said, "I didn't mean that to sound as bad as it did. I just don't want to inconvenience you."

He waved a hand. "No problem. So shall I call you later to work out exactly when we could leave for Grosse Pointe?"

Impulsively she changed her mind. "Maybe I *will* take that lift, and we can figure something out on the way."

The car pulled over and Joel got out to help Allie with the bike. The second she was sitting next to him and on the way up Brock Street to Wellington, she thought she ought to have cycled, after all. The spandex suit was hot and itchy. Worse, she feared her trusty deodorant might not have been up to the task of dealing with the twenty-mile route around Wolfe Island.

He didn't speak for a long while, adding to her discomfort. But when they were almost at her corner, he said, "If you're free tonight, I'd appreciate having company for dinner. We could make our plans then. Interested?"

And surprisingly, she was.

"THAT'S THE OWNER—Zal." Allie nodded to a heavyset bearded man walking toward the center doors of the restaurant. "He used to be a member of a 1960s rock group called the Lovin' Spoonful. Ever hear of it?"

Joel frowned. "Vaguely. So he retired from that to go into the restaurant business? I bet this is harder work." He glanced around the patio courtyard where they were sitting beneath a lattice of wisteria and vines. "Very pretty, though."

"And the food's great," Allie added.

"The name's a bit odd."

"I suppose, to an outsider. But here in Kingston, Chez Piggy is so famous no one questions the name."

Joel flipped open the menu. "Okay, so let's get into it. Prove the name right. I'm starving."

"Me, too." Allie picked up her glass of wine and sipped leisurely. It was a lovely balmy evening and she wanted to savor every second of it. Her dining experience was enhanced, she had to admit, by the man sitting across from her. Allie hadn't missed the discreet looks he'd been receiving from some of the other female patrons.

She'd met Joel outside the nineteenth-century tunnel-style walkway that led into the restaurant and had been surprised at her thrill of pleasure when he approached. His beaming smile reassured her that the afternoon's edginess had disappeared. He didn't look like a private investigator, in his pressed tan trousers and crisp, pale-yellow short-sleeved shirt, at least not like Allie's television-inspired notion of one.

His perusal of the menu gave her a chance to study him closer. He was an introvert, she decided. His dark-brown eyes, set deeply in his face, gave little away in terms of what he was feeling or thinking. Except when he raised his head and caught her in the act. Then he let her know right away that he figured she was sizing him up, and the idea obviously amused him. Allie feigned sudden interest in the antics of some children at an adjacent table.

"You don't seem like the maternal type," he remarked.

The comment took her aback. "Well, maybe not yet, but I hope to be someday."

"It's a serious job, parenting."

"You sound like you speak from experience."

He seemed to regret the opener, giving a slight shrug that she couldn't interpret. Finally he said, "Actually, I have a six-year-old son, Ben. He lives with his mother most of the time, but I see him one weekend a month and a couple weeks every summer." He paused, adding in a more somber voice, "If my schedule can work the visit in."

Allie didn't know what to say. For some reason she'd never considered that Joel Kennedy might be married with a child. Or rather, divorced with a child.

"You must miss him."

The observation hit home. He gave a brusque, "Yeah," before turning his head to signal the waitress.

After they ordered, the subject was dropped and Allie devoted her attention to the bread basket. She sighed, thinking about the long trip she'd soon be making with him.

"Something wrong?" he asked.

"No...no," she stammered, raising her eyes to his. "Just tired, I guess."

"Shall we decide when to leave? I was thinking about the day after tomorrow, if you need the time. Or," he paused, "even tomorrow, if you're finished what you had to do."

Better to get the whole thing over with. "I've actually finished what I need to do. We can leave tomorrow if you like. But after my run, which I usually do about six or six-thirty."

He gave a mock shudder. "Okay. How about I pick you up at eight? We'll stop for coffee on the way to the highway."

"Fine." Allie returned a smile, but wasn't feeling as optimistic as she had moments ago. Did she really know him well enough to spend five or six hours alone with him in a car?

The waitress arrived with their dinners, and for the next half hour they focused on eating. But after their plates were whisked away and they were lingering over coffee, Allie blurted, "Tell me more about Spiro Kostakis."

"Curious?"

"Of course. Why wouldn't I be?"

"Forty-eight hours ago you were doubting his relationship to you."

"A lot can change in forty-eight hours," she murmured, and peered down at her coffee.

"Yes. A lot can," he agreed.

Something in his tone brought her head up, but his expression was impassive. He cleared his throat. "How about if we leave the business part till tomorrow? I don't like mixing business with pleasure if I can help it."

Allie felt unexpectedly flattered that she was part of the

pleasure that night. Tomorrow would be soon enough to get the lowdown on this new family of hers.

Joel insisted on picking up the tab for dinner. "Expenses," he said, settling the matter, and because the evening was so mild, they decided to walk.

"Is it always this quiet on a Thursday night?" he asked.

"This time of year it is, because most of the university students have gone home for the summer. The weekends are busy, but the real tourist crowd doesn't arrive until June. Then all the outdoor restaurants, clubs and bars are full."

"I was watching the marina from my hotel room. I guess it's hopping in the summer, too."

"Oh, yes," Allie said, nodding. "I once spent a hectic summer working there when I was a student. The boating crowd tends to attract some pretty eccentric types."

"I don't get the draw," Joel said. "To big luxury boats, I mean."

"Some people call those huge speedboats 'babe magnets.'"

"Ouch! Expensive way to ensure a good love life," he muttered.

She laughed, but thought he'd probably never had to worry about attracting women.

They'd reached her house and now stood awkwardly in front of it. Allie briefly considered asking him in, but had too much to do. He solved the impasse by commenting, "I imagine you have things to get ready. And you have to pack for a couple of weeks."

"Really? I didn't think it would take that long."

Joel frowned. "I hope I never implied that, Allie. If I did, I'm sorry. First they have to do blood tests to see if you're a match. This is assuming Spiro is still in remission so they can go ahead with the transplant. Plus, you'll need a few days to recuperate.''

Allie's stomach gave a small lurch. She hadn't thought through the physical implications of the whole business. ''I hope this doesn't jeopardize my... I mean, I'm supposed to...''

''Your triathlon? We'll find out as soon as we get there, but I've a hunch it won't. End of June, you said?''

She nodded.

''It should be okay. Don't worry.'' He leaned forward and kissed her gently on the cheek. ''Thanks for a great evening. I enjoyed it.''

Allie simply stared. It wasn't only the unexpected kiss that puzzled her, but the stiffly presented compliment that came with it. For want of anything wittier, she said, ''Was that business or pleasure?''

A stain of red crept up his neck. ''Definitely pleasure,'' he replied. Then, turning on his heel, he said, ''I'll be here at eight.''

Allie watched his retreating back, thinking he was the oddest man she'd met in a long time. And if that was pleasure, she was thinking, what does he do to really let loose?

JOEL MADE THE CALL about ten o'clock. Their estimated time of arrival in Grosse Pointe, he'd said, would be about four in the afternoon, allowing for lunch and rest-room breaks. Spiro was pleased, as Joel guessed he would be, but reserved.

He'd asked what Allie was like, and Joel had to think for a moment. In the end, he suggested that Spiro should draw his own conclusions, but that she was definitely Katrina's daughter. Joel told him about the duplicate photograph, omitting the fact that Allie's mother had been torn out of the picture. When Spiro mentioned that the whole family would be on hand to greet her the next day, Joel felt a tug of sympathy for her. He hung up the phone and swung his legs off the bed.

Allie had no idea what she was getting into, yet still had agreed to go with him. A gutsy woman, definitely. Beautiful, too, though not in the Hollywood way. If he hadn't been such a prig about following the rules, he might still be with her, instead of alone in his hotel room.

Maybe what he really needed was a long cold shower to rid his head of Allie Newman. Though he doubted the shower would be enough.

CHAPTER FOUR

ALLIE FIDGETED against the smooth leather upholstery of the car. She was tempted to take her Walkman out of her pack and listen to it, but was afraid Joel might be offended. She certainly wouldn't be interrupting a flow of conversation, though. Since leaving Kingston an hour ago, he'd uttered scarcely half-a-dozen words. She leaned back and closed her eyes, thinking of last night.

After Joel had left, she'd been overcome by a fit of energy. She couldn't understand the tumult of emotions his leaving had produced. Or was it the fraternal peck on her cheek? Why would that bother her at all? The kiss had been so neutral it couldn't even be considered inappropriate. Allie sighed, opening her eyes just enough to sneak a glance at the man beside her.

He'd nicked himself shaving that morning, she noticed, spotting a small cut on the lower edge of his jaw. And the slightly puffy semicircles beneath his eyes indicated a rough night. Insomnia? she wondered, or had he hit the bars after leaving her? She dismissed the latter, deciding he was far too disciplined. Yet if he had been tossing and turning, what thoughts had kept *him* from sleep?

She doubted they were the same confused thoughts that had her pacing the apartment until finally she hopped on her bike and rode out to the farm. Susan had greeted her with pleased surprise, tinged with some dismay when she heard that Allie planned to leave the next morning for Michigan.

"Are you sure you can trust this man, dear? Do you feel you know him well enough for a six-hour drive? Why not take a bus?"

Allie hesitated. She felt that she could trust Joel Kennedy, although she realized, in the face of Susan's questions, that she really had no basis for feeling that way. What exactly was it about him that had produced this belief that he *was* trustworthy? Not his warm, engaging manner, to be sure.

"How do you even know his story is legitimate?"

Allie didn't like where Susan was going with this. In fact, it strongly reminded her of the old days when her father grilled her about a new date. "The photograph, remember? The one I found in Dad's papers? And by the way, did you ever find anything else?"

Susan shook her head. "Nothing but some old receipts, insurance papers and so on. Did I tell you that there wasn't a single income-tax return?"

"I guess you can't file a return if you're living under an alias." Allie fell silent then, thinking of all the different jobs her father had held. Each one probably paid in cash.

"I suppose not," Susan whispered. "It probably also explains why he refused to own a credit card and insisted on paying in cash for everything. When we bought the business together, I used his half for a cash deposit. He said he wanted the business to be in my name." Her sigh sounded sad and regretful.

Allie hugged her. "Susan, I wish he were here to explain everything. And why he did it."

"Me too." Susan pulled away, dabbing at her eyes with a tissue. "Anyway, what about this Kennedy? Have you checked to see if he really is a private investigator?"

"No, I never thought of it." Allie hesitated. She wasn't even certain she wanted to check. But Susan was looking at her, obviously expecting her to do so. "I have his business card," she said, and found it in her wallet.

"Is there an address on it?"

"No, just his name and two phone numbers. I'm not sure what state the area code represents. I guess it would be Michigan." Allie suddenly realized she didn't know very much at all about how Joel Kennedy came to be hired by Spiro Kostakis. She thought of all the questions she ought to have asked before agreeing to travel to Grosse Pointe with the man. *Too late now.*

"There's no point dialing the cell phone number, because I'll just reach him," Allie said. "I'll try the other number." After several rings, an automated voice informed her that the number was no longer in service. Allie hung up.

"What is it?" Susan asked.

"Out of service. Maybe this is an old business card."

"Maybe," Susan murmured. Her forehead was creased with worry. "I don't know about this." She thought for a moment. "What about calling Spiro Kostakis—your grandfather?"

Allie was alarmed at the idea. "I can't just call out of the blue. What would I say? This is the granddaughter you thought was dead for twenty-seven years?"

"It wouldn't be a shock. I'm sure he already knows you're coming. This Kennedy man would have called."

Allie rubbed her temples. Why were things getting so complicated? "Look, Susan, I'll be all right. I can't explain it, but I feel in my gut that Joel Kennedy isn't going to harm me. And I know he's a good driver because I've already been in a car with him." She forced a laugh, hoping to ease Susan's anxiety. Rob Newman had always posed a last question to Allie's dates just as they were walking out the door. *Are you a good driver?*

Susan's smile suggested she was willing to back off even if she wasn't happy about it. But the ride back into town gave Allie an opportunity to mull over some of their talk. She'd agreed to borrow Susan's cell phone and had assured her that she could still perform the basic karate moves she'd learned a few years ago. *Though if I really wanted to put him off, I'd just have to pucker up for a good kiss and he'd be gone in a flash.* Allie snorted.

"What?"

"Huh?"

"Is something funny?" Joel took his eyes off the road for a moment, holding Allie's gaze long enough for her to have second thoughts about his driving abilities.

"No no. Just thinking of something silly. Uh, something I read in one of my exam papers."

Something funny on a math exam? His eyes left the windshield again, back to her. He grinned. "What was it?"

Allie waved a hand. "Nothing really. Um, funny only to…"

"A mathematician?"

"Yeah," she mumbled, and turned her head to look out the passenger-side window.

Fortunately he didn't pursue the matter, but popped a CD into the player, instead. Allie leaned her head back, closed her eyes again and let the mellow cadences of a female jazz singer make the time pass just a little more quickly.

The deceleration of the car jolted her awake. Her eyes blinked open and for an instant she forgot where she was. Her neck swiveled along the edge of the headrest, first to the window, then to her left. Joel was peering through the windshield looking for a parking space in a service center, but cast a quick glance her way and smiled.

"Have a good sleep?"

"Mmm. Where are we?"

"About halfway there. I need to gas up the car and thought we'd get some lunch. I'm not sure what kind of eating places are ahead of us, but this was familiar."

Allie stared at the sign of a fast-food chain and sighed. *There goes half a day's training,* she thought.

However, the menu board inside indicated salads and vegetarian options, so she was able to order something that wouldn't cause too much damage.

"Training lunch?" Joel asked, digging into his man-size cheeseburger and fries.

"Sort of, but I'm not into fast food, anyway."

"Good for you. As for me, I eat whatever's handy when I'm hungry."

"Well, it doesn't seem to have done you any harm."

He swallowed a mouthful of Coke and said, "I noticed you had more than an edge on me the other day."

She frowned.

"The park?" he said. "The photograph?"

"Ohh. You weren't that far behind me."

His turn to smile. "You're being kind. By the way, you bring the photo?"

Allie toyed with her salad. "I forgot it."

"Seriously?"

She nodded.

He lowered the remains of his burger and stared at her for an uncomfortable moment. Then he said, "Shouldn't make a difference."

"Why the concern, then?"

"I just thought Spiro would be interested in seeing it.

Because he owns the identical one I showed you," he added.

Not quite identical, she mused, considering my mother was removed from my copy. Which was why Allie had purposely left it behind, even though he'd suggested bringing it. She didn't want Spiro Kostakis to see what her father had done.

"Speaking of my grandfather, you said you'd tell me more about him."

"I only know what I managed to pick up from some of my contacts in the business."

"The business?"

"Uh, the investigation business."

"Oh. Do you always investigate your clients?"

"I like to know something about them. You know, such as, am I going to get paid? Is the check going to bounce? That sort of thing."

"Does it happen often?"

"Often enough. Anyway, Spiro and his older brother, Niko, came to America from Greece in 1947, just after the war. They did the usual new immigrant thing at first, taking whatever jobs they could get. They saved some money and sent for their Greek fiancées to join them in Detroit. Eventually they got into the restaurant business, were very successful and opened another location. Niko took over the food part of the Kostakis empire after Spiro got into importing and exporting. By then, they'd both married and had children. Sometime in the late fifties, Spiro moved into his mansion in Grosse Pointe Farms."

"Grosse Pointe *Farms?*"

"Don't be fooled by the word *farms.* It's a very affluent area of Grosse Pointe. Anyway, a few years after that, Niko had a fatal heart attack, so his widow and son, Tony, moved in with Spiro and his wife."

"What about Niko's share of the business?"

"Good question. For some unknown reason, Spiro was Niko's beneficiary, with allowances going to his spouse and children."

"That's unusual. It must have caused some family friction."

He nodded. "The brothers probably did that as some kind of insurance when they got here. No other family and only each other to rely on."

"You'd think Niko would have changed his will after his son was born."

"I guess he never got around to it. Anyway, when Tony was in his late twenties, he married and had two boys—your cousins—George and Christo. By then, he was working his way up in the business."

"What happened to him?"

"Rumor has it he and Spiro had a major falling-out one night over money. Tony disappeared and was never seen again." Joel dabbed at his mouth with his napkin, checked the time and said, "I'll finish on the way. I promised Spiro we'd be there before dinner."

Allie followed him silently to the car. The story was unfolding like a soap opera, and she had a suspicion it was going to get even more incredible. At the same time, she was fascinated. Until she remembered that she herself was about to be drawn into it.

He remained silent for the first few miles. She decided to prompt him. "So, are you implying that Spiro had something to do with his nephew's disappearance?"

Joel turned his head slightly to look at her. "That's not what *I* was implying."

"Is seems pretty obvious, doesn't it?"

He turned back to the windshield. "Not necessarily. Apparently Tony had racked up a huge gambling debt. He also had more than a few unsavory friends. It may have been one big coincidence.''

"I don't know if I believe in coincidences."

"You gotta be kidding! After saving that old man and his dog? Wouldn't you call that a helluva big coincidence—that a topnotch athlete and a strong swimmer, the only person who could have saved their lives, happened to be around?''

"Well, yes, I suppose that was a stroke of good luck for poor Harry and Jeb.''

"Or a great coincidence.''

"You made your point,'' she murmured, and peered out the window.

"Speaking of the guy, have you seen him since?''

Allie smiled, thinking of the friendship that had grown between the three of them. "Yes, actually, I have. Harry and Jeb live in a retirement complex near the very river where they fell in. I had dinner with them twice last month. He's a darling and so is his dog.''

"I figured something like that.''

"What do you mean?''

"You don't seem the type to walk away from things. It makes sense that you'd go on to forge a friendship with the man whose life you'd saved.''

She was surprised at the pleasure his comment gave her. Then she realized he'd very skillfully digressed from his story about her grandfather and the rest of the family. "What happened after Tony disappeared?''

His head swerved her way for an instant. "Not much. His family moved in with Spiro's.''

"And Niko's widow?''

"She left Michigan after the family gave up looking for Tony and now lives in a retirement colony in Florida.''

Allie frowned. "And...do I still have a grandmother?''

"Sorry, I should've mentioned that. Vangelia outlived your mother by one year. A heart attack, I believe."

Allie thought for a long moment about people she'd never get to meet.

"So the family is pretty rich, huh?"

Joel snorted. "Rich! Baby, the guy's loaded. This Cadillac? The low end of his fleet. Like I said, don't be fooled by the word *farms* in Grosse Pointe Farms. The area used to have the summer retreats of the rich and famous. Now the places are permanent homes." He shook his head. "Old Spiro is worth millions."

"From the restaurant business?"

"Along with all the other companies he owns." Then he added, "Ironic, though, that in spite of all his money, the one thing he needs most of all can't be bought."

"What's that?"

His eyes met hers. "Your bone marrow," he whispered. "His only hope of life."

Allie turned away from his stare. She flashed back to that moment in the icy Catarqui when Harry Maguire's frantic clutching pushed her under. That was what she was feeling all over again.

THEY CROSSED the border in midafternoon, and as the car rolled over the Ambassador Bridge into Detroit, Allie murmured, "This is the first time I've been out of Canada."

"No kidding? You've led a sheltered life."

"Not really. I just haven't traveled much. Some people never even leave their hometowns."

"I guess so. It's just hard for me to imagine. Seems like I've been on the road my whole life."

"Really? Where have you been?"

"I left home when I was seventeen to join the marines."

"Seventeen!"

"Yeah, well, I left home out of self-preservation. My old man and I didn't exactly hit it off." He gave a harsh laugh.

Allie didn't know what to say, so she kept quiet.

"After the marine stint," he went on, "I worked my way through college. Majored in criminology and law."

"Did you go on to being a private investigator from there?"

"Huh? Oh, well, kinda. I decided to go into law enforcement and spent a couple of years with the Philadelphia Police Department."

"Why Philadelphia?"

"It's my hometown," he said. "My father had died and my mom needed looking after."

"Is she...?"

"Yeah, she had a stroke and died about two years later."

"Do you have brothers and sisters?"

"Yep, one of each. Both living in Philly, still in the same old neighborhood. A bit like the kind of people you were talking about. They're content to stay put with their families."

"Whereas you..."

"I cut my family ties when I was seventeen. Once you've done that, you're really only a visitor afterward."

The terse reply didn't encourage further conversation, so Allie sat silently, looking out the window as they headed east, away from the city and toward the suburbs. She didn't speak again until the car turned onto a paved road that ran along beside water.

"Oh!" she exclaimed. "Is that the Detroit River?"

"No. Lake St. Clair. Grosse Pointe borders the lake."

"So we're getting close?"

"Not far now. Nervous?"

"Of course. Shouldn't I be?"

"Perhaps."

Something in the way he said that single word alarmed her. There was warning in it, she thought. He'd turned his head her way, but his sunglasses foiled any attempt to read his expression. Too late to go back now, she thought. She decided to make light of it.

"When I was a kid and I was nervous about something—no matter what it was—my father used to say that I could always change my mind."

He nodded, his expression blank. "Good advice to remember," he said, and turned the car into a tree-lined drive fronted by brick columns supporting a massive wrought-iron gate. The gate was open and the Cadillac passed through.

Allie felt her heart rate pick up. All she could see so far was a stretch of trimmed lawn and groves of trees that stretched farther than the acreage around the farm back home. Rounding a bend in the drive, she suddenly saw the lake again. And then the house.

She must have gasped, for Joel simply said, "Tudor Revival, they call it. Built in the early thirties for some auto magnate. Six-car garage with Spiro's specialty cars over there, at the end of the west wing." His arm stretched across her face to point. "Tennis court just behind a guest house—you can see it now—and the outdoor swimming pool is next to it."

"You mean there's an indoor pool?"

"Yup. It's smaller and occupies most of a separate wing."

Huge landscaped gardens that Allie knew Susan would love edged the section of drive that wound its way to the entrance of the house. As the Cadillac coasted to a halt in front of granite steps, double French doors at the top terrace swung open and a handful of people spilled out.

They organized themselves on the steps as if choreographed. As Joel parked the car and switched off the engine, Allie moistened dry lips and glanced at him.

"All set?" he asked.

She nodded.

"You'll be fine. And remember, you're here to give them something. Not to justify whatever happened twenty-seven years ago."

She was grateful to him for that and, taking a deep breath, opened the car door. When she stepped out onto the paved drive, the group of people parted as if by silent command, giving way for a tall, thin, gray-haired man grasping a cane and walking slowly through them. Allie was thinking that particular moment was more frightening than diving into the Cataraqui after Harry Maguire. Still, pasting a smile on her face, she plunged forward.

The elderly man descended slowly to the first layer of steps. "*Koritsiemou,* Allie. My darling granddaughter."

Up close, she could see the ravages of his illness. His skin was waxen and taut against prominent facial bones, but his eyes were bright and alert, as yet undiminished by illness. His raspy greeting activated the others and they clustered around Allie. There was a hubbub of talk and some nervous laughter, mainly from Allie, she realized afterward.

Spiro introduced the others. First, Allie was presented to a slight woman in her fifties with a blend of black and silver hair, who was wearing a simple but expensive-looking black dress.

"Ephtimea—Effie—is the wife of my late nephew, Anthony, and the mother of my two great-nephews, George and Christo."

The woman stepped forward and shyly kissed Allie on both cheeks. "Welcome, my dear."

"That's George—" Spiro gestured to the man at Effie's left, "—my nephew, Effie's eldest son."

A large-framed man with the darkest eyes Allie had ever seen nodded, but didn't smile.

"And his fiancée, Lynn," Spiro continued.

The curvaceous blonde that Allie had caught a glimpse of as she'd walked up the steps strode into the center of the group and held out her hand. "Nice to meetcha," she said before backing up and taking a long draw on the cigarette she held in her other hand.

Allie saw Spiro frown, his upper lip curling in a grimace that everybody noticed except for Lynn, who was brushing something off the tight bosom of her lime-green sheath dress. Allie sneaked a peek at Spiro again. His downturned mouth tightened.

He turned to Allie and seemed to force a smile as he said, "Christo, Effie's youngest," and the shorter, hand-somer man standing off to one side leaped forward. His grin implied that he, too, had enjoyed the little scene. He grasped Allie firmly by both shoulders, planting a solid kiss first on one cheek, then on the other.

She wondered for a moment if he was going to release her, but eventually he stood back and said, "Wonderful to meet you at last, cuz. We've been breathless with excite-ment, haven't we, George?" He cocked his head to George who'd been staring intently at Lynn. Christo burst into laughter. "George! You poor lovesick puppy."

George smiled weakly at Allie, though he managed to give his brother a playful punch in the shoulder.

Spiro shook his head. "Boys, boys." He made a mock clucking sound but obviously enjoyed their antics. "Allie needs more time before she has to face the family in its true light," he said.

Christo laughed again. "Sure, Uncle Spiro, but I'm still waiting for that day myself."

Spiro wasn't amused this time. Allie noted the subtle way his chin pulled downward and his gray eyes flashed. Still, he made no response and turned, instead, to introduce the other three people waiting dutifully in the background.

"Yolanda, my nurse," Spiro said, gesturing to a stout woman in a lavender uniform. She beamed warmly at Allie, and Allie responded in kind. Then he gestured for a thin, gray-haired woman in black to move forward.

"This is Maria, who has managed my home for many years. The household can't function without her, and whatever you need or want while you are here, speak to Maria."

The older woman nodded solemnly, fixing her small, birdlike eyes on Allie, and extended a hand. *No kiss on both cheeks here.* She might have known my mother, Allie thought, unnerved by the woman's stare.

Spiro gestured last to a burly man in a navy-blue uniform standing on a lower step between the terrace and the drive. "Marko, my driver." The man merely tipped his head at Allie, not bothering to make eye contact.

"Shall we go inside?" Spiro asked, his voice sounding weary. "We'll have drinks on the back terrace in half an hour. Maria will show you to your room, Allie." He ushered Allie toward the door, his palm resting lightly at the small of her back. In the doorway, she suddenly wheeled around to see if Joel was coming, too.

He was still leaning against the side of the Cadillac, arms folded across his chest. She hadn't anticipated his parting, though realized his job for Spiro Kostakis was likely completed. Still, she couldn't simply wave goodbye without talking to him one last time, could she? She hesitated, aware that the others were waiting for her to enter.

Joel's voice rang out. "Mr. Kostakis, may I have a word with you before I leave?"

Spiro frowned. "Come to my study," he finally said, and with Yolanda's assistance, shuffled through the open door. The others filed inside, taking Allie with them. She cast another look at Joel before she was herded into the cool, dark interior of the Kostakis mansion.

LIKE BAIT TO SHARKS, Joel thought, watching Allie being swarmed by the Kostakis clan and urged inside. When she'd turned around from the threshold to look at him, something in her face caught at him, and that was when he knew his part in this family drama mustn't end. Impulsively he'd called out to Spiro. When he saw the relief wash across her face, he knew his instincts were right.

As everyone moved into the house, his brain went into overdrive, searching for some convincing reason to stay. Then he, too, headed up the granite staircase, ignoring a smirking Marko, and went inside. The foyer gleamed with polished hardwood, mahogany and oak trim and sparkling crystal. Joel had seen layouts of the house once in a trendy home-design magazine; the real thing was even more spectacular.

He'd been interviewed for the job by George at the Kostakis skyscraper in downtown Detroit, but had seen maps of the family compound. Hence his brief tour-guide recitation to Allie on the way in. Huge vases containing ornate flower arrangements were artfully placed throughout the foyer. A winding staircase swept up from the center of the hall, and Joel had a glimpse of a black skirt disappearing off the landing above. Maria, he wondered, or Effie?

There was no sign of Allie or any of the others. It was

as if the great house had just sucked them up. There sure were plenty of rooms to vanish into, Joel decided. Just then the quiet swish of rubber soles to his left drew his attention. Yolanda, Spiro's personal nurse, was walking toward him.

"Mr. Kostakis is waiting for you in his study," she said, her voice little more than a whisper.

"Where is that?"

She pointed to a doorway a few feet away. "He's very tired. Hasn't been sleeping too well because of the excitement and all. Please don't keep him. He's going to join the others for a drink and then have dinner alone in his suite."

"Thank you…uh…Miss…"

"Yolanda will do," she said, and her white teeth flashed the first real smile Joel had received from anyone attached to the estate.

Spiro was sipping something from a tall glass when Joel entered the study.

"One of Yolanda's concoctions," he explained. "Supposed to be a nutrition booster. Whatever it does, it tastes damn good." He smacked his lips and, with a hand that trembled slightly, set the empty glass on a coffee table.

Joel gave the room a quick glance, noting the same wood paneling as in the foyer and simple, but obviously expensive furnishings. Some paintings that looked familiar hung on the walls. Joel was itching to get a closer look, but the old man was watching him intently.

"You like art?" he asked.

"I do, though I don't know much about it. Are these reproductions?"

Spiro chuckled. "I hope not, considering what I paid for them. Now, Mr. Kennedy—"

"Joel."

Spiro gave a slight nod. "I suppose you want a check from me, but my nephew George takes care of the household accounts. Perhaps if you send your bill to our head office—"

"Mr. Kostakis," Joel interrupted, "I didn't want to speak to you about my fee. I've no doubt that will be fully paid in good time. It's about the job itself," he said, pausing and thinking rapidly.

"Go on."

He decided to target what he hoped were Spiro's protective instincts. "I have a few concerns about Miss Newman. Allie," he added after a slight hesitation, indicating to Spiro that a first-name basis had been struck with his granddaughter.

His ploy grabbed the old man's attention. "What concerns?"

"Well, we had a chance to get to know each other over the past few days."

"Four days," Spiro pointed out.

"Yes, but I can safely say that a kind of trust has grown between us."

"In four days?"

Joel refused to be sidetracked. "Allie is worried about the clinical procedure that may be ahead for her. She's also worried about her family back home."

"What family? You said her father was dead."

"Well, there's her stepmother."

"Stepmother!" His tone of voice virtually eliminated Susan's importance.

"Allie is very close to Susan."

Spiro waved a hand dismissively. "The woman isn't family. She isn't *blood*."

Joel flinched, but went on, "And what Allie has learned has naturally shocked her, forced her to basically reexamine her whole life. Not to mention her relationship with her father.''

Spiro made a low, snarling sound at the mention of Rob Newman, but said nothing.

''She's very fragile right now,'' Joel said, suppressing the image of Allie jogging half a block ahead of him. ''I think she'd assimilate better into her new family and feel more confident if a familiar face was around. Someone she can confide in, who of course would report any concerns to you.'' He stopped then, not wanting to overdo it.

The old man pursed his lips. ''You may have a point. I'm hoping that in time, my granddaughter will consider relocating here to be with her family. Her *real* family,'' he emphasized. ''And it has nothing to do with the transplant. That will work or it won't work. I want my daughter's child to take her rightful place in the home of her birth. I want *my* family to continue on through her. She's all I have now. So, all right. Stay another week to be a familiar face, as you say.''

Joel looked away, afraid Spiro would see the relief in his eyes.

''You can stay with Marko in the apartments above the garage. I'll find something for you to do. Make sure I get my money's worth,'' he muttered. ''I won't expect you to file an expense claim, since you'll be eating and sleeping here.''

''Of course not, sir. Thank you, you've made the right decision. Allie will appreciate it, believe me.''

Spiro rang the small silver bell on the table beside him. ''Fine. I'll expect you to keep an eye on her, too.''

''Sort of a bodyguard?''

He mulled that over. ''Sort of, but more casual. I want this to be just between the two of us. No need to offer explanations to my nephews as to why you're staying on. Am I clear?''

The request startled Joel. Something afoot in the Kostakis clan? he wondered. But it fit right in with own plans. He nodded and started to leave. Spiro's voice stopped him just as he reached the door.

''You'll be dining with the other staff in the main kitchen, or you can cook for yourself in the apartment.''

''Of course,'' Joel murmured deferentially, and turning his back on the man, allowed himself a grin.

CHAPTER FIVE

ALLIE KNEW that her chin dropped when she walked into the room, but didn't care how naive she must have looked. She'd never stayed in a five-star hotel, much less seen such a luxurious room in a private home. Maria proceeded ahead of her to fuss with draperies that hung perfectly, as far as Allie could see. Then the older woman turned around to point to a door in the corner of the room.

"En suite bathroom is through there. Extra towels on the shelves. Let me know if you need any special toiletries, otherwise the basic ones are in the cupboards."

"Thank you," Allie said. When Maria headed for the door, Allie stopped her. "Maria, were you here when my mother was a little girl?"

The woman answered, reluctantly, it seemed to Allie. "Yes, I was. I started here right out of high school. Seventeen years old. This was my first job. And the only one I was to ever have."

Not wanting to broach the subject of age directly, Allie asked, "Was my mother a baby then? Or older?"

Finally Maria produced a small smile. "Your mother was about two years old then. A beautiful little girl with platinum-blond hair, though it grew dark in time. To about your color."

"What was she like?"

Maria shrugged. "Like all pampered little girls, I suppose. Sweet, though. Until her teen years. Then she gave her parents a wild ride.''

The phrase took Allie aback. Not because she was shocked by the idea of her mother being a rebel, but by the bluntness of the comment. She'd have expected the housekeeper to be more discreet.

Not knowing how to follow up the remark, Allie simply said, ''Sometime I hope we can talk about her. There's such a…well, such a gap in my life.'' She walked to the window and gazed out across the green lawns rolling down to the lake. ''I know so little,'' she whispered.

There was a silence behind her until Maria said, her voice a bit softer, ''Maybe that's a good thing,'' and left the room.

Allie stood motionless for a moment, wondering what she was meant to infer from Maria's parting shot. Best not to let cryptic comments make her too paranoid, she thought. Especially so early in her stay.

She lifted her backpack and duffel bag from the floor onto the ottoman-style bench at the foot of the bed. Maria had mentioned on the way upstairs that drinks would be served on the rear terrace and that dress was casual. A simple skirt and blouse or a dress would be suitable, she'd added. Mr. Kostakis was old-fashioned and didn't like young women wearing jeans to family gatherings.

What about spandex? Allie had wanted to quip. Or sweatpants? She unzipped her khaki pants and pulled the T-shirt over her head on her way into the bathroom, glad she'd thought to bring both a skirt and a dress.

Twenty minutes later she had just descended the central staircase in search of the rear terrace when she bumped into Joel Kennedy. She was so pleased to see him she grabbed his forearm in greeting, causing him to stumble slightly.

"Oh, I'm glad you haven't left yet!" Allie cried. "I was afraid I wouldn't get a chance to...to..." She suddenly realized that she was clutching him as if she were the one being rescued from the Cataraqui River. "S-sorry," she stammered under his bemused grin. "I'm not usually so effusive, but really, I wanted to thank you for the drive and everything."

"Just doing my job," he said.

She felt even more ridiculous at that. Of course. Why had she assumed otherwise?

"Have you settled in?" he asked.

"I guess so. At any rate, I've unpacked." She gave a nervous laugh to hide the surge of homesickness that welled up at that very moment.

Joel placed a hand on top of hers, still clamped onto his other forearm. "It'll take a few days to get used to things. And you know Susan will manage okay. Have you called her yet?"

Allie shook her head, choked up by his unexpected show of sympathy.

"You should call her tonight. Maybe from your cell phone—for privacy," he rushed to say. "And I'll be sticking around for a few more days."

"You will? That's great." Allie knew she was in the running for Miss Inarticulate, but couldn't help herself. Was it the intensity of his rich brown eyes? Or maybe the increasing pressure of his hand on hers? The surprising reassurance of a warm touch?

"What will you be doing?" she managed to ask.

"Not sure yet. A bit of this and that."

"Is that normal for a private investigator?"

"It's kind of a special assignment," he said.

He held her eyes with his, his fingers now gently stroking the back of her hand. Allie was mesmerized. Until the clip-clop of heels on hardwood broke the spell. She jerked her hand from beneath his, returning it to her side just as Lynn rounded the corner.

"Oh, there you are! I went to your room to show you the way out to the terrace. Everyone's waiting." She gave Joel a slow once-over, then minced forward, waving her fingers at Allie. "This way," she said. "Bye, Mr. Kennedy."

He didn't acknowledge her farewell as her heels clicked away from him, keeping his gaze on Allie, instead, who remained where she was. After a moment he said, "Have a nice evening, Miss Newman," and started to leave.

"*Miss* Newman?"

He stopped midstride, giving a small shrug. "I'm staff now."

"And what were you a few minutes ago when you were holding my hand?"

His face darkened. "Thanks for the reminder," he muttered.

"That you don't mix business and pleasure?"

"Exactly." He turned and walked away.

Allie watched him go, her face hot with anger and embarrassment.

THE STRAIN OF THE DAY began to take its toll on Allie at dinner. The round of drinks beforehand was pleasant, though obviously centered around Spiro. Two uniformed female staff hovered, but didn't pour the drinks until his arrival. Yolanda assisted him through the double French doors leading to the outdoor terrace. It was a warm evening for the second week in May, but Spiro wore a cardigan over his white shirt and gray flannels. Allie thought he looked tired.

Once drinks were ordered, the others began to drift toward favorite chairs. Allie hesitated, until Spiro beckoned for her to sit at his side. One of the women pushed a wicker chair close to Spiro's for her, and as Allie sat, she caught an exchange of raised eyebrows between Effie and Christo. What was that about, she wondered. But her grandfather was talking and she quickly turned her attention to him.

His questions were polite but superficial—inquiries about her hometown of Kingston, her job at the university, even about Harry Maguire. The talk then switched to the history of the Kostakis house and its gardens. No mention was made of his illness or the possible bone marrow transplant. For that Allie was grateful.

When Maria came out to announce that dinner would be served in five minutes, Yolanda left her corner seat where she'd been reading a newspaper and stood waiting to help Spiro upstairs. Allie realized that, although her grandfather could navigate with a cane, he was unsteady on his feet, necessitating the assistance of another person for longer distances.

"I'll expect you in my study at ten tomorrow morning, my dear," he said as he was leaving. "And I hope one of your cousins will show you around the grounds after dinner."

All eyes turned to Allie, who nodded and looked away, self-conscious. By some unspoken agreement, Effie took over as host then, leading them to a dining room that was less formal than Allie expected, and sat at the head of the table. George sat at his mother's right and Lynn across from him. Christo pulled out a chair for Allie beside George's and took the one next to hers.

"Christo, you should be across from her, beside Lynn."

"Oh, Mother, let's dispense with the etiquette tonight, okay? Allie needs someone to talk to, and I know old

George there won't be any good to her. He's only got eyes for the luscious Lynn."

George reddened but said nothing.

"Then the table's out of balance," Effie said, displeased.

"Horrors!" mocked Christo. He rolled his eyes but took his place without further argument.

Allie sighed, thinking that the dining room may not be opulent, but the rules of etiquette were going to be strictly enforced. She poked at her salad, her appetite rapidly waning, and wondered how soon etiquette allowed one to leave the table.

"Don't worry," a voice at her left whispered. "Mother's showing off tonight for you. Tomorrow it'll be the usual 'wolf it down and leave as quickly as possible' routine. Even she does it." George smiled at Allie. "All this must seem very strange to you."

His comment was the second friendly one of the day, Allie noted. First place still went to Joel. She glanced around the table, looking at all the heads bent intently over their salads. If Joel was here…

"Yes, it is," she replied. "But this place is beautiful—"

"Not the house. I meant all of us—complete strangers who are suddenly supposed to be family."

"Exactly." She was beginning to feel herself thaw. "It's all so overwhelming."

"I bet. We can be overwhelming to regular folks, let alone to long-lost relatives."

"Oh, I wasn't referring to *you* when I said overwhelming. It's just that finding out you have an entirely different past than you thought—that's what's difficult to deal with."

"So you knew nothing about us until…"

"Joel told me."

"Joel?"

"The private investigator."

"Oh, right. Actually, I interviewed him for the job. On behalf of Uncle Spiro, of course. So he apparently located you in Kingston. Is that on Lake Ontario?"

"Yes. Have you been there?"

He shook his head. "No, but a friend of mine went to Queen's University and raved about Kingston."

"I teach at Queen's."

"Really? What subject?"

"Math," said Allie. "Mainly to undergrads."

"Hey, that's great. We can certainly use a math-oriented family member in our investment area."

"Oh, well…" Allie stammered. She hesitated to put a damper on the talk, which she'd been enjoying, but wanted to squelch any notion that she intended to stay.

"I'm getting ahead of the game, aren't I." He smiled again. "What I meant was, there'll obviously be a place for you here in the family business. If you want it."

"Why, thank you, George," she said, warming to him. Then she happened to glance toward the head of the table and noticed Effie staring at her. The expression on the older woman's face wasn't anywhere near as friendly as her son's.

Allie speared a piece of avocado and looked at Christo across from her. He'd been chatting to Lynn, but must have heard George's remark, as well. He returned Allie's smile, though with less enthusiasm than before.

One of the uniformed staff Allie had met earlier came in with the main course, and the bustle of plates put a halt to talk for a while, which Allie appreciated. She decided that it was her own paranoia that made her feel she was being sized up, and so she became determined to relax, rather than read innuendo into every facial expression. But when Lynn spoke, just as the staff left, Allie's resolve evaporated.

"So, didn't your father ever say anything to you about your mother or the rest of the family?"

All eyes shifted from dinner to Allie, who pasted on a smile and, in as brisk a voice as she could muster, said, "Obviously not." She kept her gaze on her plate as she began to cut her roast lamb. "Mmm," she murmured, forking a piece of meat into her mouth. "Delicious."

The others took their cue and began to eat. Allie silently congratulated herself for refusing to be drawn into a conversation she didn't want to have—not then, anyway—and enjoyed the rest of her meal.

When dessert was served, Allie declined. She'd already more than broken her training regimen by finishing two glasses of wine with dinner.

"Surely you're not watching your waistline," Effie admonished.

"In a way, though not for fashion," Allie explained. "I'm taking part in a triathlon at the end of June, and I'm supposed to be in training."

"An athlete," Christo drawled, "as well as a mathematician? Good heavens, how can the rest of us compete?"

Allie summoned a smile as insincere as his. "I'm sure where you're concerned, Christo, there's no competition at all."

His smile wavered, but only slightly. From Allie's left, George murmured, "Good one."

Effie looked uncertainly from one son to the other, while Lynn appeared to be busy with her dessert. The silence was soon broken by the arrival of coffee, which Effie suggested they take to the library. Allie followed them out of the dining room and across the foyer to a room lined with books. Large overstuffed leather armchairs and sofas were arranged in small conversation groupings.

George and Christo excused themselves to talk business in a corner trio of chairs and table. Effie picked up a piece of embroidery lying on a footstool next to a wing chair and began working on it, while Lynn sat on one of the sofas and flipped through a magazine. She glanced up when Allie sat next to her.

"I didn't mean to be rude, you know," Lynn said, "when I asked about your father. I was just curious. I mean, everyone's curious. Aren't they?"

Allie smiled at her innocent tone. "Probably. Anyway, I wasn't offended. And the answer is no, I didn't know anything." She looked across the room at the men, who were talking, and at Effie, whose head was bent over her needlework. Was it like this every night? she wondered. So quiet. So...*dull*. She couldn't imagine why Lynn and her cousins were hanging around, unless it was for her.

Lynn tossed the magazine aside and stifled a yawn. "Guess I should be going home. Work tomorrow!"

"Where do you work?" Allie asked.

"Why, for the Kostakis company. That's how I met George." She stood up, smoothed her form-fitting dress over her hips and said, "I'm in human resources." Then she cleared her throat, crooked a pinky at George and leaned over Effie to give her a quick peck on the cheek. "Night, Mrs. Kostakis."

Effie put the needlework down on her lap. "Good night, Lynn dear. Don't keep George up late. He has to work in the morning, too."

Lynn smirked. "Yeah, but he's the *boss*."

Christo laughed from across the room.

After the couple left, Effie rose and said good-night. "I

hope you sleep well tonight, Allie. You must be exhausted after such a long day. Christo, please escort Allie to her room when she's ready.''

Allie remained standing after Effie left, then turned to Christo. "I can find my way."

"Can I persuade you to stay for a nightcap? Brandy? A liqueur?"

"No thanks. I've had plenty to drink."

"Oh, yes. The triathlon. Is this your first?"

"No, I did one last year. It's a fund-raiser for the Heart and Stroke Foundation in Kingston."

"And your father…"

"Died of a heart attack."

"So it's not just a love of athletics that lures you to these events?"

She had to laugh. His nose was wrinkled as if he'd detected a bad odor. Whatever opinions her cousin had, at least he didn't bother concealing them.

Then, in a complete non sequitur, he said, "I hope dinner wasn't terribly boring. Normally we all do our own thing for dinner, except on Sundays when we please Uncle Spiro and dine together."

"And tonight?"

"We were all curious, believe me. No one needed an arm twisted to attend dinner tonight."

The frankness of his admission made her smile. "I hope I didn't let anyone down," she said.

"If you're fishing for a compliment, cuz, you can have it. We're all charmed, even though we obviously have failed to show it."

For some reason, that pleased her. But as Effie had said, the events of the day were now taking their toll. "I'm beat," she said. "And I'd like to get in a run before breakfast. Is there a special time?"

"Nope. The staff'll get whatever you want whenever you want. This place is better than a five-star resort, believe me."

"I do believe you. By the way, do you know how far it is from the house to the main gate?"

He thought for a second. "I'm not great at estimating distances, but I'd say a quarter of a mile."

"Great. Thanks." She headed for the doorway.

"I'll be happy to show you upstairs."

Allie waved a hand. "Don't be silly. I'm sure I can find the way myself. Good night."

"G'night, cuz."

Allie entered the hall, in shadows now that the sconce lighting had been extinguished. In spite of its shaky start, the evening hadn't been as bad as she'd feared. She walked a few feet before she realized she was heading in the wrong direction. If she continued the same way, she'd be back in the dining room. She stood, mentally retracing her movements from the bottom of the main staircase where she'd met Joel.

The house couldn't be *that* big, she reasoned. She took the opposite direction from the dining room, thinking if she found the sunroom and its entrance onto the rear terrace, she could easily backtrack to the staircase. Except that the hallway she took seemed to lead to a lot of closed doors, and when she opened one of them, she found herself staring at a huge laundry room. Two dryers were still running and someone had left the light on. She closed the door and reversed direction, back to the hall leading out of the library.

Maybe she'd better find Christo and get him to guide her back, after all. Retracing her steps to the library hall, she found it all in darkness. Christo had already gone upstairs.

If he hadn't passed her, Allie reasoned, then she must have gone in the completely wrong direction. Logic de-

manded that she head for the dining room, after all. She
shuffled along the hallway, unable to find a switch. Didn't
these people believe in night-lights? How did the staff get
about? *With flashlights or candles?* She stifled a nervous
giggle and, feeling her way with one arm extended, headed
into the blackness.

She'd only gone a few steps when she thought she heard
a rustling noise. She stopped, waiting for it to sound again
so she could pinpoint the direction, not wanting to bump
into someone. No sound came. Allie continued walking,
deciding to knock on any closed doors she came upon.
There. That noise again. She paused. Silence. Then she
went on, waiting for it to start up again. And it did. She
froze. Then all was quiet again. This pattern was beginning
to get to her.

She forced her feet to move a little faster, in spite of
her inability to guide them effectively. The noise picked
up speed, too, eliminating any possibility of a household
cat. Allie's eyes strained against the dark, detecting a glimmer ahead. It was more of a suggestion of light, rather
than the real thing. She rushed toward it, relieved that as
she got closer, the hint of light materialized, throwing pale
shadows onto the walls and highlighting shapes of objects
along the way.

The hallway ended abruptly in a ghostly neon glow emanating from beneath a closed door. Allie hesitated, her
determination to knock for assistance suddenly faltering.
How ridiculous would she look? she wondered. *Help, I
can't find the way to my bedroom!* She started to leave.
Whatever was behind that door, it wasn't the central
staircase. She turned on her heel and collided with a
warm body.

SURPRISE HAD RENDERED her speechless. Or so Joel
thought, until she began to sputter as if she'd fallen into

one of the pools and was coming up for air. And when the various synapses finally started to work again, all she could spew out was an accusation.

"You've been following me!"

"Well, no," he began, "not really. I was just going in there to take a case of Perrier water to the kitchen. I didn't even see you until I rounded the corner."

"What corner? I didn't see any corner!" Her eyes darted left and right.

"Behind you, just to the right of the door." He pointed.

She followed his index finger, noticing then the alcove and the corridor extending from it. "Where are we?" she asked.

He picked up the wobble in her voice and didn't tease her anymore. "In the east wing of the house on the ground floor. That door leads to a pantry and storage area. The corridor there—" he tipped his chin in the direction she'd been looking "—ends up in the garage. I'm staying in the apartments above."

"How do you know your way around so well? Isn't this your first time here?"

Joel paused. She was just a bit too quick. "I've seen a map of the place."

"A map? You mean *you* got a map? *I* didn't."

He smiled at the woeful complaint, but how to get out of the slip? "I told you—I read an article about the place."

Her expression was skeptical, though she seemed to accept the answer.

"Can I escort you to your room?"

"Please," she whispered.

He wanted to wrap his arms around her at that moment. The self-assured woman he'd witnessed over the past few days seemed to have vanished, leaving behind a waif. The fatigue circles under her eyes darkened in the light spilling out from under the door.

Joel put a hand to the small of her back and guided her along the hallway she'd come from. Her skin seemed to pulse under the silky fabric of her blouse, electrifying his hand.

"It's such a big place," she was saying, though all he could think about was the warm hollow beneath his palm. "I thought I'd get back with no problem at all. I even turned down Christo's offer to show me the way."

"*Christo?*" That grabbed his attention. Joel forced himself to sound noncommittal. "Oh, yeah? Well, the house is an odd design. Get someone to show you around in daylight, and it'll be a lot easier the next time."

"How come the house is so quiet? It can't be more than ten."

"Maybe because of Spiro's illness. The boys probably go elsewhere for action, and that leaves only Effie, who seems to be a pretty solitary type."

"Well, I have to say it's slower than Kingston on a Wednesday night in the winter."

He chuckled. She seemed able to bounce back from any situation, which was a good thing. When they arrived at the library, Joel explained the route back to the foyer and the main staircase. "I should leave you here, I suppose," he said in a loud whisper.

"You mean you're not going to escort me to my door?" she asked, grinning up at him.

And of course he did, because he wanted to extend his time with her by even a few minutes. Heaven only knew why. They'd both still be here in the morning. It was just something in the air. The delicate fragrance that wafted from her as she moved. The swish of her skirt and her impossibly filmy top. The whole outfit looked as though it had been made from cobwebs or parachute silk. A strong gust of wind and... He thrust his mind away from thoughts of the clothes blowing off that lithe body.

"Yes," he murmured, and reached down to take her hand in his. As they ascended the wide circular staircase, she stumbled once against him. Instinctively he brought his free arm up to steady her, inadvertently brushing her breast as he did.

"Sorry," he said, and abruptly pulled his hand from hers, pretending to search for the light switch at the top of the stairs. But what he really wanted to hide was the sudden and unexpected trembling in his hands. The overpowering desire to bring his fingers up through her hair, which swung loose on her shoulders. And after that, slide them down the length of her back, through the flimsy fabric of her blouse....

"Mine is the third door on the left," she whispered, and moved ahead of him. Her door was already open when he reached it, just behind her. She'd found the switch inside, and in the rosy glow from a bedside lamp, he could see a slice of four-poster, quilt-covered bed, pillows plumped invitingly against a dark wooden headboard.

Just what I need, he thought. *A solid visual to remember when I'm trying to get to sleep on my own narrow cot above the garage.*

"Thank you for showing me the way. Otherwise I might have ended up sleeping in the garage, instead of here."

She meant it as a joke, of course, but the fact that he himself was sleeping there hit both of them at the same time.

"I mean, I...uh...you know..."

Joel smiled. He touched a fingertip to her chin and, tilting her head forward, kissed her on the forehead.

"I do know," he murmured. "G'night, Miss Newman," and walked away as quickly as he could.

ALLIE'S ARM snaked out of the bedcovers to fumble for her watch and the source of the beeping. She dragged the watch over and blearily tried to read its face. The time was right on—seven o'clock. No more lying in bed. She scissored her legs out and over the edge and paused there, letting her blood circulate.

Sunlight streamed through the sheer draperies, dappling the pale-lavender walls with pink and indigo blotches. The room was crisp, all set for a photo shoot. Allie was reluctant to leave it for the uncertainty of the day ahead. Passing the full-length mirror next to the chest of drawers, she stopped to take a long look.

A restless sleep had spun fine rattails of hair all over her head. The pale-blue circles under her eyes—always a giveaway to her father and Susan when she'd been out too late—would fade by noon. Reaching up, she grabbed her nightie T-shirt by the ribbed neckline and pulled it up and over her head.

Friends had always complimented her on her trim figure. Medium-size breasts, flat stomach and toned, shapely legs. Nothing to complain about there, she decided, studying herself with an objective eye. Yet it was, in the end, just a body. Fit and healthy, for which she thanked her genes and her training regimen. But shouldn't a thirty-year-old be glowing? Shouldn't that skin have the sheen of a much-polished, much-loved piece of wood?

She stepped right up to the mirror, eyes drawn to an invisible place in the center of her forehead. But not invisible to her, for she could still feel the warm pressure of his lips there. An ever-so-faint tingle. Allie wished her whole body was sparkling just like that tiny spot. She took a deep breath and headed for her bathroom.

Five minutes later she was out the front door and warming up on the granite terrace. Maria had encountered her on the stairs and reminded her that she could have breakfast at any time, but that Mr. Kostakis was expecting her promptly at ten. Her cousins had already driven into Detroit for the working day, and Mrs. Kostakis only came down at lunch.

The estate was quiet except for the distant buzz of a lawn mower. An automatic sprinkler system spurted on and off as she loped along the gravel shoulder of the drive, passing a parked limousine and the same Cadillac she and Joel had driven in from Kingston. She turned her head sharply to the left and right, but didn't see him. Her feet crunched on the gravel edging until she cut behind the limo onto the asphalt.

As she picked up speed, her body took charge, finding its rhythm while her mind let go. Except for competitions, when every cell had to be on full alert, Allie considered running a form of meditation. The air by the lake was clean and fresh, much like the air along the waterfront in Kingston. She wished she could jog along the lake itself and decided to ask if there was such a trail in the area. Even if she had to cycle or drive there, it would beat running up and down a paved driveway every day. Cycle. She wished she'd brought her bike now, although when she was packing, she really wasn't anticipating a stay longer than a week, in spite of what Joel had said.

Joel. There you go again. He was a funny guy, really, seeming to shift from being kind and thoughtful to distant and aloof. He was undeniably handsome, yet his features alone wouldn't be templates in a plastic surgeon's office.

And that great smile. It only seemed to appear when he forgot himself, Allie thought. And why was that?

A rabbit dashed across the pavement in front of her, and Allie swerved, but didn't lose pace. The drive curved sharply ahead and just as she reached the elbow of the curve, a car roared from the opposite direction, surging out of the bend. It had taken the curve too fast and, confronting Allie, braked hard. Allie leaped onto the shoulder.

The car's rear end fishtailed, spraying gravel. Clumps of it struck Allie, and she raised her hands to protect her face. The impulse prevented her from noticing a dip in the drive's shoulder, and she set her right foot down awkwardly, causing her to fall backward. The car barely slowed as it regained the paved section of the drive and continued to race toward the house. Allie lay sprawled on the gravel for a long moment, then managed to sit up, gingerly feeling her leg and right foot.

The sound of another car rounding the curve was enough to send her scrambling farther into the trees. The car took the bend at a normal speed, however, slowing down as Allie came into view and braking with a squeal yards away. Allie looked up, but the sun was in her face.

Feet dashed across the asphalt and gravel. Allie heard labored breathing and then a large shadow fell over her and she found herself squinting into Joel Kennedy's pale face.

"Are you all right? What happened?" He knelt at her side.

"I'm fine. The other car didn't hit me. I tripped and fell." Her voice rose a bit. "But that wouldn't have happened if that idiot hadn't been going so fast."

"Who was the jerk, anyway? Did you get a look?"

"No. I don't even know what kind of car it was. Something fast and sporty, I think. And red. Can you help me up?''

He rose and placed his hands under her armpits. She carefully set her right foot down, easing onto it slowly. No pain. She gave a sigh of relief. The triathlon was still on.

"Maybe you should get a lift back with me, just in case," he suggested.

She decided to take the offer. Not because she'd hurt herself, but because the incident had shaken her, especially once she considered what might have happened had she been running in the center of the drive.

Joel wrapped an arm around her waist as they headed to the car, a dark blue station wagon, an older model.

"Is this yours?" she asked.

"Yeah," he said.

"Are you sure?" she teased.

"Of course. Why wouldn't I be?"

"You seemed to hesitate." Then she said, "I'm only kidding, Joel. Don't look so serious."

He stopped walking, grasped her shoulders and turned her slowly to face him. "You could have been hurt back there. I *am* serious, Allie. And I'm bloody mad at the fool who was driving that car. I intend to find out who it was right away."

"It's okay," she murmured, wanting to ease his anger.

"No, it isn't okay." His voice rose. "It's..." He stopped to brush a strand of hair away from her forehead.

The little spot on Allie's forehead started to tingle again, but this time Joel bypassed it completely. He lowered his head as he tilted hers back and placed his mouth gently, but solidly, on hers.

CHAPTER SIX

IT WAS THE PERFECT CURE, Allie decided, for a near miss. But his lips—*great* lips—were no sooner clamped on hers, his tongue running swiftly across their surface, than he broke off.

Contact lost, she wanted to quip, but his knotted eyebrows and flushed face ruled banter out at that particular moment. He took a big step backward as if afraid she might lunge at him.

"I'm sorry," he said. "I shouldn't have done that. It was out of order and it won't happen again."

She almost expected him to swipe at his mouth, ridding himself of all trace of her. His high-handed tone offended her. Was he implying he had to be in control because *she* couldn't be? That one kiss from him and it would be game over for her? Just like that?

"Maybe I should walk back."

Joel ran his fingers through his hair. "This isn't going the way I wanted it to."

"Obviously not. Maybe you ought to have tried last night in the dark."

"Tried what?"

Allie sighed and waved a hand. "Forget it."

"Please, Allie, get in the car. Let me drive you."

And because she was tired of quibbling, she did. Gum wrappers and empty Coke cans littered the floor. Her left foot slid out from under her on one of the pop cans and she plunked herself unceremoniously on the seat. As he climbed in the driver side, she asked, "Does this car double as a garbage can?"

He ignored her at first, turning on the ignition. "Sorry for the mess. I spend a lot of time in it, as you can see."

She looked around, not bothering to hide her disgust. "Like when you're on a stakeout, you mean?"

The car rolled forward, taking the drive at a snail's pace, but he kept his eyes on the windshield as if he was tackling Detroit rush hour.

Finally he said, "Stakeout? You know the P.I. lingo, I see."

"I've read a few detective novels in my life," she muttered.

She found his grin somewhat patronizing. The house was in sight now. Allie scanned the area in front of the garage to the left of the house, but saw no red sports car. Indignation about the incident rose in her again, although she had to admit that if the kiss hadn't been so abruptly terminated, she might have almost forgotten about the car. At least for the rest of the day. But humiliation was all she was left with after both her morning run and her morning kiss. She sighed.

"Sure you're okay?"

"I've suffered worse spills than that one, believe me."

"It's not the spill I'm worried about."

"What then? The *kiss?*"

The car came to a halt behind the limo. Joel turned his head toward her, an expression of incredulity on his face. "I'm not worried about the kiss," he said.

Allie reached for the door handle and pulled down. The door creaked open. She nudged it with her foot and, as she got out, craned her head around to say, "Maybe you ought to be. Worried, I mean."

He looked puzzled.

"About the kiss," she prompted. "'Cause I've had much better." She jumped out onto the drive, slamming the door behind her to preempt any comeback he might have made. She entered the house, priding herself on not looking back, and met Maria on the staircase. The housekeeper was coming down with a bundle of sheets in her arms.

"Ready for breakfast, Miss Newman?"

"Just about. In the dining room?"

"If you like." The housekeeper smiled. "But the others tend to eat in the sunroom or the kitchen itself. Less formal."

"The kitchen's okay by me," Allie said. "I just have to shower and change."

"Twenty minutes, then?"

"Yes, that'll be great. And, Maria?"

The older woman turned.

"Please call me Allie."

That drew a faint smile. "Of course," and she continued on her way.

The kitchen was a good choice, as Allie soon discovered. It was a big sunny room with original brick exposed on two walls. Lots of spanking-new stainless-steel appliances adorned the room, all looking so identical Allie couldn't tell which one was which and mistakenly tried to get orange juice from the built-in convection oven. The cook, Liz, and her helper-cum-maid, Ruth, giggled as they watched. They also insisted on making her a full breakfast, in spite of her protestations that she normally had only a bowl of granola.

When she finished, Allie realized it was time to meet her grandfather in his study. Ruth showed her the way, and as she walked through the quiet halls, Allie couldn't help but think the house was more like an institution than a home. She didn't encounter a single person en route, although she had the impression that a bustle of activity was taking place behind several closed doors. The one person she was afraid of meeting was Joel, and there was no sign of him at all.

She was still smarting from the embarrassment of that damned kiss. Did he think she was such a pathetic, lonely person that she needed some bolstering? Or that she hadn't been kissed lately and might have forgotten what it was like? True though that may be, she admitted grudgingly, he had no business assuming she wanted to be kissed by him or that she'd even like it. Which—humiliatingly enough—she had.

Yolanda opened the study door at her tap, greeting Allie with a warm smile that helped ease some of her nervousness about the meeting with her grandfather.

"Here she is, Mr. Spiro," the nurse's rich voice boomed. She winked at Allie and said, "He was fretting a bit, but I told him you'd be here on the dot of ten. And so you are. See, Mr. Spiro? All that fuss over nothing. Where do you think she'd have gone? Nothin' much to do round this place any time. Or have you already found that out, Miss Allie?"

Nonplussed, Allie stammered, "I...uh, I've only been here since yesterday, so I'm afraid..."

Yolanda patted her on the arm on her way out the door. "Don't mind me, honey. I'm just a tease and a meddler, as your grandfather likes to tell me." Before she left, she said to Spiro, "Don't forget you have an appointment after lunch in the city, so we'll have to do your blood work a bit earlier today."

Spiro scowled from the chair behind the desk, but Allie realized there wasn't much heat behind the look. Chuck-

ling, Yolanda swished through the door, closing it behind
her. There was a brief, uncomfortable silence that Allie
tried nervously to fill.

"Your home is beautiful and so is my room."

He continued to stare at her for a few seconds longer,
then said, "You're the spitting image of your mother. Got
any of your father in you?"

Allie felt a quick flare of anger. "I imagine so, given
the laws of nature."

He emitted an impatient harrumph. "Your daddy broke
all the laws of nature when he abandoned your mother,
betrayed me and stole you away from your family."

"If you asked me to come here so you could bash my
father, you may as well save your breath. I'm sure you
need every bit of it, anyway." She started for the door.

"Where're you going?"

"To my room to pack."

His sunken eyes almost jumped out of his head. "You
just got here! What about the blood test? It's all set up for
Monday. Or is that how you're going to get what you want
from me? By holding that over my head?"

"I'm not holding anything over your head and there's
nothing you have that I want."

Incredulity sputtered from him. "Come *on.* You want
my money, just like everyone else. Join the line."

Allie shook her head. She didn't know whether to laugh
or be really ticked off. "I assure you that I neither want
nor need your money. Until a few days ago, I wasn't aware
that you existed, let alone had any money that I might lay
claim to. As for the blood test, I agreed to go through with
it and I'll stay until the results are in. But if you think I'm
going to allow you to bad-mouth my father, think again,
Mr. Kostakis."

There was a long, strained silence. His eyes never left

her face. At length, he said, his voice less strident now, "I can see your father in you. No—" he raised a palm to fend off a retort "—I'm not going to bad-mouth him, as you put it. You've got your father's spunk and maybe his Irish temper, too." Spiro opened a drawer behind the desk. "Here, take a look at this. There was a time when I loved your father."

The hand holding out a framed photograph was shaking. Allie walked over and took it from him. It was a wedding photo of her parents. She'd never seen one of her father when he was that young. The mustache and dark-brown hair that was thicker than she could remember were a surprise. He wore pinstripe tails and was more formally dressed than she'd ever seen him in her life.

Her mother was breathtaking in a Shakespearean-style wedding gown with a high bodice. A tiny beaded cap was perched at the back of her head, and her hair was long and flowing. Princess hair, Allie thought. Standing behind the groom, one hand on his shoulder, was a beaming Spiro. Also younger, he looked robust and healthy, his black hair and mustache as thick as her father's.

"She was beautiful."

"From the beginning, even as a baby. People would hold her and almost be in awe. Of course, what we forgot was that she was also an ordinary little girl."

Allie sat down in a chair on the other side of the desk and continued to study the picture.

"Haven't you seen one like it before?"

"I haven't seen any wedding photographs of my parents." She paused, adding in a softer voice, "Until the other day, I'd never seen a picture of my mother."

Spiro shook his head sadly. "If only we had known then…" He stopped, apparently overcome by the past.

"About her drinking problem?" Allie had to say it, had to get everything out in the open.

His nostrils flared. "Who told you there was a drinking problem?"

"Joel Kennedy."

"How would he know *that?*"

Afraid she might be breaking a confidence, Allie hesitated. Too late now, she told herself. "Apparently he did some research into the family background after he was hired."

Spiro sat still for a long time, his hands steepled over the bridge of his nose. When he spoke, his voice was husky. "He had no right to do that. But I suppose eventually you'll learn all about us—your family." He inhaled raggedly. "My wife, Vangelia, and I couldn't have any other children after Katrina. So our daughter became our little princess. We denied her nothing."

He fell silent for a moment before continuing, "When she was in high school, in her sophomore year, she was arrested for driving under the influence of alcohol. She claimed it was a first time and that some friends had pressured her into drinking. In our desire to believe, we accepted her story. Over the years, however, it became clear that she had a problem. She dropped out of college after she met your father and tried to get sober. We sent her to the best rehabilitation centers available. And she was sober for a long time." He paused again, inhaling deeply. "Your grandmother and I were overjoyed to see the change in her. She was madly in love with Eddie. After they got married, she continued with some college courses, but then she got pregnant."

Spiro looked across at Allie, his eyes haunted. "You must understand that everyone was ecstatic. A new life, new hope for Katrina and all of us. The problem was, it was too soon. She hadn't found anything to replace what alcohol had given her. At least, that's what the specialists said. And we went to them all."

"My father was working for you at the time?"

A raised eyebrow. "Yes, I suppose Kennedy told you that, too. Eddie was my right-hand man. I trusted him implicitly. As much as I'd trusted my brother, Niko."

"But?"

His face told it all. The anger, the sense of betrayal. Allie's mouth went dry. Bad enough that the mother she never knew had been an alcoholic. She didn't want her memory of her father tarnished, too.

Spiro must have sensed that he'd revealed more than she wanted to know. He seemed to sag into himself, as if giving up the fight. "What's done is done," he said. "Let's return to the present, a far more important time for me." A weary smile. "Indulge an old man and allow me to show you off, my dear. Tomorrow we go to church for a special mass that I've arranged, and I want you to meet some dear friends of mine."

Allie sighed. That just about wrapped up the weekend. "And the blood test?"

"Monday morning at a private clinic near here."

"How long before..."

"The results? A couple of days, maybe less."

"That seems fast."

"Money can't buy me good health, unfortunately, but it can get me the best health care. Now, my dear, if you'll get Yolanda for me, I must rest before my appointment this afternoon."

Allie wanted to say something more, to proclaim her happy childhood in defense of her father, but she saw that Spiro was exhausted. What was the point, anyway? No amount of justification could change the past.

She was at the door, her hand on its carved wooden knob, when he said, "I want to forgive your father, my dear, even now. But he betrayed my trust. He ran out on his wife—my only child—and he took the one thing that might have meant salvation for her. *You.* I can't forgive that."

Allie's eyes stung with tears. She grasped the doorknob and pushed, brushing past Yolanda as she rose from the chair she'd been sitting in outside the study. She scarcely registered Yolanda's "All finished then, Miss Allie?" and charged blindly along the hallway.

She was heading for the safety of her room, but was diverted by the sudden appearance of Maria, coming from the solarium. Allie made a quick left, ending up in the same wing of the house where she'd bumped into Joel last night. The laundry room was straight ahead, she recalled, and would be a good place to compose herself before returning to the main area of the house.

She opened the door and stuck her head inside. A waft of humid, steamy air greeted her, but all the machines were still and the room was empty. At the sound of loud, angry voices nearby, she paused, waiting to see if the people were heading her way, but let the laundry door swing shut when she recognized one of the raised voices as Joel's. Curious, she followed the arguing around the corner to the door that Joel had indicated led to the garage. It was ajar, and when she heard her own name, she moved closer to the gap.

"Allie was on the road! How could you not have seen her, you bloody fool?"

The driver of the mystery car?

"I didn't know it was her! She was right on the curve as I was going into it. The trees hid her."

"You were going too fast! And you were in the middle of the road, for God's sake."

The anger in Joel's voice dropped to disgust. Allie craned her neck, peering around the edge of the door to catch a glimpse of Joel's back. At least, she figured it was Joel. His shirt looked familiar.

She couldn't see the other man at all. But what she could see was the fender and hood of a bright-red car. The same car that had nearly run her down that morning.

"What's the big deal, anyway? Nothing happened! Jeez, what're you so uptight about?"

"Because the whole thing could've ended right there, fella. Our reason for being here. Give that five minutes of thought, will ya?"

Allie frowned, trying to make sense of Joel's last comment, when he abruptly wheeled around to leave. She let the door ease back into place and scurried to the nearest hiding place. The laundry room.

She made it just as she heard the garage door slam shut. Then she heard the sound of footsteps on the tiled hall floor, heading her way. Now that she was here, Allie wondered why she hadn't simply walked back to the main wing. How could she explain being in the laundry room? The question occurred to her at the precise instant the door opened and Joel marched into the room.

"What the hell are *you* doing here?"

"I…I thought I'd do some laundry."

"Oh, yeah?"

"Is that so hard to imagine?" she countered.

"Not at all, except that we just got here yesterday. Have you run out of clothes already?"

What was that to him? she wondered, buying into her own fake excuse. "I suppose I could ask the same of you. I doubt you were hired to do laundry."

"Nope," he said curtly, walking over to one of the dryers and popping open the door. "But there *is* a load of rags to pick up for Marko. The chauffeur?" he prompted.

Was Marko the man he'd been arguing with? Allie wanted to find out what he'd meant by the last remark she'd heard, but hated to admit she'd been eavesdropping. She started to leave.

"So where's your laundry?" he asked, pulling out a heap of multicolored rags from the dryer.

"Oh, I haven't brought it down yet. I, uh…just wanted to check things out first."

He stared at her. Allie squirmed with discomfort, knowing that he knew she was lying. Clutching the mass of rags in his arms, he set them down on top of one of the washing machines and took two steps toward her. He was so close to her she could feel the heat from the dryer still emanating from him.

"Was there something *else* you came down here to check out?"

"No," she murmured, turning her head slightly away. "I guess I'd better get back. It must be time for lunch." She took a step away, but he reached out to grab her wrist.

"Are you okay?" His voice was softer now.

"Of course." Her answer was a bit more strident than she'd intended. She returned his stare. "If you don't mind…"

He released her. "You look like you've been crying," he said. "Your eyes are red."

"The heat."

He pursed his lips, thinking. "I found out whose car almost ran you down this morning."

Allie stiffened. Was this some kind of test? Did he suspect she'd been eavesdropping? "Oh?" She made herself sound indifferent.

"The car belongs to Christo."

But the other man's voice hadn't sounded like Christo's. She waited for Joel to clarify his statement, but he didn't add anything more. Just stared.

Unsure of herself and of him, Allie decided her best option was to leave as soon as possible. He was keeping something from her. What and why she'd eventually discover. For now, she wanted only to escape the stifling humidity of the room and Joel Kennedy's unrelenting gaze. She headed for the door, and this time, he didn't stop her.

JOEL WATCHED the door close behind her. Her face had been a dead giveaway. She'd seen or heard something, but what exactly he couldn't say. Still, he knew she hadn't been in the laundry room the whole time. And what the hell was she doing down here, anyway?

He was ticked off, but more at himself than her. He had a feeling he should've acted as if nothing had happened. As if he believed her story about laundry. Maybe then she'd have come right out and confronted him about whatever she might have heard. But then, maybe she hadn't really heard anything at all.

Nah, she heard something. He rubbed his face, his mind racing about what to do. He slapped a palm against the top of the washing machine. Damn Pat for being such a hothead. He could blow the whole operation if he wasn't reined in.

Joel took in a calming breath. Maybe he should let things hang for a while. Let Allie mull over what she might've heard and wait until she came to him about it. He knew she would. As he'd told her, she wasn't the type to walk away from something. He picked up the basket of rags and headed for the door, resolved to come up with a plausible version of whatever part she'd heard when the moment arrived. It was only a matter of time. Then he swore again, realizing that time wasn't exactly on his side.

ALLIE SPENT part of the afternoon prowling about the vast estate. She had a solitary lunch, taken in the solarium at Maria's suggestion. Midway through the afternoon, Allie decided she'd never last two weeks. She wandered the grounds, admiring the many varied flower beds. If Susan had been there, she'd have identified the perennials by their Latin names.

Allie watched the two gardeners digging a new bed adjacent to the outdoor pool and asked the younger one what they planned to plant there. He hesitated, then looked at the older man, whose weather-beaten face and rough hands indicated a lifetime of digging.

"Sam? What's going in here? I forget."

The old man raised his head, an expression of frustration in his face. "Succulents, mainly, and hostas over there in the shade."

The younger man turned back to Allie and grinned. "My first season on the job," he explained.

He wiped his forehead with the bandanna sticking out of his shorts pocket. He had short, curly, blond hair, and his glistening bare chest suggested regular workouts at the gym. "How do you like this place? Pretty impressive, isn't it?"

"Yes, though there's not a lot for me to do." Allie frowned. There was something familiar about him. He was watching her so intently she felt uncomfortable. She glanced across the lawn at the empty swimming pool. "I guess it's too early for a swim."

"In this part of the country, for sure. But there's an indoor pool."

"Right. I forgot. Thanks for the reminder."

She started to move away, but halted as he added, "The sliding glass doors leading to the pool are at the west end of the terrace. I think you get to it inside from a set of stairs near the kitchen. There's a Ping-Pong table and another billiards table down there, as well. And a state-of-the-art sound system."

"For someone new to the place, you seem to know a lot."

"I'm observant," he said.

"You gonna yak all day?" Sam asked, looking up at them. He was still on his knees, spading small plants into the soil.

"Better get back to the job," the younger man said.

"Thanks a lot…uh, sorry, I don't know your name. I'm Allie," she said, sticking out her right hand.

"Hi, nice to meet you. Though I already knew your name from the staff. I'm Patrick—or Pat, as everyone calls me."

Allie waved and headed purposefully toward the house. Pat the gardener, she realized now, sounded like the man Joel had argued with in the garage. She took the solarium entrance into the house, wanting to avoid the garage wing and Joel Kennedy, and was bounding up the main staircase when she encountered Effie, descending.

"I was just coming to look for you," Effie said. "I've got some photo albums I think you'll be interested in. Come, we'll go to the library. It'll be cooler there."

Allie meekly followed the older woman. Once in the library, she wished she'd thought up an excuse to avoid the picture-album presentation. The events of the day so far had drained her of the desire to discover any more facts about her family. She'd heard enough already.

But Effie was intent on giving Allie a visual history and began with photos of Spiro and his brother, Niko, when they were new immigrants to America. Allie found the pictures interesting, but she felt no emotional tug. She might as well have been examining old photographs of strangers for all these people meant to her. Her curiosity was finally aroused when Effie opened her own wedding album.

"There's your mother," Effie said. "She was my maid of honor. Wasn't she beautiful?"

Allie stared at the group portrait, identifying her mother even before Effie pointed to her. The lump in her throat stopped her from answering. Forever young, she was thinking. Then she spotted her father, standing at the end of the line of groom's attendants.

Tall and lanky, he hadn't yet assumed the bearlike shape that middle age would bring. He had a lot more hair, too, like in his own wedding picture, which Allie had seen that morning. Allie smiled. Rob Newman had always been anxious about his receding hairline, conferring frequently with Susan or Allie on ways to conceal it.

"I had my dress made in New York," Effie was saying. "It was an Oscar de la Renta."

Allie focused on the bridal couple. Effie had made a lovely bride in her designer gown, but anyone could see that the star of the wedding party had been Katrina Kostakis. "It's gorgeous," she said, knowing the older woman was waiting for a comment. "Do you still have it?"

Effie glanced up, her eyes shining. "Yes, I do. It's all packed away. I'd always hoped to have a daughter who would wear it, but that wasn't to be." She looked back down at the album and fell silent.

"Maybe Lynn would wear it," Allie suggested.

Effie gave a faint smile. "I think Lynn's style may be a little more…modern."

"Your husband was very handsome," Allie said. Tall

and dark, Tony Kostakis was a younger version of his uncle. Allie squinted at the photograph. The groom stood at an angle beside his bride, Effie, his face turned her way. But he almost seemed to be gazing beyond her, at the maid of honor—Katrina, his cousin.

"He was *very* handsome," Effie murmured, her eyes downcast. "I was the envy of all the young eligible women in the community."

Allie didn't know how to respond to that, for it was obvious that the distinction hadn't made Effie's life any happier. After a long moment Allie observed that Tony resembled his uncle.

"He wasn't anything like Spiro!"

The vehemence in her voice startled Allie.

"He was warm and charming," she went on. "He could tease a bad mood out of anyone, even Uncle Spiro."

"How did he die?" It was a natural place for the question and Allie couldn't resist asking, in spite of what she knew from Joel.

The album slammed shut. Effie stood up. "He disappeared one night." She looked down at Allie, her face a tight mask. "The same night your father left with you." She gathered the albums in her arms and headed for the door.

Speechless, Allie watched as Effie closed the door behind her.

CHAPTER SEVEN

ALLIE WAS IN HER ROOM, still mulling over Effie's parting words, when Maria arrived to announce that predinner drinks would be served in the library, rather than on the terrace. The thought of sipping a glass of wine and smiling politely at people obsessed with the past was more than Allie could bear. She pleaded a headache.

"Would it be possible to have a tray in my room?" she asked the housekeeper.

Maria shot her a doubtful look. "Mr. Spiro will be eating in his room, but he wants the family to gather for dinner."

"Then perhaps if I skip the cocktails?"

"If you wish," Maria said, her face pinched in disapproval.

Before she reached the door, Allie asked impulsively, "Maria, I'm afraid I might have upset Effie today."

The housekeeper paused.

"She was showing me her wedding pictures and I asked her when her husband died. I assumed he was dead because she kept referring to him in the past tense. Was I wrong?"

"No, her husband's been dead for many years."

"How did he die?"

"She didn't tell you what happened?"

"Only that he disappeared."

Maria turned her face away and shrugged. "Mr. Spiro

had his lawyers declare Mr. Tony dead a few years back. Something to do with liquidating money and getting some stocks released to Miss Effie.'' She turned to leave, then added, ''If he's not dead, then where is he?''

And Allie, having no reply to that, silently watched the door close behind Maria. She lay back on her bed, trying to put together some of the pieces of the family puzzle. Joel had told her that Tony's disappearance could have been connected to a gambling debt. If so, wasn't it a co-incidence that it occurred the same night her father decided to run away with her? That would be too convenient, Allie figured, despite what Joel had said about coincidences on the drive to Grosse Pointe.

Not only that, but there were so many different accounts of the same story. Coming to Grosse Pointe definitely hadn't clarified many of the questions that she had about her family. Just the opposite, in fact. Mysteries and puzzles seemed to be replicating like crazy. Even Joel had his own version of her family's history.

Thinking of Joel, she wondered where and what he was doing. She thought back to the argument in the garage. He was seriously annoyed at the person driving the car and had implied that Allie could have been hurt. What had he said? *Then they'd have no reason for being there.*

Allie closed her eyes. She vowed to confront Joel Kennedy the next time she saw him.

DINNER WAS A REPEAT of the night before, except that Spiro showed up for dessert, which he insisted on being served in the library. From the dismayed faces of the staff, Allie could tell this instruction was an inconvenience, though of course no one protested.

As the others took their usual places, Spiro said in an

aside to Allie, "Glad to see you're feeling better, my dear."

I bet he keeps tabs on everything that goes on around here. Allie's face colored, but she offered no further excuse for her absence at the cocktail hour. While plates of pie and ice cream were being passed around, Allie wandered about the room checking out the book collection. It was an eclectic one, she noticed, and also one that contained quite a few hardcovers in pristine condition. Did anyone read the books, or were they just for show?

"Feel free to help yourself to anything in here, Allie," Spiro said. "After my wife—your grandmother—died, I'm afraid the books began to gather dust. It seems no one has time to read anymore."

Allie turned away from the shelves to look across the room at Spiro. He'd been tracking her every move, while the rest of the family sipped coffee and started their desserts. She also noticed that when he'd made a point of saying "your grandmother" Effie and Christo had exchanged glances.

She took her seat and picked away at her dessert, though she had no real appetite for it. Then she remembered what Pat the gardener had told her about the pool. "Mr. Kostakis," she began.

All eyes turned her way. Christo smirked and George looked embarrassed. Lynn gave a little giggle that produced a frown from Effie. Only Spiro seemed unfazed.

"*Koritsiemou*—my dear—I know it's difficult getting used to family members who are still virtual strangers. But it would please an old man very much to hear you say 'Grandfather.' When you feel comfortable with it, of course. Until then, 'Spiro' will do."

Allie smiled, grateful for his sensitivity. "Thank you,

Spiro,'' she said. ''I wonder if I could use the indoor swimming pool while I'm here.''

''Of course, my dear. This house is your house, as much as it is all of ours. After we've finished, Christo will show you where the pool is.''

That silenced everyone until the dessert plates had been cleared. Spiro must have given Yolanda some signal, for she suddenly rose from her corner chair and came to assist him to his room. He was midway to the door when he raised a finger and addressed the room.

''I forgot to mention that I'm hoping everyone will have an early breakfast at nine so that we can all go to church together. I know this is unusual, but so are the circumstances. I'd like all of us to attend mass prior to the blood test on Monday. Then we'll have a traditional Greek dinner with some of our old family friends to introduce them to Allie.''

Christo expelled a blustery sigh. Otherwise, no one said a word except Allie, who murmured, ''Oh, that would be very nice.''

Yolanda continued walking Spiro to the door, but was halted again, this time by Effie.

''Did your meeting at the lawyer's go well today, Uncle Spiro?''

''Very well,'' he said gruffly, then jerked his head at Yolanda, who helped him through the door.

The silence that followed was deafening. At last Effie rose from her chair, turned to George and said meaningfully, ''Now you know.''

As soon as she left, Christo muttered, ''So is she saying the rest is up to us, bro?''

George's face reddened with anger. He gestured to Lynn and, without a word, stormed out of the room.

Allie looked at Christo, who offered no other explanation than, "Family business. Come, I'll show you how to get to the pool."

He seemed harassed and Allie said, "I can find it on my own tomorrow. There'll be someone up early, I'm sure. Especially if breakfast is at nine."

"Yeah, the royal summons," he said bitterly. "It's okay, let's go now. Just along the hall from here, past the kitchen and down to the lower terrace. It won't take long."

Allie followed meekly, wishing she hadn't asked about the pool in the first place. It was only eight o'clock, but the house was already closed down for the night.

When she commented on that, Christo turned his head to say, "It's Saturday night and the help is supposed to get off early. Everyone but Maria and Marko live off the premises. But bringing the dessert to the library took extra time, so they probably blasted out of here as soon as they could."

"That explains the long faces. You'd think Spiro would be more considerate."

Christo stopped walking. "One thing you gotta know about Uncle Spiro. He pleases himself first, then others. If there's a difference of opinion, you can guess who's gonna win out." He stared at Allie for a moment before adding, "I have to hand it to you, though. That whole speech of his about what to call him? Of course it was his not-so-subtle way of telling you to call him Grandfather, but you called his bluff good." He laughed, shaking his head. "Pretty cool, Allie. Coming right back with 'Spiro.' Just to let him know you weren't gonna be told."

"But that's not why I—"

He cut her off. "Doesn't matter. That's the message you delivered, kiddo." He resumed leading the way down a set of stairs beyond the dark kitchen to the lower level.

Great, Allie thought. *I seem to have joined the club. Spiro versus the rest of the gang.*

When she walked through an inconspicuous door leading into the pool area, Allie gasped. The room had more square footage than her apartment in Kingston. Christo flicked a light switch and spotlights bathed the pool in bright white light.

"If that's too blinding," he said, "you can dim them." He rotated the knob and the room transformed from something akin to a search-and-rescue operation to a romantic candlelit rendezvous. Underwater pool lights cast abstract shadows that shifted at every ripple on the water's surface.

Allie circled the pool, noting the spotless ceramic tile floor, the two change rooms with louvered doors, large tropical plants and flowering shrubs situated just so. Deck chairs and tables added to the overall effect of a Caribbean resort.

"It's amazing!" she said. "Training here will be truly a pleasure."

"For the triathlon?" Christo asked. He was leaning against the change-room door and seemed faintly amused at her enthusiasm. "Involving what? Three different things?"

She nodded. "Swimming first, then cycling and running last."

"Good God, sounds horrible. Always in that order?"

"Usually. Better to do the swim when you're fresh—less chance of drowning," she added, laughing. "And if you collapse while you're running, you don't have as far to fall."

He shuddered. "Better you than me, as the saying goes." He flicked off the lights and motioned toward glass sliding doors opposite the pool. "Shall we take the back way?"

He unlocked the doors and waited for her. When she reached his side, he said, "You know, Uncle Spiro had the pool put in for your mother. It was part of the renovations done when she was about ten or eleven years old."

"Really?"

"Yeah. Apparently she was quite a swimmer, too. Maybe that's where you get it from."

It was the first positive thing, other than about her physical beauty, that Allie had heard about her mother. "Did you know her?"

Christo shook his head. "Vaguely. I was only about seven when we moved in here. About the time you and your father vanished."

Allie noted that he didn't mention his own father's disappearance.

"I remember getting into trouble because of you," he said.

"How?"

"I think I pulled your hair and made you cry. Uncle Spiro was very angry. You were the apple of his eye." His gaze fixed on her face. Then he reached out his arm to touch her hair.

Allie shivered, unnerved by the intimacy of the gesture. "Well, I guess you've grown out of that habit," she said, forcing a lightness she wasn't feeling into her voice.

He got the message. He dropped his hand to the door mechanism and slid it open. She brushed past him, stepping outside to fill her lungs with the cool night air.

He was hard on her heels. "Care for a walk around the grounds?"

Allie turned sharply. "I don't think so, Christo. And actually, I'll find my own way back. Thanks for showing me the pool."

His face showed he was doing some mental math. Figuring things out, she hoped. "Fine by me. Good luck with the workout tomorrow. See you at breakfast." A jaunty wave and he slouched off into the darkness.

Allie sagged against the doorjamb. *What was that all about?* She squinted into the darkness and decided to take the inside route to her room, after all. Turning around to go back in, she caught the distorted reflection of a man looming behind her.

IT WAS MORE of a gasp than a scream, but it was enough to make him extend an arm as if to physically stop her. "It's me—Joel."

"Do you always have to come sneaking up behind me?"

How to account for his presence now? "I was just checking to see that all the doors are locked," he improvised. "Part of my job."

"Couldn't you have announced yourself?"

That got him. *As if she'd have noticed.* "I didn't think you'd hear."

"What's that supposed to mean?"

"You were cheek by jowl with Christo when I came along."

Her mouth moved silently. Indignantly, he thought. She finally came up with a defense. "We were not. At least, it wasn't how you're suggesting. That's disgusting," she added.

"Why? He's a good-looking guy."

"We're cousins!"

"Second? Third? I don't think it matters much."

"Let's get back to why you're following me."

He grinned. Sharp as a tack. "I already explained. Want an escort to your room?"

She looked about and, perhaps deciding he was the only one around, nodded.

"Inside or out?" he asked.

"Out, please. I could use some air."

"I *guess.*"

She ignored that and waited while he locked the door. Then he held out a hand, which she took—surprisingly—and helped her climb the gently sloping hill that led from the lower terrace to the main floor of the house. Her hand fit nicely in his. Her skin was soft and cool, but not damp. He wondered for a second if the rest of her skin felt like that, but pushed the thought away.

When they crested the hill and reached the main terrace, she let go of his hand. The letdown he felt startled him. *You're losing it, Kennedy. Stay focused on the job.*

"Beautiful night," he murmured, gazing up at the stars as they walked.

She tipped her head up. "Mmm," she agreed. Then, as if suddenly remembering something, halted in her tracks, arms on her hips and asked, "This morning you said Christo's car was the one that almost knocked me over. But you didn't say that he was driving. Was he?"

"Did you ask *him* if he was driving?"

"No, but it obviously wasn't him or you'd have spelled it out more clearly. So who was it?"

He hesitated, then sensed he couldn't put her off any longer. Besides, what did it really matter now? "It was one of the staff here. Christo asked him to pick up the car from the dealer where it was getting a tune-up."

"Patrick?"

He frowned. "You've met Pat?"

"This morning just before lunch. He and Sam were digging near the outdoor pool. Why didn't you just tell me it was him, instead of making a big secret out of it?"

He felt a surge of heat. She had a way of twisting things. "I wasn't keeping it a secret. I didn't think it mattered. Besides, I didn't want to get him in trouble."

"Oh." She seemed to mull that over for a moment, then said, "I won't mention it to anyone. I guess now he'll be more careful."

"He better be," Joel muttered.

He continued walking toward the solarium, knowing it was unlocked, because he'd left that way when he saw Christo leading Allie down to the pool wing. At the time he'd been merely curious to see what they were up to and feeling the need for some night air.

Giving up cigarettes four months before a big job had been a mistake, he reckoned. Though he felt some satisfaction at knowing he hadn't yet caved in to the urge. Unless continued proximity to Allie Newman drove him back to the wicked weed.

When they reached the French doors of the solarium, he stopped. "I guess you can find your own way from here," he said, half hoping she'd ask him to lead her all the way.

But she didn't. Instead, she said, "Patrick was the man you were talking to in the garage."

"So you *were* listening!"

"You said something I didn't understand."

"Go on," he said, knowing what was coming.

"It was a reference to me. That if something happened to me, there'd be no reason for you to be here."

"And?"

"Well, what did you mean by that?"

She was totally maddening and desirable at the same time. He was torn between kissing her or throttling her. Instead, he forced himself to stay neutral. In control. "I think it's pretty obvious, don't you? If you're no longer on the scene, then my job here is finished."

Silence. Moonlight flickered in her face at every wave of the tree branches behind him. Her hair glistened like silver in the ghostly light, and her eyes were more luminous than ever. Joel watched her mouth shaping words he wasn't even listening to, her lips full and inviting.

"Why would you say something like that to Patrick?"

Tossed from his trance, Joel could feel his blood pressure rising. *Calm down, Kennedy. You're letting her get to you.* "I don't know. Jeez, why the third degree? He probably asked me why I was so ticked off. Anyway, it's obvious, isn't it, that if you were no longer here I'd be out of a job?"

"Is that your job? To watch over me?"

"Yeah, that's right. Spiro asked me to stay on till you felt more comfortable here."

"Well, I feel very comfortable here, so any time you want to leave, go ahead." Then she spun around and marched through the French doors.

Sensing he'd just blown the whole thing, Joel rubbed his face and stood motionless, watching her fade into the shadows of the house. *How the hell did that just happen?*

ALLIE HADN'T BEEN in her room long when she heard a discreet tap on the door. For an insane second she thought it might be Joel. Though heaven only knew why she imagined it might be him, or that she'd even *want* it to be him.

Still, when she'd slipped her hand in his, it had felt so very right. She couldn't understand the effect the man had on her. Talk about approach-avoidance conflict, she thought. One moment she was dying to have any kind of physical contact with him at all, and the next her inner warning radar beeped like crazy. The guy was definitely big trouble and to be avoided at all costs. *So why am I constantly on the lookout for him?*

More physical activity ought to eradicate such futile thinking, Allie had decided. She'd set her watch alarm for six and had just shed her clothes prior to showering when a faint knocking at the door sent her scrambling for a robe.

She was surprised at her disappointment when she opened the door to Lynn. George's fiancée, too, was ready for bed, though she wore a long, clinging negligee over a matching nightgown. "Hope I'm not disturbing you," she said. "But I couldn't sleep and I saw light under the door."

Allie let her in. "You didn't go home tonight?"

"Not much point, since Uncle Spiro wants everyone to be here at nine for breakfast and then church."

"Does that have to include you?"

Lynn widened her big baby blues at Allie. "Well, as George's fiancée I guess that does include me. I mean, I know more about the family than...well, than you do."

Allie conceded the point. Lynn wandered about the room, scanning the bureau and Allie's meager collection of toiletries and other personal items.

"You didn't bring a lot of stuff, did ya," she said.

"No. Why?"

"Does that mean you don't plan on staying?"

"I never intended to stay longer than the blood test and whatever comes after it."

"Really?" Lynn set down a jar of moisture cream to gape at Allie.

"Of course. Why should I stay? This isn't my home. Besides, I've a job and an apartment back in Kingston."

"That's the place. I forgot the name. In Ontario, isn't it? Near Toronto?"

"Not really. East of Toronto. Anyway, I have a life there, believe me."

"That's what I've been saying to George and Christo.

But they think otherwise. No doubt because of their mother, you know.'' She walked over to where Allie was standing. ''Effie thinks you plan to stay forever, I think. She's all uptight about it.''

''Why? What's the big deal?''

Lynn pulled an incredulous face. ''Can't you guess?''

''No. Should I be able to?'' Allie was tiring of the game, wishing Lynn would leave so she could go to bed.

''Everyone thinks you're here for the money. You know,'' she prompted at Allie's blank look, ''Spiro's money. When he dies. They think he's going to change his will, leaving everything to you, instead of George and Christo.''

Allie was stunned. ''That's ridiculous. Why would he? He hardly knows me.''

''Exactly. But you're his blood. That's all that matters to him.'' Lynn walked in a tight circle around Allie, as if sizing her up. ''So, is it true?''

''Is what true?''

''That you're going to try to get him to alter the will in your favor.''

''Look, I've no idea where you or anyone else got the idea. A week ago I didn't know Spiro and the rest of you even existed. This is all new to me. And very overwhelming.''

Lynn shrugged, casting her a disbelieving look. She moved toward the door, where she paused to say, ''Just so you know, we're not going to sit back and let that happen. You know? George and Christo, they've worked really hard all these years to please their uncle and get where they are in the business. They're not about to let it slip away from them because some long-lost granddaughter shows up out of nowhere. So you can forget about it. Do the blood test and whatever—be a big hero all over again if you want, then leave us alone.'' Lynn opened the bedroom door and left without a backward glance.

Allie was dumbfounded. The first thought that came to mind was that she was only partway through her first weekend in Grosse Pointe with her new family. *What more could possibly happen?*

CHAPTER EIGHT

ALLIE DOVE into the azure water and came up in the center of the pool. She started right into her laps, not bothering to count them because she'd decided to keep swimming until she was too tired to continue.

The pool area had been locked when she'd arrived at seven, but the kitchen staff were already preparing breakfast, and one of them had unlocked the door for her. By the time her workout was finished, Allie had eased out most of the kinks from last night's insomnia. She headed for the change room and had just stepped out of her bathing suit when she heard a door open and close.

She waited for the person to announce his—or her—presence, but when no one did, called a hello herself. No response. *Must be my imagination,* she thought, toweling herself briskly. A clinking sound, like keys, stopped her. Again she waited.

"Is someone there?"

Allie dropped the towel to the floor and turned to retrieve her clothes from the hook. But they were gone. Someone was playing a joke on her and it wasn't very funny, she thought. She was wrapping the towel around her when the outline of a form appeared through the louvers of the door.

"I'm just getting changed," she announced, thinking someone was about to burst in on her. "I'll be right out."

She heard steady breathing. The silhouette gradually

faded, as if the person was slowly backing away. Allie waited, listening for a closing door, but the only thing she heard was the pounding in her ears. Anger quickly replaced the fear that had gripped her. She thrust open the door.

The first thing she noticed was the opened glass sliding door leading to the lower terrace. The interior door through which she'd entered was still closed. Allie's heart rate picked up as she realized that someone might have come in through the sliding doors while she was swimming. She wouldn't have noticed. The idea that someone was watching her the whole time sickened her.

She tightened the towel around her and padded around the pool in search of her clothes. After a few seconds of looking under every chair and behind every potted plant, she eventually discovered them beneath a cushion. They'd been folded neatly and a scrap of paper rested on top of them.

Scrawled in large block letters were two words: GO HOME.

The note shook in Allie's hand. This was no joke, she realized.

"I think you're supposed to use the change room."

Her head pivoted sharply. Joel Kennedy was standing in the doorway leading from the house. He held up his hands. "Hey, I didn't mean to scare you. What's up? You look like you've seen a ghost."

She couldn't speak, just watched him as he walked the full length of the pool to where she stood.

"Allie?" His voice lowered. "What is it?"

She held out the note.

He skimmed it and stuck it into his shirt pocket. "Where did you find this?"

"With my clothes. Someone..." she stammered,

"someone came in here while I was swimming. He...I don't know, it could have been a woman, but he must've been watching me. Maybe the whole time." She shivered. "When I got out, my clothes weren't in the change room. I thought someone was playing a joke on me." Her voice cracked.

"Look, you're cold. Go get dressed." He set his hands on her shoulders, guiding her like a child to the change room. "I'll be waiting right out here. I won't leave."

Allie wanted to lock the door when she was inside, in spite of the fact that it was Joel out there. Maybe, her paranoid self suggested, it had been *him* watching the whole time. The way he'd stared at her just now had made her feel the towel she wore was transparent. She caught her pale face in the mirror. *Get real, Newman. What reason would he have for wanting you to leave? You're his meal ticket.*

She unhitched the towel and reached for her underwear, keeping her eyes on the louvered door the whole time she dressed. Her mind sorted through other possibilities. Christo had seemed strange the other night. If he wasn't her cousin, he could have been hitting on her. *Face it. He was.*

Then she remembered the late-night visit from Lynn. Hadn't she more or less been passing on the same message as the note? And Lynn had a motive for wanting Allie to leave. She was engaged to the man designated as Spiro's successor. For that matter, Allie reasoned, the person could have been George himself. Though she didn't consider him a serious suspect. He was too nice. Still, what about that little fit of temper last night in the library?

Allie blew out a mouthful of sour air. *Get a grip, girl. Suspect? Motive? Next thing you'll be playing detective. Or investigator.* Her mind drifted again to Joel, waiting outside the door. What had prompted him to come along when he had?

She slipped into her track pants, pulled on the T-shirt and stooped to pick up her wet bathing suit and towel. When she came out, he was standing at the glass sliding doors.

"Were these closed when you came in here?"

"Yes. I came in the way you did."

"Did you notice if they were locked?"

"I didn't go anywhere near them. I went straight into the change room."

He walked toward her. "Well, my bet is that the mystery man—or woman—came in through them."

"I pretty much guessed the same thing," she said.

She forked her fingers through her hair, realizing she'd forgotten to bring a brush. Joel's eyes tracked her hand as it pulled through the knots in her hair, fanning it out from her head.

Had he stood outside the change room door like that, too? she asked herself, catching his stare. Just watching? Discomfited, she whirled around, aiming for the door.

He reached out and grasped her shoulder. "I think we should talk about that note."

"What made you show up here, anyway?"

His face suggested she was asking a ridiculous question. "I told you yesterday, didn't I? I'm supposed to keep an eye on you."

"Yes, you did. But I also told you not to bother. So why does it seem that everywhere I go, you turn up?"

"Sorry it seems that way."

His breath warmed her face. Slightly fruity, she thought, like chewing gum. She tilted her head back, defiant. "If you have to follow me around, then please be more obvious about it. I...just...don't...like...surprises."

He inched closer at each word, his chin just about even with her nose, his mouth at her forehead. "I didn't get that," he murmured.

She froze. Were his lips brushing her brow? Or had a strand of hair fallen across her forehead? She lowered her eyes, saw the rise and fall of his Adam's apple. The tufts of black hair poking up through the opened neck of his denim blue shirt. The edge of the scrap of paper sticking out of his shirt pocket. Dry-mouthed, Allie took a step back—out of range, onto neutral ground.

"Just let me know if you're going to be showing up, that's all." Allie began to move to the door.

"Doesn't that defeat the whole purpose?"

"What *is* the purpose, Joel? You tell me. And please, not the bull manure about making me feel comfortable."

He smiled. "I like that in you, Allie. No beating around the bush." Finally he got around to answering her. "You know that Spiro's worth a lot of money. I don't know the particulars of how his estate is set up, but I imagine George and Christo expect to inherit the family business at least. Suddenly along comes a complete stranger—a possible rival to that inheritance. You figure it out."

"But part of the reason I'm here is to save his life."

"Yeah." He paused a beat. "And therefore..."

"Someone might not want me to do that?"

"Possibly."

The conclusion Allie came to was a sobering one. How far would that someone go, she asked herself, to make sure of that? "I think I'd better call the police," she said, and headed for the door.

"Don't do that!"

His alarm stopped her. "Why not? Isn't that the sensible thing to do?"

"Just that I know Spiro. The worry of it, the publicity,

would be very stressful. What with the test tomorrow and all…''

''But shouldn't he know that someone has threatened me?''

''He will. But I think you should wait until after the test. I'm here to watch over you. That's what he hired me to do, remember?''

''Did he think something like this might happen?''

''I don't know. Really,'' he said emphatically at her shaking head. ''But Spiro wouldn't take chances with you. Maybe he's worried some reporters might get wind of the story—you know, how you were recently found by the family, saving the wealthy patriarch and so on.''

''You sound like a reporter yourself.''

''I know how they operate.''

She could understand his point about her grandfather. ''All right. When the test is over, we'll talk to Spiro and then let him decide about the police.''

''In the meantime if you get any more notes—or if anything at all happens that upsets you—you're to tell me right away. And I'll come with you when you're training.''

She had an instant mental picture of him jogging at her heels and couldn't resist a smile. ''Sure.'' At the door, she turned around to ask, ''How did you know I was going to be swimming this morning?''

''Spiro told me.''

It was her turn to frown. ''He did?''

''Didn't you tell him over dessert in the library? That's why he had Christo show you the pool.''

''Right,'' she murmured, realizing that what she said—and did—was obviously going back and forth between Joel Kennedy and her grandfather. And she was not at all pleased about it.

THE REST OF THE DAY passed in a blur for Allie. Mass at a Greek Orthodox church was both mysterious and fascinating. Mingling on the steps of the church afterward afforded her a chance to witness Spiro's obviously high status in the community. Yolanda finally forced him away from the well-wishers and people who seemed to be either requesting favors or seeking permission for something.

The late-afternoon dinner was an extravaganza of food and drink. Spiro was in his glory at the head of the table, basking in the reverence accorded him by his guests. The room was full of wealth and power—businessmen, judges, doctors and lawyers—and all were Spiro's friends and family members. Allie had no doubt that each and every one of them would have been all too willing to help one of their own win custody of his granddaughter. For the first time she had a sense of the despair her father must have felt at the threat of a custody fight with Spiro. A lump formed in Allie's throat. No wonder he'd run.

By the end of the meal, Allie's head was spinning with the names and faces of dozens of people curious to meet the long-lost granddaughter. She was a hit with his friends, but more importantly, she noticed she'd won over Spiro himself. And for some reason she couldn't comprehend at all, this pleased her.

The single jarring note came at the end of the day after the last guest had departed. Spiro had retired to his own suite as had Effie, and George was about to drive Lynn home. Allie was returning from the kitchen with a bottle of spring water. She planned to jog around the grounds to work off some of the meal.

Christo was huddled in deep conversation with George, waiting for Lynn to come out of the main-floor powder room. At Allie's approach to the main staircase, the two quickly broke apart.

"Not retiring for the night already?" Christo asked.

"No. Just getting ready for a run," she said.

His smirk suggested a run after the day's events was obviously the last item on his agenda. Allie wondered if they'd been talking about her. If Spiro had noticed the fuss she was creating amongst his friends, so had they. She thought of Lynn's remark and Joel's suggestion that someone might not want the transplant to occur.

Had the person in the pool room been George or Christo? She was about to say something to set their minds at ease regarding their precious inheritance, but the powder-room door at the end of the foyer swung open and Lynn flounced their way.

"Off for the night?" Lynn asked, echoing Christo's own comment. "Tiring, isn't it?"

Allie's mind went blank.

"Working a room," Lynn explained.

Behind her, Christo stifled a laugh. Allie colored and, without a word, headed for the staircase. She heard the door open and close behind Lynn and George, then Christo's amused parting comment as she ascended the stairs.

"And a good time was had by all."

RUNNING WAS great therapy. After two warm-up sprints around the tennis court, Allie jogged across the lawn in the direction of the drive. Her Walkman was securely tucked into the waistband of her shorts and she'd just popped in the latest Dave Matthews Band recording.

The days were increasingly lengthening. It was almost eight, and nightfall was still at least half an hour away. Joel had said he would accompany her whenever she trained, yet he was nowhere to be found when she'd gone looking for him. Marko had pulled such a blank face that she wondered if he knew Joel was even staying in the garage apartment with him. She finally decided to run without him.

When she reached the main gates, she turned onto Lakeshore Drive, the road outside the estate. There was still enough light for her to be clearly visible, and besides, this section of the neighborhood was quiet and sedate, like many of its palatial homes. Driving to church that morning, she'd spotted a marina and yacht club about a quarter of a mile from the Kostakis compound. There was a public beach beyond them that would be a good turning-around place. Altogether, it was a mile run. Okay for today, she thought, but she knew tomorrow she would have to start more vigorous training.

About a hundred yards past the main gate, Allie spotted a gray van parked on the shoulder of the road ahead of her. She slowed down, crossing to the opposite side of the road. Colliding into car doors that abruptly swung open was a hazard for runners. Once past the van, she crossed over again to the right and increased her pace, pushing herself for the last quarter mile to the marina.

Strings of lights along the eaves of the marina's buildings lent an air of festivity to the place. The clubhouse at the end of the spit of land where the marina was situated glowed against the indigo backdrop of water and sky. The parking lot suggested a full house for dinner that night. Allie wondered if Spiro or anyone else in the family belonged to the club. If her mother had loved swimming, perhaps the family had once been members.

There was so much she didn't know about both her parents. Her father had once told her his parents, as well as her mother's, were both dead, but now she realized that might not be true at all. Somewhere she might have yet another whole new family to meet. That possibility was too daunting to consider.

She focused, instead, on the road, staying on the yellow line that ran between the asphalt and the gravel shoulder. Rounding a bend, she saw an expanse of shadowy landscape on her right—the public beach. Target in sight, she picked up speed, getting her second wind. The beach's parking lot was empty. Or so she thought, until she trotted into its center and turned in a tight circle, running lightly on the spot.

It was much darker now. If she had difficulty seeing, then so might drivers—time to head back. There was a single car parked in a corner opposite her, and passing it, she saw that it resembled Joel Kennedy's. She approached it for a better look. It had to be his car. There was the same dent in the front passenger side, the same sagging exterior rearview mirror. She bet if she opened the door, a flood of gum wrappers and empty pop cans would pour out onto the lot.

So where was he? Investigating on a dark and deserted public beach? Her curiosity was now in high gear. Allie slowed to a brisk walk and headed for the pavement leading from the parking lot onto the beach itself. As she rounded the corner of a closed refreshment booth, she saw the shape of a man silhouetted against a spill of moonlight. She moved onto the damp sand and slowed her pace to a near halt.

He was standing in profile to her, his right arm raised to his head. She wondered for a moment what he was doing, until she got close enough to see that he was talking on a cell phone. She stopped, watching him nodding and gesturing with his free hand. The conversation must be an engaging one, she decided, judging from his body language. It occurred to her in that split second that he might

be talking to a woman. Which might explain why he'd
driven all the way here to make the phone call—privacy.
Maybe—and she didn't like the idea, though it made more
sense—he'd arranged to meet a woman and she hadn't
turned up.

He turned suddenly, catching sight of her in the light of
the moon. The arm at his ear froze momentarily and
abruptly swung down. He plodded toward her.

"Surprise," she said for want of anything more rational
to say.

"What the hell are you doing here?"

She was tempted to giggle, but the ill temper wafting
from him deterred her. "Just out on a run," she said.

"Here?"

"Well, *to* here. I ran from the house to here."

"In the dark? Are you crazy?"

That did it. "I guess I must be. And crazier still for
taking your promise to come with me seriously and spending the fifteen minutes of extra daylight I might have had
in a fruitless search for you." She began to turn around.

He grabbed her shoulder. "You're not going to run
back, Allie. I'm driving you."

"I haven't done my whole run," she protested, hoping
that didn't sound like a whine. "Anyway, what are you
doing here? Aren't you allowed to use the phones at the
house?"

"Huh?"

"Talking on your cell phone at a beach. What's that
about?"

"I drove here to watch the sunset," he said.

"Why the cell phone?"

"Come with me," he said, ignoring her question. "You
can run before your appointment in the morning." He
pulled on her arm to lead her away.

Which annoyed her most of all. It was so patronizing. "I can manage on my own, Joel. That's what you aren't getting. I ran here because I've done similar runs at home all my life. At least, for the past ten years. I know how to be careful and I'm not a child. Please don't treat me like one."

He let go. "I want to drive you back."

The expression in his eyes defied argument. Allie nodded and followed him to his car. His footsteps made deep troughs in the wet sand, and she kept her eyes on the ground, thinking it would be easier if she followed his tracks. On the way she spotted a scattering of wadded-up gum wrappers. He'd been here a while, she figured, to chew that much gum. Either that or he'd had no dinner.

He unlocked the car and she climbed in, tossing a crumpled McDonald's bag lying in the middle of her seat to the floor.

"Here," he said, "give me that," and carried it to a nearby trash can. Once back, he turned on the ignition and the engine coughed into action, settling into an erratic chug. As they drove out of the lot, he glanced across at her and asked, "How was dinner?"

Allie flashed back to the scene with Lynn and Christo. "Okay," she murmured, peering out her window.

"Only okay? I popped by the kitchen this afternoon for a preview. Looked pretty impressive to me."

"Oh, the food was wonderful."

"But the company was lacking?"

"Why the questions?" she asked, exasperated.

"Just making polite conversation, Allie. Isn't that what you do in those circles?"

"Don't play games with me, Joel. I'm not in the mood."

He waited a moment. "Did something happen?"

Wanting to talk about it, she replayed the last part of

the evening for him. He made an exaggerated meowing sound when she repeated Lynn's remark.

"Don't spend another second chewing over that," he advised. "Lynn's a minor player here. Chalk it up to low self-esteem enhanced by someone like you suddenly dropping into her life."

"How could I be a threat to her? She's engaged to my cousin."

"Get with it, Allie. Your second or third cousin. And you a possible heir to a fortune."

"I'm tired of hearing about that," she muttered, averting her face. "I don't even want to think about it. All I want to do is get the test over with, do the transplant if it comes to that and go home. End of story."

The car rattled down the dark road. Every now and then Allie caught a glimpse of lights hidden behind stone gates or thickets of woods. Those lights glowed from opulent mansions, the grandeur of which most people had never even imagined. *I'm going to one of them right now. And Joel is suggesting that someday I might be a permanent part of all this? No way. Not in a million years.*

They approached the main gates, and Allie, remembering the van, craned her neck to look for it.

"Looking for something?"

"There was a van parked outside the house, past that bend. I thought it was a strange place for someone to leave a vehicle, out on the main road."

He checked the rearview mirror. "Seems to be gone. Probably a couple of teenagers making out in the back. This looks like a good place for that. All those nooks and crannies." He fixed his gaze on hers. "One piece of advice, Allie. Don't make a lot of plans just yet. A lot can happen. Keep your mind open to possibilities."

"What's that supposed to mean?"

He shook his head, obviously frustrated at her incomprehension, and said no more. He drove up to the house. The front spotlights were still on, but a lot of the house was already in darkness. When he braked the car, Allie quickly slipped out, but he caught up with her before she reached the steps.

"Remember what I said, okay? I'll be waiting here for you at…what time?"

"The test is at nine. Seven?"

A weary sigh. "Seven it is. Can we make it a short run? Or should I drive? Like a pace car?"

Allie smiled, in spite of her low mood. "Whatever you want," she said. "Good night, Joel."

"Good night, Allie."

She trotted up the steps to the front door, feeling his eyes on her the whole way.

JOEL WAITED until the front door closed behind her. Even then, he gave her another ten minutes to reach her second-floor bedroom. He felt as if he'd stepped into quicksand. The more he tried to pull himself out, the deeper he sank. The last time he'd felt so conflicted was after his ex left him, taking Ben with her. On the one hand, he was glad to return to a serene life again. Yet losing Ben was a high price to pay.

When the ten minutes were up, he climbed back into his station wagon and headed to the main gate. The car was definitely on the way out, he knew. His ex had taken the newer model, leaving this one for him. Maybe he ought to have used a company car, instead, but he liked the freedom of having his own, as junky as it was.

Unlike his car, his apartment in Philly was virtually spotless. Probably because he was never in it. The job in Detroit was temporary, lasting at most half a year. If nothing solid came out of the case by then, it would be reviewed and probably closed. For that reason, he'd put off finding a place to live, using hotels, motels and, occasionally, his car.

Joel grinned, recalling Allie's disgust at the mess. The discipline that made her a good athlete likely carried over into the other areas of her life. He could imagine her office at the university. She was probably one of those people who actually used organizer books, as opposed to tearing pages from them to jot down notes that were subsequently lost.

He and Allie could not have been less alike. Still, his job would definitely be easier if they were on friendly terms, even if being friends was bound to be a liability in the long run. He turned onto Lakeshore Drive and scanned both sides of the road. The van should be around somewhere.

Allie's unexpected night jog likely convinced them to change locations. He headed north, back toward the beach. If they'd shown up on time, none of this would be necessary. Then he felt a chill just thinking about how he had turned around to see Allie standing only feet away.

He'd received the warning phone call from the van mere seconds before she appeared. What if she'd arrived at the beach just as the van was pulling up for the meeting? Joel swore, vowing to chew out whoever had been watching the main gate. Yet deep down, he knew the person he was really angry at was himself. He'd promised to be around to go running whenever she did. He wasn't and she went by herself.

That was typical of Allie Newman. He was getting a clearer picture of her now, for sure. She was not someone to be taken for granted. And forget about calling the shots.

He sighed again. Maybe that was what appealed to him. That, along with the other more obvious traits.

Joel spotted the van on the curve before the Grosse Pointe Yacht Club. He took his foot off the accelerator and let the station wagon glide to a halt behind it. He got out, spilling a handful of debris as he did, and crunched along the gravel shoulder to the rear door. Joel tapped three times.

"It's me," he said.

CHAPTER NINE

SHE DIDN'T MAKE the run. Late-night dreams kept Allie tossing and turning for hours. She struggled from bed when she heard a discreet tapping on her door.

"Restless night?" Maria asked. The housekeeper walked in with a breakfast tray and set it on a small table next to the armchair near the bay window.

Allie mumbled a greeting that Maria interpreted as a request for the time.

"Eight o'clock. Mr. Spiro says his car will be waiting out front in one hour exactly."

No room for argument there, Allie thought. She waited for Maria to leave before slumping into the armchair. The breakfast, like all the meals in the house, was plentiful and attractively presented, but what Allie really yearned for was a bowl of homemade granola. The craving prompted a search for her cell phone.

"Susan? It's Allie... I know, the test is this morning, but I was just sitting here wishing for some of your granola and thought I'd call now.... No, nothing's wrong. Just that, well, I've been finding out more about Dad...and my mother.... Yes, I understand that I'm only getting one side of the story, but to tell you the truth, it's a story I'm not sure I want to hear, if you know what I mean.... No, everyone's been wonderful, but I think the two cousins I told you about are worried that I'm going to steal their inheritance or something.'' Allie laughed, wanting to make light of it.

Then she frowned. Susan was just too quick. ''No, honestly, Susan, I'm fine and I was only kidding…. Yes, as a matter of fact he's still here.'' She hesitated, unable to explain what Joel's role was without alarming the other woman. ''He's helping out around the house…. I know it doesn't make sense, but he's persuaded Spiro to keep him on at least until I leave.''

Another laugh. ''Good grief, I hardly know the man. Come on!… Yes, I know I said he's very good-looking, but he's not my type…. Okay, I promise to phone when I find out the results. Then hopefully I'll be home as soon as possible after that…. Love you, too. Bye.''

Allie stared at the cell phone in her lap. Susan did get some strange ideas. How she could think Allie might be attracted to Joel was unimaginable. She unfolded her legs and got up. Perhaps after a shower she'd feel more inclined to tackle some of the lavish breakfast. Allie pulled off her nightie and padded into the adjoining bath. This was one luxury she knew she'd miss when she was back home. Along with the freshly laundered towels that magically appeared every day. She stepped into the glass shower stall and ran the water.

It wasn't until she'd finished that she realized someone was knocking on her bedroom door. Maria, no doubt, returning for the breakfast tray. Allie knotted one of the towels around her and called out, ''Come in,'' through the open bathroom door. She wanted to tell Maria that she planned to eat the fruit portion of breakfast and rushed out of the bathroom to find Joel standing in the bedroom doorway.

''I thought it was Maria,'' Allie said.

''Sorry.'' He stared at her for a moment before shifting

his gaze to the window. "You didn't show up for your run."

"I slept in. Sorry, my turn to apologize." Beads of water dripped down the back of her neck onto the floor. "I better get dressed."

He started to back out the door. "Right, but I'll be driving you to the clinic. Spiro had a rough night, apparently."

"Oh."

"Right," he repeated. His eyes moved back to Allie. "Your...uh, towel is slipping," he told her as he pivoted around and disappeared through the door.

Allie peered down at her bosom, too much of which had overflowed the boundary of fabric. Her face heated up. *You're so cool, Allie Newman.*

Half an hour later she was striding along the hall to the staircase when she bumped into Christo emerging from a door near the landing.

"Today's the big day," he said. "Nervous?"

"It's only a simple blood test."

"I wasn't referring to the actual test."

He inched closer. Allie got an unpleasant whiff of stale cigarette breath and pulled her head back.

"I meant, today or tomorrow—soon—you'll find out if you're really one of us. If you *qualify*."

"I think that's already been established," she said, brushing past him to continue down the stairs. Allie kept her pace along the hallway to the massive oak front door and onto the stone terrace fronting the house. The pounding of her heart against her rib cage was almost painful, and she had to stop to catch her breath. Joel climbed out of the driver's side of the Cadillac parked at the foot of the steps.

"You all right?"

She could only nod. He opened the passenger door for her and she got in, too breathless to protest.

Once he was back in his own seat, he glanced across at her and remarked, "You look like you just ran the qualifying heat for a race."

"More like the gauntlet," she muttered.

"Say again?"

"Never mind. It's okay. Just a small verbal encounter with my cousin."

"George?"

"Christo."

"Figures. What did the twerp have to say?"

She laughed, coming down from the adrenaline rush. "Nothing important, trust me."

"If he said something to bother you, tell Spiro. That'll put a stop to it."

"I think that would make things worse," she said.

He thought for a moment, then commented, "You didn't go looking for them. Remember that."

Allie turned from fastening her seat belt. "How could I have done that, Joel? Gone looking for them? Considering I didn't know any of them existed."

"Yeah, well, you've got a point there," and he turned over the engine.

She stared blankly out the window. He'd merely been trying to reassure her. Make her feel better. *Comfortable. Just doing his job.* She sighed. The comfort of home and Susan's plain-speaking, sensible self was what she really wanted.

"Look," she began, "I didn't mean to sound unappreciative. It's just that…well, I haven't had a great morning so far." She had a regrettable vision of herself in a sagging towel. "First, not getting any sleep. Then I practically exposed myself to…to the world. Christo's nasty little gibe was the limit. That's all.''

He didn't say anything for a long moment, steering the car through the main gate and onto Lakeshore Drive. Then he glanced her way and quipped, ''Not exactly the world. It was only me. And,'' he added, ''it was a nice exposure.''

She had to laugh. ''Yeah,'' she mumbled, and feeling her face color, looked out the side window. The scenery passed in a blur, though a part of her again registered the opulent beauty of the neighborhood. There was old money here, she was thinking. She wondered how Spiro and his brother had fit in as new, rich Greek immigrants. Had social acceptance been an issue? Was that what had driven her mother to marry Eddie Hughes?

Not that she knew anything at all about her father before Kingston. But she was curious. Before she left Grosse Pointe, she'd try to find out something about the young Eddie Hughes and where he came from. For herself and for Susan, too, so they could complete a portrait of a man they'd loved so much.

Her eyes teared up. No matter what she might discover, she knew he'd been a good man. A warm, loving father. He'd never let her down, not once. If only he'd told her the truth—his own story—before he'd died. Allie dug into her purse for a tissue.

''Something wrong?'' Joel managed a quick glance from his driving. ''Are you crying?'' The car swerved. He slowed down, eased onto the gravel shoulder and gently braked. He reached out and touched her cheek, brushing away the dampness. ''Homesick?''

Allie dabbed at her eyes. ''I'm not usually like this,'' she said. ''Maybe it's anxiety about the test and all.''

His fingers lingered at her jaw. ''It's just a normal blood test. More likely, it's the whole thing. You've got information and emotion overload. Starting from when I walked into the health-food store last week.''

She smiled. ''That's for sure.''

He didn't smile back, but focused, instead, on lightly tracing an invisible line along the curve of her jaw and down her neck. Then he ran the finger lightly around as if drawing a collar above the scooped top of her dress. Allie held her breath. The finger came to rest in the small hollow at the base of her neck.

Allie broke the connection, turning her head slightly and straightening so that he had no choice but to remove his hand. ''We can't be late,'' she mumbled, unable to look his way.

He put the car into drive and eased onto the road. Allie was grateful for his silence. She couldn't handle a half-hearted apology any more than her body could tolerate that feathery touch without responding. *Can people spontaneously combust?* She thought she'd just come dangerously close to finding out.

Her fantasy about what might have happened had she not stopped him came to an abrupt end when the car braked at the first intersection. A gray van was making a turn on her right, and as it did, she recognized the driver. It was Patrick, the gardener's helper.

''That driver!'' she said, pointing to the van, which was rapidly disappearing from view.

Joel gave her a dazed look. ''What?''

''The guy driving that van. It's the gardener. You know—Patrick.''

He peered where she pointed. ''Didn't catch him. What's the big deal, anyway?''

His nonchalance was irritating. He wasn't getting it. ''That's the van I jogged by last night. Remember? We were looking for it on the way back, but it had gone.''

He shrugged. "Doesn't it make sense that a gardener would be driving a van?" He thought for a minute. "Maybe he's running an errand for someone at the house."

Allie frowned. His interpretation sounded so much more rational than hers, but she persisted. "Why would he be parked outside the estate last night, down the road? As if he were hiding."

"Maybe he *was* hiding," Joel said. "Maybe he had someone in the van with him and he didn't want anyone to see them."

"Like a woman?"

"Or even a *married* woman."

Allie searched his face. Was she looking for evidence of truth, she asked herself, or waiting for the first crack to appear? Whatever. His impassive stare was impossible to read.

"You could always ask him," he finally said, turning his attention back to driving.

The car glided through the intersection as Allie tried to imagine how she might frame such a question. She glanced across at Joel. He seemed so unperturbed by the whole thing that she now doubted her perspective. But she noticed a tiny muscle movement along the right side of his jaw, as if he was chewing on something. Both hands were now wrapped tightly around the steering wheel.

His responses about the gray van had been almost glib, but she couldn't shake the feeling that he was just waiting for her to prove him wrong, that any moment she would connect the dots. Except she wasn't getting any idea about the hidden picture at all.

She was still pondering this puzzle when Joel made a left turn and, seconds later, pulled the Cadillac into an unassuming plaza. A large, dark-brown brick building with a simple sign reading The Sullivan Clinic dominated the plaza. There were small landscaped gardens on either side of the clinic, each featuring a miniature water fountain. Wrought-iron benches—empty, Allie noted—added to the picture of serenity in the midst of suburbia.

"Where shall I meet you when I'm finished?"

He looked surprised. "Don't you want me to go in with you?"

"And hold my hand? As you said, it's a simple blood test."

"Okay. I'll wait on one of those benches," he said, nodding his head toward one of the parkettes.

She was halfway through the door when she changed her mind. Turning around to beckon for him to come in, she saw that he was still in the car, talking on his cell phone. Disappointed, but at the same time relieved that she hadn't embarrassed herself for the umpteenth time that day, Allie entered the clinic.

When she emerged twenty minutes later, she felt as though she'd been to a spa. The hushed luxury of the clinic was unlike any other medical center she'd ever visited. The attentive staff had treated her like a valued client, rather than a patient. On leaving, she noticed a wall of brass plaques, each one commemorating a generous donation to the clinic. And there it was, she thought. The reason for the VIP reception. Spiro Kostakis and Family.

Allie was still contemplating the by-products of wealth when she spotted Joel sitting on one of the benches with his arms crossed, surveying the water fountain as if it were a marvel of nature.

"Lost in thought?" she asked.

He jumped. "I didn't hear you coming."

"Obviously." Allie sat down beside him. "Pretty, isn't

it? In spite of the artificiality of it all.'' She gestured to the landscaping.

"Yes. I guess patients are meant to sit here and find a bit of peace.''

"Before taking out their checkbooks,'' she quipped.

"No doubt.''

He grinned at her and she had a sudden image of a twelve-year-old boy.

"How did it go?''

"All right, I guess. I had a lot of papers to fill out and they took a brief medical history.''

"And when do you get the results?''

"A couple of days. They have their own lab facilities out back, so patients don't have to wait long.''

"Money buys anything.''

She gave him a sharp look. "You don't really believe that, do you?''

"Most of the time I do.'' He seemed embarrassed by the admission, adding, "Though sometimes I'm pleasantly surprised.''

"But not often,'' she said.

"It comes with the job,'' he said.

As if that explained anything. Changing the subject, she asked, "What were you thinking about just before I joined you?''

He turned his head back to the water fountain. "My son, Ben. He fell into a fountain like that when he was two. We were visiting friends and, well, it happened in an instant. Our backs were turned and bingo!''

In spite of the nonchalance in his voice, Allie could see that the memory still affected him. "Scary. Does he remember it?''

"I doubt it. He loves water, so it didn't traumatize him that way. It scared us, more than anyone.''

She tried to imagine the two other people in his story. Ben and the unnamed ex-wife. Then she tried to set them into a picture of the Joel Kennedy she'd gotten to know in the past week and couldn't do it. For some reason, her image of him was always a solitary one. Standing alone on a beach. Sitting lost in thought on a bench. Cramped into a car he obviously treated as a second home.

"You miss him."

His head swung her way again. "Every day."

Impulsively Allie leaned over and kissed him on the cheek. He brought his hand up, feeling the spot. Then he reached over, clasping her behind the neck to draw her to him. His lips were firm and soft at the same time, she thought, opening her mouth to his and sinking into the moist, sweet taste of him. Juicy Fruit gum, she decided.

His fingers sifted her hair, as he pressed her closer to him. A groan. His tongue pushed deeper into her mouth, exploring every part of hers until, finished with that, he moved his lips down the length of her neck to the hollow at her throat. She gasped, wanting more. Wanting his lips, fingers and tongue everywhere.

Reality broke through. The sound of a car crunching its way into the parking lot. Then more sounds that Allie only half heard—a door slamming, followed by an exaggerated clearing of the throat. They sprang apart, like two teenagers caught by an outraged parent. Or, judging by the pinched expression on the older woman's face, like two people sharing an illicit tryst. The woman sniffed, skirting the bench. When the door to the clinic closed behind her, Joel and Allie laughed.

Allie looked away first, but it was Joel who said what they were thinking.

"I've been wanting to do that for days." He paused. "But—"

"It won't work," she said, anticipating him.

A longer pause. "No. Sorry. I should have—"

Allie leaped to her feet. "Forget about it, okay? One thing I learned years ago—regrets are useless. It happened. It's over. End of story." She headed for the car, smoothing out her dress as she walked.

"Allie!" He followed her, grabbed her arm as she opened the door. "If it's really no regrets, then you shouldn't be angry. We both wanted it to happen and it did. That's all there is to it. Neither of us is hurt. Right?"

Reluctantly she raised her eyes to his. But when she echoed him, whispering, "Right," she had to look away.

IT SEEMED TO BE a pattern, he thought. Their parting. Her—slamming a car door and marching, shoulders straight, up the steps and inside. Him—guiltily watching her back as she put distance between herself and the car.

It was a nice back, too. Compact. Strong. Joel sighed, sensing he'd never get the chance to place his hands on that back again. The scene on the bench had been the line drawn in the sand, so to speak. Now he wished he'd been more restrained. But that first kiss of hers—the one telling him she knew what he was feeling—had unraveled all his resolve.

God only knew what might have happened if that older woman hadn't come along. Joel shuddered. How could he have been so reckless, so oblivious to anything but the woman in his arms? What if Pat had decided to drive by the clinic? Or if Spiro had changed his mind and come by in the limo with Marko?

The front door closed behind Allie, and Joel, shifting the car angrily into drive, headed for the garage. Two of the doors were open when he pulled up. Marko and another man were at the far end of one of the garage bays, huddled in deep conversation. Curious, Joel sat in the Caddie and watched.

Marko had his back to Joel, shielding the other man. Although Joel couldn't hear what was being said, it was obvious the two were arguing. Marko was waving his arms about as if refereeing a basketball game.

Joel didn't care for Marko and he knew the feeling was mutual. Marko had greeted him with hostile suspicion the afternoon Joel moved into the apartment above the garage. Fortunately, they'd managed to stay out of each other's way, though Joel suspected Marko wouldn't tolerate his presence for long. Which was okay because Joel hoped he wouldn't be *around* for long. After what had happened in the parkette, that was just as well, too.

He was about to get out of the car when Marko spun around and stomped into the house through the inside door. The other man—George, Joel saw now—watched him go, his face an angry red, then headed for his silver-gray Jaguar parked in the adjacent bay.

Curiouser and curiouser, Joel thought, wondering what those two were up to. It would have made more sense if the other man had been Christo. Now *he* was definitely a guy up to no good.

The Jag's engine roared to life, and Joel got out of the Caddie before George noticed him. He popped the hood and pretended to be inspecting the interior as the Jag reversed out of the bay. He kept his eyes on the engine in front of him, but his ears tracked the Jag as it purred to a halt a few yards away. There was the soft hum of an electric window followed by George's voice.

"Back from the clinic already?"

Joel looked up, feigning surprise. "Yep."

"So how'd it go?"

Joel shrugged. ''No idea. Miss Newman said it would take a day or two.''

Without another word, George zipped the window back up and continued on his way. Joel pushed the Caddie hood down and watched the Jag shoot toward the main gate. George should have been at the office that morning bright and early, as was his custom. Maybe he stuck around waiting to see if the test results would be immediate. The whole house seemed to be on edge about the damn blood test.

No wonder Allie was feeling stressed out. He wondered what would happen if it turned out she wasn't a match, after all. Would even Spiro still want her around? It wasn't as if the old man had spent the past twenty-seven years searching for her.

Then the next question. *What if she was a match?*

ALLIE TAPPED on Spiro's bedroom door. She hadn't been in this upstairs wing of the house apart from the brief tour Maria had given her on the way to her room the first evening.

The house extended into two branches from a massive two-story central section taken up by the foyer, the living room, the attached solarium and the library. The south ground-floor wing led to the dining room, the kitchen, Spiro's study, and various storage rooms and pantries, with the indoor pool and games room on the lower level. Above that wing on the second floor was the master bedroom with a smaller connecting room.

The opposite wing on the second floor accommodated rooms for George, Christo and Effie, as well as two guest rooms, one of which was Allie's.

Although Spiro hadn't been feeling well that morning,

she knew that telling him about the test was the right thing to do. Yolanda answered the door and gave her a big smile.

"Hey, Miss Allie, nice to see you. Everything okay?" Her dark-brown eyes were warm and probing at the same time.

A friendly face, Allie thought, is great medicine. No wonder Spiro liked to have her around as much as possible. "I'm fine, Yolanda, thanks. Would it be possible to see Spiro? Or is he resting?"

"Your grandpa's just had an early lunch, and he's been waiting anxiously for your return. Come in."

Allie squeezed past Yolanda and followed her through a small anteroom into Spiro's main room. He was sitting in an armchair in front of the bay window that overlooked the rear of the estate and the St. Clair River. It was a breathtaking view.

"Beautiful, isn't it?" he said to Allie.

Yolanda moved noiselessly by to pick up the lunch tray at his elbow. "You'll have to do better than this, Mr. Spiro, if you're going to be well enough for that transplant."

He made a clucking sound and waved a hand, dismissing her. Yolanda returned the clucking sound, adding, "to you, too," and with a hearty laugh, breezed out through the door.

"She enjoys harassing me," he complained to Allie.

"Somehow I think you like it."

He raised an eyebrow and pointed to another chair. "Pull that up and face me. Then I can look at you and you can enjoy the spectacular view behind me."

"The view can wait. I prefer to look at you."

"Not much in this old face to look at anymore, I'm afraid."

"Are you fishing for a compliment?"

His laugh quickly erupted into a coughing fit, and Allie, sorry she'd made the quip, rushed to pour him a glass of water from a pitcher on the table. She waited for him to sip and the spasm to finish. Then she took the glass from his wrinkled, trembling hand and set it on the table.

"Not your fault. This happens all the time," he managed to gasp. After a long moment, their gazes locked, he said, "I see your mother in you. Before she was...sick. She had those same smart comebacks."

Allie opened her mouth to apologize, but he held up a hand. "No, no," he said. "I like it. Always did. That's how she wrapped me around her finger. But all that gumption fizzled out of her when..." He looked down at his lap, fussing with the knotted border of the small blanket across his legs.

"She was sick?"

He raised his head. His eyes were distant and watery pale. "Not sick. Addicted."

"I think it's the same thing," Allie murmured.

"Is that the current thinking? In our day, it was a shame. Something to hide."

"That didn't help the person."

"No, it didn't. I often wish... But you can't turn back the clock, can you."

She shook her head, knowing exactly how he was feeling. She had wished so many times in the past week that one could. They fell into a momentary silence, each lost in thought. Allie's gaze shifted to the window, the perfectly landscaped lawns and the sparkling river beyond.

"I imagine your wife enjoyed this," Allie said at last.

"My wife—your grandmother—was a shy person, and yes, she did love this room. I've done little to change it since her death."

"How did she die?"

"Heart attack. Only a year after the car crash that took your mother." He looked away. "It was all too much for her. Losing you, then Katrina. She lived for the two of you."

Allie fought the flood of guilt that swept over her. *As if I asked to be taken away!* But she let it go, knowing at once that what had happened could never be changed or made right. No regrets, she reminded herself, and thought immediately of this morning at the clinic.

"I see I've upset you. I don't mean that as a reflection on you, my dear," Spiro said. "Any blame for the past rests with me."

Allie's eyes cut back to him. "No, Spiro. It's never just one person's fault."

"I think old age is naturally a time of reproach. The sand is running out of the hourglass, and now, too late, I can see more clearly what I might have done. But you're right. We shouldn't dwell on the past. As I said before, it can't be made over." After a moment he asked, "How was this morning? Did they treat you well?"

"Like a guest at a luxury spa," she said.

Amusement glinted in his eyes. "Good. They get enough money from me."

She knew he was waiting and so quickly added, "The results won't be ready for a day or two."

He nodded. "And what about you?"

"Me?"

"Have you made a decision yet? Whether you want to go ahead if you are a match?"

"I would help anyone in trouble."

Another nod. "Like that old geezer in the river."

Allie looked down to hide her smile. Harry Maguire was at least ten years younger than Spiro.

"I take your silence as a yes, then," Spiro murmured.

"Of course," she said, raising her head. "How could you think otherwise?"

"I may be your biological grandparent, but we're still strangers."

Disputing that would have been pointless. She suddenly thought of something totally off track. "Can you tell me anything about my father's parents? Where he came from?"

Spiro tilted his head to one side as if looking at some peculiar object. "I know very little. He's from northern Michigan. Met your mother at Wayne State University. When he graduated, I took him into the firm. He was smart. A quick thinker and talker." He paused a beat. "Quick to anger, too."

"Not when I knew him," she put in.

He shrugged. "People change, mature. I imagine the events around his leaving here would have affected him profoundly."

Allie mulled that over. She wasn't certain how to interpret it. What were the events, other than leaving a wife ravaged by alcohol and taking a three-year-old with him? She wanted to ask, but noticed for the first time how far Spiro had sagged into the cushions, deflated, it seemed, by their talk.

She stood up. "I should go and let you rest. I'll let you know as soon as I've heard from the clinic."

He sent her a tired smile. "They've been instructed to inform me first."

Of course. She ought to have known.

"Shall I send for Yolanda now?"

"Please. And, Allie…"

She turned around.

"Whatever the results, I want you to know how very

happy I am that I've found you. That a dying old man's prayer has been answered."

A lump formed in Allie's throat. She managed a wobbly smile. "Thanks for saying that. I'll see you later... Grandfather."

Light transformed his face. She had a glimpse of a young Spiro—handsome and vibrant. Then she softly closed the door behind her.

CHAPTER TEN

ALLIE SHOWED UP in the dining room for dinner at the customary time and was surprised to find it empty. She wandered toward the kitchen and was met halfway by Maria.

"Miss Newman, sorry I forgot to mention it. Your cousins are dining out tonight, and Miss Effie wants a tray in her room. She suffers from migraines, poor thing. Where would you like to eat?"

"What about my grandfather?"

"Mr. Spiro usually dines in his room, but if you'd like to wait in the solarium, I'll go ask him."

"Fine." Allie made her way to the solarium. It was filled with the rich, golden sun of early evening. The windows were open and a fresh, pungent breeze swept in from the river. Allie chose one of the wicker armchairs with its plump chintz cushions and picked up a magazine from the glass-topped coffee table next to it. It was a business magazine and didn't hold her interest, so she stood at the glass door leading to the terrace and gazed out at the river. She was standing there when Spiro arrived with Yolanda.

"Nice in here this time of year," he remarked, taking his customary seat, "and in winter. But in the middle of summer, we tend to avoid it. Even with central air, the room heats up."

"It must be nice in the fall, too, when all those trees by the river have changed color."

"It is, but not as spectacular as I imagine the trees are where you come from."

"I think Northern Ontario is better for autumn color, but the countryside around Kingston can be beautiful, too."

He nodded, seeming interested in the small talk. "I hope you're enjoying your stay here, in spite of the...unusual circumstances."

Allie couldn't resist a smile. He sounded so formal. "Of course I am. The house is amazing and the food is wonderful."

He smiled at this. "But it's not home."

"No. But it *is* beautiful," she hastened to add.

Spiro turned to his nurse, who was fussing with the venetian blind on one of the windows. "Yolanda, could you find Maria and tell her that Allie and I will have dinner in here? Oh, and have her bring a bottle of champagne. Is that all right with you, my dear?"

Allie sensed he wanted this to be an occasion and she quickly agreed. She sat in the chair beside him. "I think this is one of my favorite rooms," she said. "But the library is my next."

His eyes gleamed. "Mine, too. When the boys got older and started using it more, I set up shop in my study. We don't have a so-called family room, but the television and stereo set, or whatever you call it now, are built into cupboards in the library."

"I never noticed."

"No one uses the library much anymore. They've all got televisions and what have you in their own rooms. So, there you are."

She realized how lonely it must be for him. For all of them, in a way.

"I'm glad you like the house," he went on to say. "I'm

hoping you'll come back and visit—after all of this is over,
I mean.''

The invitation startled her. She hadn't really been thinking ahead to more than the end of the week. By then, she
figured, she'd know the test results and would be preparing
for the transplant. The only problem was ensuring it all
happened well before the triathlon.

"Of course I will. Why wouldn't I?"

"Grosse Pointe is a long way from Kingston and I know
you're busy there—helping out in that health-food store,
teaching at the college. Participating in triathlons.'' He
paused, leaning forward in his chair. ''I've decided to
change my will. Now that I've found you, you must have
a part of all this.'' He made a circular motion with his
hand.

Before Allie could open her mouth to protest, Maria
swished into the room with champagne and glasses. She
brushed past Allie, accidentally bumping the corner of her
chair, and plunked the tray down loudly onto the coffee
table. Spiro gave her a sharp look, but said nothing as she
deftly uncorked the bottle and poured two flutes.

When Allie took her glass from the housekeeper, she
was shocked by the anger she saw in the woman's face.
And she knew then that Maria had overheard Spiro talking
about his will. *This is only a small example,* Allie thought
with dismay, *of what I can hope to receive when the word
gets around.*

She wasn't surprised when Ruth brought their dinner
trays. Maria, the young woman explained, had taken ill
and gone to her room. Spiro didn't seem surprised, either,
though Allie noticed his expression of disapproval. They
ate their dinners in silence. But it was a comfortable silence, Allie decided. The kind families often fall into.
Oddly enough, the comparison didn't displease her.

When dinner trays were collected, Spiro asked Allie if she'd like dessert with a game of chess in the library. The invitation thrilled her. Mainly because she hadn't played chess since her father had died. She mentioned this when she told Spiro she'd love a game.

"I won't be as challenging as your father," he said, though obviously warmed at her enthusiasm.

Allie tucked her arm through his on the way to the study and set up the game while he watched. They played, their dessert and coffee untouched on a side table until Yolanda arrived with Spiro's nighttime medication. They took a break from the chess, and this time Allie watched as Spiro swallowed pill after pill. She lost count eventually, but realized how sick her grandfather was. The desire to help him overwhelmed her, and she had to get up to browse the bookshelves so he wouldn't see the emotion in her face.

As Yolanda left, she whispered to Allie that Spiro needed to be in bed by nine and it was almost that now. Allie nodded and as soon as the nurse left, began to make yawning sounds.

"Has Yolanda put you up to something?"

"Well, obviously no one puts anything over on you," she teased.

He grinned and shook a bony index finger at her. "And don't you forget it." They smiled at each other. At last Spiro said, "She's right though. Time for bed. Besides, I suspect you've won the game already, and I've appointments first thing in the morning. By the way, how's your training going?"

"I was lazy today. But I think I'll go for a swim tomorrow." Then she remembered the last swimming venture and frowned. "Or maybe a run."

"Take that private investigator with you. Kennedy. May as well earn his keep. Once the test results are in, I guess

I'll let him go. Unless—'' he looked at Allie ''—you want him around longer.''

Heat rose in her face. ''I can't think why I would,'' she replied.

As Allie got up to leave, she impulsively stooped down and kissed Spiro on the cheek. ''Good night, Grandfather, and thanks for the chess game.''

''Thank yourself,'' he blustered, ''seeing as how you wiped me out. Can't even let a sick old man win one game of chess.''

Allie grinned and went to tell Yolanda that Spiro was ready to go upstairs. The evening had been an emotional one, and Allie felt too restless to go directly to her room. As she passed through the living room, she decided to check out the view from the solarium by moonlight.

The moon was lush and luminous above the darkness of the St. Clair River. Allie opened the solarium door and stepped out, walking along the terrace to where the lawn began. The warm, southern evening breeze invited a stroll. She headed out onto the lawn for a panoramic view of the river and the lights on the far Canadian side. A pang of homesickness struck again. There was so much to tell Susan when she returned to Kingston. Especially about her increasingly conflicted feelings about Spiro.

Was he really as benevolent as he appeared? Or were the bantering and philosophizing simply part of an act—a means to manipulate others and achieve his goals? She couldn't tell and wasn't sure she wanted to know. All she knew for certain was that Spiro Kostakis was wealthy, powerful and used to getting his way.

Allie turned to go back inside, but found the solarium door locked. She swore, realizing she'd closed it herself without checking the lock. The rooms were in complete darkness, though she could see a faint glow of light in the foyer. She knocked briskly on the glass and waited a few minutes before accepting that she'd have to go around to the front door of the house. Considering that her cousins were out and Effie and Spiro were upstairs in their bedrooms, she doubted she'd raise anyone by knocking at a *back* door.

The walk was easy, well lit by a few security spotlights. She aimed for the garage wing, thinking that maybe Marko or Joel were in, but as she approached, saw that there was no door from the garage to the outside. She walked behind the garage, glancing at the apartment above it as she did. The windows were dark.

The front door was now her only choice. She reached the end of the garage and rounded the corner. The tennis-court lights were out and with the moon hidden by the house at this end, Allie was suddenly in total darkness. She slowed her pace, afraid of stumbling.

She'd taken only a few steps when she paused, sniffing the air. A hint of cigarette smoke drifted around her. Either someone was nearby or had been standing there having a smoke recently.

"Hello?" she called. "Is anyone there?"

Silence. Allie continued walking. Then froze. Somewhere to her right, a branch cracked in the stand of fir trees between the garage and the tennis court.

"Who's there?" She was angry now, thinking how eerily similar the moment was to the episode in the swimming-pool change room. Was it the same sick person? Her pace quickened and so, too, did the rustling in the bushes. When she stopped or slowed, the sounds followed her lead. Someone was playing cat-and-mouse with her.

She was halfway to the end of the side of the garage now and could plainly see, in the light from the front of the garage, part of a parked vehicle. It looked like Joel's station wagon. Allie began to jog, aware of the irony in considering that dilapidated car some kind of refuge. The instant she picked up speed, so did the person behind and to her right.

The pounding in Allie's ears merged with her steady puffs of exhaled air, but she could still hear the running behind her. But as she approached the corner of the garage, she sensed that the person behind was lagging. That didn't slow her down, though. She broached the corner, rounded it and slammed into a body.

JOEL FELL BACKWARD against the front bumper of the car.

"What the...?" was all he could get out, breathless. When his vision cleared, he saw that he hadn't been rammed by a charging bull, but by Allie Newman. All five foot seven and 130 pounds of her, or so he estimated. The humiliation of being knocked over by someone a good six inches shorter and quite a few pounds lighter was almost as bad as hearing what she had to say. Almost.

"Someone was chasing me!" she blurted. "I was trying to get back into the house and—"

He held up a hand to slow her down.

"Did you see anyone?" she asked.

Still leaning against the car for support, he shook his head. "No. But you pack quite a wallop."

"Sorry. I didn't know you were there and I was running as fast as I could."

"Well, I'd say you're in damn good shape for that triathlon." Joel wiped a hand across his face, feeling as if he'd just awakened from some bad dream. "Tell me what happened."

"After dinner I felt too revved up to sleep so—"

"Where was dinner and who'd you eat with?"

She stammered. "In...in the solarium with my grandfather. Then we had dessert in the library and played a game of chess and after I left I wanted to go for a walk so I decided to go out through the solarium door but I didn't know it was on lock and—''

''Whoa! You're still revved up. I'm surprised you have enough energy left after pummeling me like that.''

Her laughter tinkled into the night. ''Do you always exaggerate?''

''Oh, yeah? Ever been hit in the solar plexus with a battering ram? 'Cause that's exactly what it was like, believe me.'' Her face sobered. ''Just kidding,'' he said. ''Go on, but one sentence at a time please.''

Before she got to the end, he already had a couple of suspects lined up. The first he discounted at once. He and Pat had been having a chat by the side of the garage just fifteen minutes or so ago. Pat had taken the opportunity to have a smoke, and Joel had worked his way through at least two sticks of Juicy Fruit while they'd filled each other in on the day's events.

Or most of them. Joel had judiciously edited the bench scene with Allie. When they'd parted, Pat was heading for his car. So that eliminated Pat. ''Did you call out or anything?''

''Twice.''

''Tell me what you said.''

She frowned.

He could tell she was thinking his questioning was a waste of time.

''Something like 'Who's there?' and, I don't know! Is there any point to this? Doesn't it make sense to go look for him?''

''In case he's sitting in one of those deck chairs on the terrace waiting for us to show up?''

An exasperated sigh this time, but she got the point.

Nevertheless, Joel intended to have a look around as soon as she went inside. And one glance at her face, pale under the harsh garage light, told him she needed to do just that.

"Are you okay, Allie?"

She nodded, but when he moved closer, he saw that she was on the verge of tears. He took her hand and drew her close, tilting her chin so that her eyes had to meet his. The expression in hers—a mix of fear and defiance—tugged at him. She couldn't admit a weakness, he thought. The tears that threatened were angry, as if she was ashamed of herself for letting someone frighten her.

"I don't understand why this happened," he began, not sure where he was going, but trying for a nonchalance he wasn't feeling. "Someone's playing a game with you—I think to frighten you back home."

"That's what you said the other day, after the pool thing."

"Right."

"And you said not to call the police because Spiro might get upset."

"Yeah, I did." He'd had no business making light of the whole thing. For being more afraid of jeopardizing the operation than of what could happen to Allie.

"You're supposed to be a private investigator." She paused long enough for him to guess what was coming next. "So why aren't you investigating these incidents?"

She was right. "Look, I did make some inquiries after the pool thing, but came up with nothing. I still have the note and if you want to call the police, well, that's up to you. You can give them the note."

She stared at him, obviously not liking what he was saying, because she slipped free of his hands on her shoulders. "I'll wait until the results of the test come back. Then

I'll think about the police. Right now, I'm going up to bed.''

''I'll come with you,'' he said, adding quickly at the expression on her face, ''I mean, I'll walk you upstairs.''

''I think the worst is over for the night, don't you? Besides—'' she shot him a chilling look ''—it's probably better not to place me in a situation where I might be tempted to repeat my performance of this morning.'' With that, she flicked her eyes over him as if he were some microorganism on a culture plate and walked swiftly through the garage toward the inner door that led into the house.

Put in my place again, Joel thought. He waited until the door clicked shut behind her before going in search of Marko. He didn't have to go far. The brawny chauffeur was sprawled on the couch in the apartment above the garage, eyes glued to the television. The small living room was in darkness but for the flickering light of the screen, until Joel flicked the light switch, bringing Marko to his feet.

''What the...? Turn off the light!''

Joel ignored the order and took his time getting to the couch. ''I was here about ten minutes ago,'' he lied, ''looking for you. Where were you?''

The big man shrugged. His eyes narrowed, making them smaller than usual. ''Getting some fresh air,'' he said.

''Yeah? Looks more like you were getting some exercise—which is probably a good thing, Marko. You're all sweaty.'' He sniffed. ''Smelly, too.''

''You don't like it, leave.'' He sank back onto the couch, but kept his eyes on Joel. ''Be nice to have the place to myself again.''

Joel glared at him. He itched to deck the guy, certain he'd been the one scaring Allie. The why eluded him, but after witnessing Marko's talk with George, Joel wondered if there was more than a simple chauffeur-employer relationship between them.

"You'll pay big time, Marko, if I find out you've done anything—you hear me?—anything at all to bother or frighten Allie Newman."

The beady eyes scoped his. "I'm not sure why you're bringing that chick into this conversation. It's kinda interestin', though. You think because you found her, you got some kinda claim on her? Is that what this is all about?" His broad face split in a leer.

Joel's urge to plant a fist in that beefy face was strong. Instead, he bit the inside of his mouth and headed for the door, Marko's guffaw bouncing around the room as he left.

Ten minutes later the station wagon was speeding down the drive. Joel glanced at the big house in the rearview mirror. Allie's room was at the back, so there was no way—short of actually going inside—of telling if her light was out or not. He wished he'd taken her to her room, after all. Maybe… *Nah, don't torture yourself, pal. It's like she said this morning—no regrets. No anything. That's what she was really saying.*

He slowed down to pass through the gates. They were always open, even in the dead of night. Spiro had told him he was too old and sick to worry about someone stealing into the estate to harm him. Perhaps once he heard what happened to Allie, he would change his mind.

As he turned left onto Lakeshore Drive, Joel realized he ought to tell the others what had happened. He didn't want to, because he wasn't sure what the response would be. *Wait and see,* whispered the tiny voice inside him. Half a mile down the road he spotted the van, tucked between two pine trees off the shoulder. He drove a few yards past it, parked, then walked back. The door swung open at his knock.

The third man on the team, Mike, was chomping on a hamburger. Cheeks bulging, he waved a hand in greeting. Pat was already at the helm, earphones on. He signaled for Joel to join him.

Joel climbed into the van and sat on a stool next to Pat. "Whatcha got?"

"Nothing too exciting. Spiro got a phone call right after Allie left. It was George asking for a meeting with him first thing in the morning. He sounded real edgy. Oh, and, uh, you might wanna hear the post-dinner tapes. Your name came up—but not in vain." He grinned.

Joel heard Mike chortle behind him. "I know you're dying to fill me in, pal."

A snort from Mike. Pat took off the earphones and said, "Have a listen yourself," so Joel had no choice but to go along with them, though he knew he was being set up.

He listened to the library tape and fought to keep his face impassive when Spiro's offer to let him go was so indifferently received by Allie. The morning grapple at the clinic must have seriously ticked her off. When he finished, he shrugged and handed the earphones back.

"Obviously I haven't worked hard enough on my image."

Mike spluttered and Pat laughed.

"I heard you *never* had trouble with the ladies, Kennedy. You must be getting old or something," Pat joked.

Joel returned Pat's grin. "What can I say? Next to you, we're all old-timers." Joel had just offered a not-so-subtle reminder that it was Pat's first undercover. The younger man flushed.

"Hah! Good one!" exclaimed Mike, crawling over cables, empty food containers, crushed pop cans and technical equipment to resume his seat next to Pat. "So let's review. Meeting first thing in the morning—where? The study?"

Joel pursed his lips. "Maybe his bedroom. Yolanda usually gives him his massage right before his bath, and that's at eight-thirty. Spiro's a stickler for routine. Plus, I bet he resented George calling him after his bedtime."

"Yeah. He said so." Mike cast Joel an appraising glance.

"We've got a bug in the bedroom, haven't we?"

Blank looks. Joel swore. "Jeez, you gotta be kidding. I thought you were in charge of the bugs." He directed this at Pat.

"I did the library, dining room and study. No one thought of the bedroom. I mean, the guy just sleeps there. A lot."

"You were supposed to do it when I was in Kingston. That was the whole point of your going undercover. To set bugs and taps. You led me to believe it had been done."

"It *was* done. Just not the bedroom. Maybe they'll meet in the study. Makes more sense."

"Not first thing in the morning. Spiro doesn't go downstairs till after the massage, the bath, the shave and breakfast. That would be at least nine, and you said George has set it up for—what time?"

"Eight-fifteen. Said he had a meeting in the city at ten," Mike replied.

Joel noticed how Mike was avoiding looking at Pat. Distancing himself. Not wanting to get involved in the guy's screwup. Except that now they *all* were.

"My bet's on the bedroom," Joel said, fixing his eyes on Pat.

"So...now what?" Pat looked from Joel to Mike and back to Joel.

There was anger in his eyes, Joel thought, plus a refusal to accept blame. But he had to be careful not to blow things at this point, not to goad Pat into another blunder.

"Take the night to think of something," he suggested. "I'll meet you at the gardener's shed at seven." Joel headed for the door. When he reached it, he turned around to say, by way of appeasement, "Maybe I'll try to come up with an idea, too."

Then he opened the door and stepped into the dark night.

CHAPTER ELEVEN

THE NEXT TWO DAYS passed in a blur for Allie. She worked out, thumbed through several of the books in Spiro's library and surreptitiously looked for Joel, but failed to see any sign of him. Their last encounter had been the day of the fire alarm. She'd gone for a run just after six-thirty and, returning an hour later, was startled to find the family members clustered at the top of the terrace steps. Except for George, they were all in dressing gowns and slippers.

A bleary-eyed Christo filled her in, complaining that the alarm had gone off and "that private investigator—what's his name?" had banged on all the bedroom doors insisting everyone leave the house immediately.

Right after she'd jogged up to the front steps, Joel himself appeared to announce that there was no sign of either fire or smoke. The alarm, he'd said, must have been triggered by a short circuit, and everyone could go back inside. As Allie started to follow, Joel had gestured for her to stay behind.

"What time did you set out for your run, Allie?"

"About six-thirty. Why?"

"Just wondered if you saw any unusual characters lurking about."

"No, but I thought you said the alarm was some kind of electrical problem."

"Yeah, it appears that way. I just wondered if you'd noticed anyone on the estate grounds."

She'd had to think about that because there always seemed to be someone working outside. Finally she said, "I don't remember seeing a single person today." Then she'd tried to brush past him.

"I just want you to know that I'm taking what you said the other night seriously. About doing more investigating. Checking out unusual incidents," he clarified.

Her first thought was that he was teasing her, but his eyes searched her face in an apparent quest for approval.

"Well, for this particular incident, maybe a phone call to an electrician is the best option," she said, trying not to sound too sarcastic. This time as she went to pass him, he let her go. She hadn't seen him since.

Now, the third morning after her blood test, Yolanda knocked on Allie's door with the news that Spiro would like to take her out for lunch.

"Your grandpa said it would be someplace special so to wear a dress." Yolanda pursed her lips. "But you wear whatever you like."

Allie smiled. "What time does he want me to be ready for lunch?"

"The limo will be waiting for you at the front door at twelve-thirty."

"Sharp."

Yolanda flashed a grin. "*Always* sharp, honey. You got it."

Allie closed the bedroom door behind her. She didn't have to wonder what the special occasion was about. The blood-test results had to be in.

HER GUESS WAS CONFIRMED twenty minutes into lunch. Spiro had taken her to his favorite Greek restaurant in downtown Detroit. He'd been quiet during the drive into the city, occasionally pointing out sights and landmarks of interest. Allie had found herself doing most of the talking, and the conversation flowed naturally. She'd recounted some of her childhood on the farm, told him her father had established a carpentry business in Kingston and eventually also became known as a canoe and kayak maker. She'd also told him about Susan entering their lives and how she'd filled the role of mother. Spiro had winced at that, but didn't stop her from continuing. It was as if, she realized later, he couldn't hear enough. And during all of it, he'd listened attentively, a thoughtful expression on his face.

After they'd ordered and the steward had poured a glass of wine for Allie, Spiro said, "The clinic phoned this morning with the test results."

Allie set her wineglass down.

"You're a match," he said.

Even though she'd suspected this was what he was going to say, a strange sensation, akin to wooziness, floated through her. She managed a wobbly smile. "Okay. When?"

"You still want to go through with it?"

"I said I would."

"Yes, my dear, you did. But I want you to think about it tonight and give me your answer tomorrow. I won't hold you to any previous commitments," he said, smiling. "The procedure comes with some discomfort to you, I understand. So if you want to change your mind—"

"No! I said I would and I will. When?"

"I'm in remission and you've already passed the physical with flying colors, so the clinic can do it the day after tomorrow."

"Saturday?"

"Yes." His brow creased with concern. "Are you certain?"

Allie reached out a hand to pat his, resting on the edge of the table. "Yes...Grandfather. I'm very certain."

His smile was one that would come back to haunt Allie in the days ahead.

ALLIE WASN'T SURPRISED to receive word of predinner drinks that night. Spiro had warned her that he'd have to tell the rest of the family. When Maria came to her room about four o'clock, the housekeeper seemed distant.

"Maria? Where will drinks be served?" Allie asked as the woman turned to leave.

"Didn't I just say?"

"No, you didn't."

"The library. At five-thirty." She paused in the doorway to ask, "Is there a special occasion you're celebrating?"

Allie hesitated. It wasn't her place to reveal the test results. "Why do you ask?"

"He told me to open a bottle of some expensive champagne he'd been saving and to use the Waterford crystal. That's usually for guests, not just family."

"Perhaps he's going to announce some news," Allie evaded.

"Mmm. Perhaps." She hesitated for a moment, then drifted through the doorway.

Allie arrived in the library early and browsed through the shelves of books while she waited for the others. One section of an end shelf was devoted to leather-bound yearbooks, and Allie, curious, took one out. It was a high-school yearbook, and when she turned to the pages of graduates, Allie discovered her mother's photograph. She stared at it, awed again by her mother's beauty. Her dark hair flowed dramatically over the black gown, and unlike many of the other female grads, Katrina wore a minimum of makeup.

Allie began to flip through the pages, searching for more photographs. There were several. Her mother on the swim team. Again, on the soccer team. Allie's jaw dropped. *Soccer. Who'd have thought?* There she was again, beaming from the midst of a cluster of performers from the school's production of *West Side Story,* and last, a random shot of Katrina with a gang of students at a football game.

Allie leafed through until, satisfied there were no more pictures, closed the book and replaced it on the shelf. Her hands trembled as she fingered the yearbooks from Wayne State University. There were four of them and she knew her parents had met there. She hesitated, wondering if she'd have time to look through another before the others arrived. A voice from behind made the decision for her.

"You can have those, if you like."

Allie spun around.

Spiro was standing in the doorway. "She wasn't always an alcoholic," he said, using his cane to propel himself to his favorite chair. "In those books, she still had promise." He propped the cane against the side of the chair and, placing his palms on each of the arms, lowered himself slowly into the seat.

"I was hoping to find one with both my parents," Allie said. She left the shelf and took a chair next to her grandfather.

He nodded. "You should. The last one, I think. Their graduating year. She met your father that year, but they weren't really an item until the end of it. I remember the first time she brought him home." He fell silent. "Young Eddie Hughes. I knew as soon as he walked in the door that he came from poor Irish stock."

Allie felt the hairs on the back of her neck bristle until he added, "Only because it took one to know one. He had the same drive and awe of wealth my brother and I had when we came to this country."

"But my father was born here."

"I know. When you've grown up poor, meeting the rich is like entering another country, believe me. I still had the feeling the first time I went to the Grosse Pointe Yacht Club. I couldn't believe that I was actually a member of such a place."

"My father wasn't the type to be ashamed of his background."

"But he didn't tell you anything about his family, did he."

His keen eyes drilled into hers. Allie averted her head. "Not much. He told me his parents were dead."

Spiro waited a minute before saying, "And well they might be, by now. But when he and your mother married, his parents came to the wedding."

"What were they like?"

"Simple, plain folk. In awe of this place and the wedding itself, but decent and hardworking. Nothing to be ashamed of." He sighed. "We were all proud of young Eddie." His voice dropped.

Until he ran away with your granddaughter. The conclusion was obvious. Was she ever going to understand what had happened?

"My dear," Spiro said, reaching over to pat the back of her hand as if to make amends. "Remember what I've already told you about rewriting the past? It can't be done. You know he was a good man. You lived with an older Eddie Hughes, and I lived with a younger one. One that was more impetuous and hotheaded. They were both your father. You have good memories of him. At my age, I think that's all that matters."

Yes and no, she thought. But it always comes down to this. *I was deprived of a mother and a family I never got to know.* An overwhelming sadness flowed through her. When she looked at her grandfather again, she saw that he recognized what she was feeling.

"Come, give an old man a hug," he said, his voice husky.

And she did, crouching awkwardly at his side and leaning against the arm of the chair to support her weight. She kissed his cheek.

"Before the others come," he went on to say, smiling gently at her, "I want to tell you that I've changed my will to include you. I know you insist on having nothing, but I think you'll be content with what I've planned."

"Grandfather, I—"

There was a gentle tap at the door. Maria was standing on the threshold, a tray of champagne flutes in her hands. She looked from Spiro to Allie, just getting to her feet after crouching to hug him.

"Ruth's coming with the champagne and appetizers, Mr. Kostakis. Where would you like me to put this?"

"Wherever you like, Maria. Why so formal? You've delivered plenty of trays to this room."

The woman's face flushed as she set the tray on a high wooden table across from Spiro. "I didn't want to interrupt," she muttered, and left the room without another word.

After a moment Spiro said, "I don't know what's gotten into that woman. She's been very peculiar lately. Always hovering over me."

"She's worried about you, as we all are."

He smiled indulgently. "By the way, I've some photograph albums I want you to take back to Kingston with you. Spend some time with them, and when you come for a visit, we can go through them together." He caught something in her face, adding quickly, "You will come to visit, won't you?"

Allie whispered, "Of course," uncertain if the prospect pleased or intimidated her.

The library door swung open all the way as Ruth entered with a tray of appetizers. Christo was right behind her, bearing the champagne in a bucket. He frowned when he caught sight of Allie and Spiro.

"I thought you said five-thirty. It's just that now."

"We got here a bit earlier," Spiro said, motioning for Ruth to set the tray next to the one Maria had brought.

"Did we now?" Christo murmured, his eyes fixed on Allie as he walked over to the table. "What a coincidence," he said in a voice only Allie could have heard.

The others arrived, including Lynn, whom Allie hadn't seen since the Sunday of the open house. Her greeting was cool as she swept by Allie to sit close to George. Effie appeared, looking drawn and pale. When Ruth left, closing the door behind her, Spiro asked George to uncork the champagne and pour.

The room was dead quiet while everyone watched George pass the flutes around. Allie, knowing what Spiro was about to say, felt the tension mount inside her. Her face was already warming up in anticipation.

"I've some wonderful news," Spiro began, holding his glass aloft in a trembling hand. "The test results show that Allie is a match!"

Four pairs of eyes shifted as one from Spiro to Allie. Her smile would have been warmer, she knew, if the expressions in those eyes had been happy and congratulatory.

But she read in them emotions varying from caution to outright suspicion, in Lynn's case.

And worry, Allie guessed, worry that I'm about to rob them of their inheritance. Knowing, too, that he'd also changed his will, she looked away, peering down at the hand clenched around her wineglass.

It was George who spoke first, clearing his throat loudly. "That's great, Uncle Spiro. When will the procedure take place?"

"Saturday morning. Unless either Allie or I come down with the sniffles, of course. Then it'll be on hold." His soft chuckle echoed in the silent room.

Allie was appalled and embarrassed for Spiro at their obvious lack of joy at his news, but couldn't think of anything to say. Once again, George took charge.

"I don't think we need to worry about Allie coming down with anything, judging from the training schedule she's been following. She has to be the most fit of all of us."

All eyes turned her way again and Allie's face reddened.

"As for you, Uncle Spiro," George went on, "I know you're in good hands with Yolanda." A slight pause. "Where is she, by the way?"

"She left early. Some special event at her daughter's school. Besides, I can get myself to bed. I've been feeling better in recent days than I've felt in a couple of years. Shall we have dinner now? I'm starving."

Everyone stood, but it was Allie who took the cane and helped Spiro to his feet. Grasping her arm in his, he led the way to the dining room. In spite of Spiro's good humor, dinner was a subdued affair. Only Spiro ate heartily. The most, Allie thought, she'd seen him eat since her arrival. As soon as the dessert plates were being cleared, people began to rise and make excuses to leave.

Effie began the exodus, pleading a migraine. Lynn announced that she had an early-morning conference call and stood expectantly, waiting for George to get the message and take her home. As he left, he turned to Spiro to ask, "I'd like to see you, Uncle Spiro, before you go to bed. We still haven't had the talk we'd scheduled the other day, the morning of the fire alarm."

"Very well. Come to my study at nine. I asked Marko to help me upstairs about nine-thirty so..."

George nodded. "I'll be back by then." He and Lynn left without another word.

"I think I'd like to sit in on that meeting tonight, too, Uncle Spiro," said Christo.

A glint of amusement shone from the old man's eyes. "Of course." Turning to Allie, he asked, "What about you, Allie? Would you like to be at the meeting?"

She knew at once he was having a joke at Christo's expense, but she didn't feel like being part of it. She murmured no and, turning her head aside, saw the alarm in her cousin's face. Then he left.

"Allie, my dear, will you help me back to my study? And since you've chosen not to attend this very important meeting, I'll give you some of those photograph albums now."

"Do you *want* me to come to this meeting, Grandfather?"

Spiro laughed. "Heavens, no. I've a feeling they want to ensure my affairs are in order before the transplant operation on Saturday. Just in case."

"It's not a life-threatening procedure, is it?"

"No, my dear. Certainly not for you. And if it's successful, as we hope it will be, then I've nothing to worry about, either."

Allie held out an arm for him and, as they slowly walked

out of the room, thought about the very real possibility that the transplant might not work. She glanced at her grandfather's face in profile and realized, for the very first time, that what she was feeling deep inside was affection.

JOEL LIFTED THE EARPHONES from his head and leaned back against the interior wall of the van. He was exhausted. A day fueled by coffee, stale doughnuts and gum didn't bode well for the morrow, though he knew the sick feeling in his gut had nothing to do with his physical health. It was already eight-thirty and Allie had just accompanied Spiro to his study. George and Christo were due in half an hour. Joel figured they were hot to straighten out a couple of things. Like, did Spiro intend to change his will? He hoped that this conversation would produce what they needed to keep the operation going. If not…well, Joel didn't care to go there.

The van door flew open and Mike barreled in. "Sorry I'm late. Had to take my son to a soccer game and it went into overtime. Can you believe it?"

Joel rubbed at his face and downed the last of his Coke. "Where's Pat? He's supposed to relieve me at nine."

"Dunno. He'll turn up. Give the kid some slack, why don't you? Besides, it's just past eight-thirty." He lumbered, stooped, over to the chair next to Joel. "Anything interesting?"

"The old man's changing his will."

Mike's eyes popped. "No kidding. Jeez. That should get things stirred up. Do the boys know yet?"

"No, but they must suspect. The test results show she's a match and the transplant's set for Saturday."

"Hey, things are moving at last. This just might be the catalyst. Right?"

"That's what I'm worried about."

Mike gave him the once-over. "That's what we want, isn't it? Some action? Otherwise, the operation's put out to pasture."

Joel closed his eyes. "I'm worried about Allie."

"Allie?" Mike grinned. "Ah, I get it. You've established a bond. No more Miss Newman. It's *Allie* now." His voice drawled the last sentence, teasing.

Joel was too tired to respond, even though he knew Mike was angling for a comeback. He handed another pair of earphones to Mike and said, "Battle stations."

Another grin. "Aye-aye, Cap."

Joel checked his watch—exactly eight-fifty-five—jotted the time down on the clipboard in his lap and checked the tape. He and Mike placed their headsets on and tuned in to Spiro's study.

Spiro: *Come in. Oh, Christo. Where's your brother?*

Christo: *He just called on his cell phone. He got held up in some traffic coming back from Lynn's place. He'll be another ten minutes.*

Spiro: *Well if he's too late I'm going to bed. My routine has already been shot to hell with Yolanda taking off early. Maybe you can tell me what's so important you gotta keep your old uncle up past his bedtime.*

Christo: *George and I are worried about you.*

Spiro: *I know you are. But the operation's standard these days. Either it works or it doesn't. If it does, I get maybe another couple of years. If it doesn't…who knows.*

Christo: *It's a gamble, true, but you gotta take it. Right, Uncle Spiro?*

Spiro: *Sure. So what else is bothering you?*

Christo: *One thing I want to bring up is this private investigator, Kennedy. What do we need him for? Did you know he's been camped out in the hallway upstairs the last two nights? Ever since the day of the fire alarm.*

Spiro: *I know he has. He came and got permission to be there.*

Christo: *What for?*

Spiro: *Apparently the electrician I called in said there was nothing wrong with our system. So someone must have…*

Christo: *Pulled the alarm?*

Spiro: *That's what Kennedy thinks.*

Christo: *Someone from here? That's ridiculous. What would be the point?*

Spiro: *Kennedy doesn't know, but he offered to stand guard up there, keep an eye on the hall. If the alarm goes off in the night, at least he can help me get out. Not to mention the rest of you.*

Christo: *I think it's unnecessary for him to be there now. Besides, it's an invasion of our privacy.*

Spiro: *Okay, okay, you may be right. Hand me the house phone and I'll call him, tell him to forget about it. (Pause) No answer. Tell you what, when Marko comes to take me up to bed, I'll tell him to let Kennedy know.*

Christo: *Thanks, Uncle Spiro. And do we even need him around at all anymore? I mean, he's served his purpose. He found Allie for you.*

Spiro: *You're probably right. I thought he'd be a familiar face for her, but she seems to have settled in just fine.*

Christo: *I'll say.*

Spiro: *What's that supposed to mean?*

Christo: *Nothing. Just that it's like she's always been around.*

Spiro: *And I do hope she always is around—a lot. I've asked her to come back and visit, after the operation. There's one other thing. Damn. Who's that?*

Christo: *I'll get it. (pause) Maria, with coffee for us.*

Spiro: *Maria, I wasn't expecting this, but thank you. Set it right there. As I was going to say, I'm changing my will. The papers will be signed tomorrow.*

Christo: *Was there a need for that, Uncle Spiro?*

Spiro: *What did you think I'd do when I found my long-lost granddaughter? Not acknowledge her at all?*

Christo: *But we had everything worked out. The transition from you to George at the office, starting when you got sick. He's worked damn hard, Uncle Spiro.*

Spiro: *I know he has. Why do you think he's going— Maria! Are you still here? We're fine. And can you have breakfast ready for eight sharp?*

Maria: *Yes sir. Oh, here's Mr. George now.*

George: *Uncle Spiro, I hope Christo apologized for me.*

Christo: *Uncle Spiro was just talking about his will.*

George: *Oh?*

Spiro: *George, don't just stand there with your mouth gaping. Sit down. You boys will get your fair share, believe me. Just that Allie will get something, too. She's my grand-daughter, after all. Now, I'm too tired to go on with this talk. Get Marko for me, will you? He's waiting in the hall, I think.*

George: *Uncle Spiro, if we could just discuss this—*

Spiro: *Not now, George. Another time.*

There was a knock at the door and Marko came in to take Spiro upstairs. When the study door closed, Joel raised the headset from his head and looked across at Mike.

"You're toast, buddy," was all his partner said.

THE SEPARATION between dream and real life was a blurred line until the pounding at Allie's door defined it.

The door burst open, and Allie's eyes, blinking in the stream of early-morning sun that fell across her bed, took several seconds to adjust.

Yolanda was standing beside her bed, her eyes wide with fright and shock.

"Yolanda! What is it? What's the matter?"

"Oh, honey." The nurse choked up. "It's your grand-daddy—Mr. Spiro. I...I'm afraid he's...he's passed away."

Allie shot up. "Passed away?"

Yolanda extracted a tissue from her dress pocket. "Yes, honey. Mr. Spiro is dead."

CHAPTER TWELVE

LOOKING BACK, Allie couldn't recall throwing on a robe or even going to Spiro's bedroom with Yolanda. She did remember the strength of the nurse's arms. And later she conjured up George's face as he met them at Spiro's door. His face had been ashen, his eyes haunted. She recalled the pronounced lines across his thirty-something forehead, as if he'd aged since being awakened with the news half an hour earlier.

He held out his arms to Allie. The hug was brief, but his hands squeezed her shoulders reassuringly, and Allie impulsively turned her face to kiss his cheek. Christo arrived then with his mother, and his mouth pursed in disapproval when he saw them. George ushered them into the room.

Spiro was lying under the covers, his eyes closed and his face tranquil in death.

"He was so peacefullike, I thought he must've been having some nice dreams," Yolanda said, bursting into tears.

Allie wrapped an arm around Yolanda and moved with her to a love seat opposite the bed. She couldn't take her eyes off Spiro, expecting him to rise any second and ask what everyone was staring at.

No one else was crying, though Effie dabbed at her eyes and daintily blew her nose. Allie's own emotions were battling inside her. Shock and disbelief were winning out, temporarily, over grief. She knew that would come later when she was alone. For now, she needed to know what had happened.

"Who found him? You, Yolanda?" she asked.

Increased sobbing from the nurse, which Allie took as confirmation.

When Yolanda was able to speak, she said, "He told me to come in whenever I wanted this morning, but I was already feeling guilty about leaving early last night, so I made a point of getting here at my usual time—six-forty-five—for his massage at seven." She stopped to blow her nose. "If only I'd stayed till his bedtime. At least I could've seen if anything was different with his condition."

Allie glanced around the room. All eyes were on Spiro. "How did he die?"

"Good God, it's obvious isn't it? He died of leukemia." Christo's voice oozed sarcasm.

"But he was in remission."

"So, it was something else. Some organ breakdown from the chemo he's had or the pills he took. Who knows? He was seventy-eight years old."

Yolanda raised her face from the wad of tissues she held. "Allie's right. Mr. Spiro was in remission and there was nothing wrong with his heart—not that I knew about."

A chilled silence filled the room. Finally George asked, "Are you suggesting…?"

"We should call the police," Allie said.

There was a barely muffled expletive from Christo. "Call his family doctor—someone has to sign a death certificate, anyway. But calling the police right now is ridiculous. Come, Mother. I'll take you back to your room and have Maria bring you breakfast there."

As he escorted Effie from the room, he paused long

enough to glare at Allie, then turned to George to repeat, "Call the doctor, George. I'll inform the office and people there."

After they left, Yolanda blew her nose loudly one last time. "He was a good boss. Tough and demanding, but fair and generous, too." She heaved a sigh. "Maybe his heart couldn't take the strain, after all."

"But you said his heart was okay," George reminded her.

"It had to be something to take him away in his sleep. If not his heart, what?" Her question went unanswered.

George rose and said, "I'll call the doctor now. Would you two like breakfast? Or at least coffee?"

"Coffee would be good," Allie murmured. She stood up and reached for Yolanda's hand. "Come, we'll go to the kitchen and get some coffee."

"If you don't mind, Miss Allie, I'd like to sit with Mr. Spiro until the doctor comes."

Allie nodded and left the room. The impact of what had happened was just starting to hit. As she walked, dream-like, along the hallway, all the countless experiences she'd never have with her grandfather filled her mind. By the time she reached the foyer, she could scarcely see through her tears.

She didn't realize she was heading directly for Joel until his voice stopped her. "Allie? What is it?"

"My grandfather's dead," she blurted, and flung herself into his arms. She buried her face in the hollow between his neck and shoulder. His hand at the back of her head held her gently to him. For the first time since she'd awakened to Yolanda's terrible news, she felt anchored to something familiar. She stayed there long enough to soak his cotton shirt with her tears.

When she raised her head, she saw him in a blur through eyes she knew were red and swollen. His smile was tender.

"Are you all right?"

She nodded and started to speak, but his index finger touched her lightly on the mouth.

"Wait," he said. "When you're ready, you can tell me what happened."

Allie took a deep breath, calming herself. "Yolanda came to wake me early. She said Spiro was dead. I went with her, and George was just coming out of Spiro's bedroom."

"Was he alone?"

"Yes, but then Christo and Effie arrived."

"Did you all go into the room together?"

"Uh-huh."

"Did you notice anything different from the last time you were in there?"

"No."

"Anything lying on the floor? Tipped over on a table? That's what I mean."

"No, no. I didn't notice anything. Why? What are you thinking?"

"It's okay. I'm just asking questions that someone else might ask later. Now's a good time because your memory is fresh."

"Someone like the police?"

"Who knows? But don't worry now. Why don't you go get dressed, then have something to eat. I've a feeling it's going to be a long day."

Before she pulled away from him, he bent to kiss her on the top of her head. "Bye for now," he murmured, his voice husky.

He turned sharply, heading for the hall leading to

Spiro's study. Allie watched until he disappeared, then went upstairs.

IT WAS A LONG DAY, as Joel had predicted. When Spiro's doctor arrived, he conferred with George before announcing that he'd decided to call the coroner. This caused a stir, which Allie first heard about from Maria.

Tight-lipped, the housekeeper informed Allie that the doctor had requested that all members of the household stay on the premises until the coroner arrived and had a chance to talk to them.

"What are my cousins doing right now?"

"Mr. George is calling friends and business associates of Mr. Spiro's. Mr. Christo is playing tennis with Mr. George's fiancée, and Mrs. Kostakis is resting."

And I'm sitting in the solarium reading magazines, Allie thought. All present and accounted for and no one seriously grieving over Spiro Kostakis. The realization filled her with dismay. Surely Spiro deserved more. But what? Weeping and wailing hadn't been his style, either. She just wished one of them gave the *appearance* of caring.

She glanced up, realizing Maria was still there. The housekeeper was staring out the solarium windows.

"Maria? Are you all right?"

"Hmm?" Her pale face turned to Allie.

"I asked if you were all right. Maybe you should get some rest yourself. Or go somewhere."

Maria frowned. "And where would I go, Miss Allie? This is the only home I've known."

"I meant, go visit a friend or relative. Just get away from this place for a bit after the coroner's talked to you."

"I've got no relatives and my only friends are here, in the kitchen. Ruth and Liz. And they'll be taking turns seeing their own families today. Likely tomorrow we'll all be getting ready for a funeral."

"Not if there's an autopsy."

"I don't see why the coroner had to come. Anybody can see Mr. Spiro died in his sleep. He was an old man with leukemia."

"I don't know why, either, Maria. But I do know that I had lunch with my grandfather yesterday, and he was alert and vibrant and looking forward to the transplant." Allie stopped, unable to say more.

After a moment Maria muttered, "People are always stirring up things. Can't leave well enough alone."

She left the solarium before Allie could ask her what she meant. She tossed the magazine aside and decided she ought to take the advice she'd tried to give Maria. Except that she, too, had nowhere to go. Until she thought of the swimming pool. A half hour of laps was exactly what she needed.

JOEL MET GEORGE at the door to Spiro's study.

"Mr. Kennedy," George began, "I wasn't expecting to see you again."

He looked embarrassed. Perhaps he was afraid of some kind of confrontation? Joel wondered.

"I had to pick up a few things and heard the news about Mr. Kostakis. I'm very sorry."

George gave a preoccupied nod, as if he had more important things on his mind.

"Is there anything I can do for the family?"

"Uh, no, I don't think so. But thank you. Do we owe you any money?"

"Marko said there'd be a check for me this morning. I didn't get a chance to talk to Mr. Kostakis yesterday, so I hoped to—"

George interrupted him. "Yes, it was a shock for all of us. I'll let you get your things, then, and be on your way. Leave your address and I'll see that a check is sent out as soon as possible, if that's okay with you. Do you have a ride into the city?"

"Yeah, I've got my car. I noticed that the doctor's arrived. Has he said anything about how your uncle died?"

"Not really, but he's decided to call the coroner."

"Oh?"

"I assume that's standard if there's no obvious sign of death."

"So the doctor's ruled out a heart attack?"

"He can't determine that without an autopsy. He just said Uncle Spiro had no known heart condition so…"

"He thinks there should be an autopsy."

"I guess so. God, I suppose that also means the probation of Uncle Spiro's will might be delayed." An anxious frown creased his brow.

"Is that a problem for you?" Joel asked.

George gave him a sharp look. "No, of course not. Why should it be?"

Joel shrugged, though he guessed the question had been rhetorical.

"Fine, then, Mr. Kennedy. Nice to have met you and thanks for doing such a great job of finding Allie. It meant a lot to my grandfather." He added, "Though it all came to nothing in the end unfortunately."

"Nothing?" Joel had a nasty suspicion he knew where the guy was heading.

"I mean the whole transplant thing. It's all irrelevant now, isn't it."

"Maybe. But you found your cousin," he pointed out.

The frown again. "Yes, so we did." Another sigh.

Joel wondered how much of a complication Allie now

posed for her cousins. George retreated into the study, closing the door behind him. Joel had been given his walking papers and had no good reason for hanging around the house. But he didn't want to leave without seeing Allie and offering some kind of explanation. Not the whole story, of course, but something that might redeem him in her eyes in the days ahead.

And he knew he'd need a whole lot of good luck to turn things around now. The news of Spiro's death—which Marko delivered just as Joel had stepped out of the shower—had been a blow. And not only to the operation. Joel had liked the old guy, in spite of what he knew about the Kostakis family.

He was almost at the main foyer when he met Maria, carrying a tray of dirty dishes to the kitchen.

"Mr. Kennedy," she said. "I heard you were leaving us."

Word certainly got around, he thought. "Yes, I am, Maria. Just collecting the last of my things. Have you seen Miss Newman recently?"

"No, I haven't. Shall I give her a message if I do?"

"No, it's okay. Maybe I'll see her on my way out. Bye Maria."

"Goodbye—and good luck, Mr. Kennedy."

Joel went out the door and stood on the terrace for a minute, scanning the front lawn for any sign of Allie. She might have gone for a run or for a swim. He decided to check in with the guys again, then make up some excuse to come back to the estate. This might be his last chance to put something right. It was more important now than ever, since everything else had been blown to hell.

MIKE GAVE JOEL a warning sign as soon as he opened the van. Joel's eyes flicked from him to a third man sitting at the controls. *Damn.*

"Steve," he said, nodding at his boss.

"Hi, Joel. Doesn't look too good, eh?"

"A setback."

Steve snorted. "Yeah, right. A big setback, fella. Mike'n I've been discussing our next step."

Joel frowned. "I hope you planned to include me."

Steve waved a dismissive hand. "No need to get on your high horse. I've just heard the tape from Kostakis's bedroom."

Joel swore under his breath. He hadn't heard it all himself yet, and now plans were already being made.

"Here, give us your take on it." Steve handed Joel a pair of headphones.

When Joel was ready, he nodded to Mike who ran the tape. A knock on the door. Marko coming in to help Spiro get ready for bed. *No bath tonight,* Spiro said. *He'll shower in the morning.* Some heaving and grunting sounds as Marko obviously helped the old guy into pajamas and bed.

Then Spiro told Marko that he'd decided he didn't need Kennedy on the payroll anymore, that he'd have a check waiting for him in the morning. Joel twitched at mention of his name, not daring to glance at Steve. Before Marko left, Spiro asked him to have Ruth bring him a cup of hot milk. A door closed and there were sounds of Spiro settling in bed.

"This is it?" Joel asked Mike.

Mike shook his head. "Not yet. I'll fast-forward to the part we want you to hear."

Another knock at the door, followed by Spiro's voice.

"Come in, Ruth."

"I've brought your milk, sir. Shall I put it on the night table?"

"Yes, Ruth. Then I'd like you to do me a favor. See that file on my desk? Could you bring it over to me?"

Some rustling sounds, followed by Ruth's voice.

"Here you go, sir. Anything else?"

"Stay a minute, Ruth. I want you to witness this for me."

More papers shuffling. "Here, you sign this one. Right at the bottom, on the line marked by an 'x.'"

"May I ask what I'm signing, sir?"

A chuckle. "Not to worry, Ruth. It's not a loan guaranty, it's my will. I've changed it and have decided to sign it tonight, instead of tomorrow. Guess I don't want anyone to try to change my mind."

"Oh, no sir. That wouldn't be very likely."

A laugh from Spiro this time.

"So, right here, sir?"

"Yes, Ruth."

A pause. "Terrific. Thanks, Ruth, I appreciate it. Saves me some trouble tomorrow. Now if you'll put this folder in the bottom of my dresser, I'd appreciate it."

"Anything else, sir?"

"No. If you see Maria, tell her I don't wish to be disturbed again tonight. Oh, and, Ruth, this business between us—the witnessing—please keep that confidential for now."

"Yes, sir. Good night, then."

The sound of a door closing.

"Well, well," Joel said, "the old guy signed the will last night, instead of today. Wonder what made him do that?"

"Like he said, maybe he was worried that the boys would put more pressure on him not to. Anyway, it's not finished yet. The next bit's what's really important. There's a gap of about an hour of tape time, so I'll fast-forward again.'' Mike fiddled with the machine.

Joel watched Steve while he waited for the tape to spin to the designated spot. The fact that his boss had shown up so quickly meant the operation was probably going to be shut down. He wasn't worried about himself. There was always another job, another operation. But what about Allie?

When Mike gave the signal, Joel put the headphones back on. He heard the click of a door opening and closing. There was a swish of movement. Whoever had entered the room had done so stealthily. Then, a sound of startled fear. From Kostakis? Joel heard a muffled word, but missed it. He motioned for Mike to replay.

''I can tinker a bit. Hang on a sec,'' Mike said. He raised an index finger, indicating *go*.

Joel straightened in his seat, every auditory nerve on alert.

Rustling—sheets thrown back? That word again. *You*—

Muffled sounds followed by silence. A quiet so long Joel thought it was over. But no. There was movement again—the door opening and closing.

Mike switched off the tape. ''That's it,'' he said.

''The time?'' Joel asked.

''Spiro's nephews left about nine-twenty, followed by Marko twenty minutes later. Then we got Ruth coming in for—what? Ten minutes? Then an hour of snorting and snuffling from Spiro before the door opens.''

''So, no heart attack,'' Joel murmured.

''Unless he had one while someone was trying to kill him.''

Steve snorted.

"I heard the doctor's called in the coroner," Joel said.

"Yeah, we picked that up."

Joel looked across at his boss. "What now?"

"We're closing down. This place is gonna be crawlin' with cops. Last thing we need is to have someone wonder what our van's doing here."

"But we've put so much into this. Months of background work."

"And what've we got to show for it, Kennedy? Zip. That's the recommendation I'm making to the boss. Money's tight these days. You must've known the operation wasn't going to last much longer, anyway, given the little bit we've gotten so far."

"What about the girl?"

Steve frowned. "The girl?"

"Allie Newman. The granddaughter."

"What about her? She's not our problem."

"If Spiro *was* murdered, she may be at risk."

Steve shrugged. "So maybe she'll just go home to wherever you found her. Where was it? Someplace in Ontario?"

"At least let me take her home."

"What the hell for? Your job is done. No one's going to expect you to show up. Besides, we have to debrief."

"You mean we're just going to toss away the chance of getting back that money? Almost a million bucks?"

"Win a few, lose a few, Kennedy. You've been in the game long enough to know how it's played. Pack up here, get rid of the van and meet us in Detroit. We'll debrief there, then you guys can take some R and R. I'm sure you're ready for it." Steve stood up. His face said the discussion was over.

Behind his back, Mike made a throat-slitting gesture to

Joel, warning him to keep quiet. The van door closed behind Steve.

A long moment passed before Joel muttered, "It may be over for him, but it's not over for me."

"Oh, God," moaned Mike. "I was afraid you'd say something stupid like that."

ALLIE HIT THE WATER in a perfect racing dive. She came up midway along the length of the pool, flung her hair from her eyes and began the first lap. The water was just the right temperature, not too cold, but brisk enough to refresh.

She focused on the swim, clearing her mind of all else. Back and forth. Back and forth. Not until her limbs were heavy with fatigue did she slow down, then tread water until she felt ready to come out of the pool. She bobbed under one last time, emerging just at the ladder. Placed two hands on the sides and heaved herself up and out.

Joel was standing on the platform waiting for her.

"Care to pass me that towel?" she asked.

He followed her arm, saw the towel lying across the back of one of the patio chairs and went for it. She caught the towel when he tossed it and rubbed it across her face. By then, he was standing in front of her again, though at a judicious distance, avoiding the drops of water that flew as she dried her hair.

"Good workout?"

"Very." She avoided his eyes, reluctant to talk about Spiro. She needed more time. The cool air in the room hit her and she shivered. Teeth chattering, she made an awkward pass at her back with the towel. Joel plucked it from her hands.

"Here. Let me."

He briskly dried between her shoulder blades, then

down her back and started to move toward the calves of her legs when she stepped forward.

"I'm okay," she protested. "I can do it."

He wrapped the towel around her, turning her to face him. The heat emanating from him was inviting. There was a small pulse beating at the base of his throat, a few tufts of black hair poking up from the open neck of his shirt. Allie knew if she allowed herself to inch forward, her mouth would be level with that hollow. And from someplace deep inside her came the urge to do simply that.

But instead, she stiffened. This was neither the time nor the place, she thought.

"You should get dressed before you get a chill," he said huskily.

She turned to go.

"Wait a sec. I've come to tell you that I've been let go. As of last night."

"But…" She couldn't get the words out, because her teeth were clacking against each other.

"It's okay, Allie. I was expecting it. But I want you to call me if you need me—about anything. Anything at all. You've still got my card?"

She nodded.

"Okay, the cell-phone number on it is valid. All right? If you need to call me, I'll get the message. Even if you have to leave a recording."

Allie dug her fingers into the ends of the towel, clutching it tightly against her chest. "Where are you going? Back to Detroit?"

"Detroit? Oh, yeah. Eventually. But I may stay in this area for a day or two—writing up my report and so on. Just that I won't be here at the house. So if anything comes up that feels weird to you—anything at all, you understand—then I want you to call me right away." He set his hands on her shoulders, forcing her eyes on his. "Got that?"

"Yes, but..."

Ignoring her, he dropped his hands and walked rapidly toward the pool-room door. Allie stood, shivering and waiting for him to turn around and come back. When he didn't, she made for the change room. Her mind, eased temporarily by the swim, was now whirling with questions.

LATER THAT AFTERNOON, Yolanda knocked on Allie's bedroom door to say that the coroner had ordered an autopsy.

"They've come to take him to the morgue," she sniffed. "Poor Mr. Spiro. He went through so much with his cancer treatments, and now there's no dignity for him even in death."

"But isn't it a good thing in a way? To find out how he died?"

"I suppose. Guess I just wish his death had been obviously natural so that this wouldn't have to happen." Yolanda walked farther into the room to where Allie was sitting in an armchair. "You okay, honey? How're you holding up, anyway?"

Allie gave her a grateful smile. The nurse was the only person, other than Joel and Susan—whom she'd phoned almost immediately—to express such concern. "I'm fine, but how are you? You worked for him a long time, didn't you?"

"I wasn't hired until early last year, when Mr. Spiro had to undergo a second round of chemo. He'd been in remission for almost a year when it came back. After the chemo, the doctors told him a transplant was his only chance. They didn't even hold out much hope for that." She shook her head. "Poor man. When Miss Effie saw

that magazine article and remarked at dinner how much
you looked like your mother, Mr. Spiro got her to show
him the article right away. I think he was up half the night
phoning people. Someone eventually suggested he call a
private investigator.''

"And that's how Joel Kennedy was hired?"

"In a roundabout way. A business friend of Mr. Spiro's
called about something else and happened to say he knew
someone who'd recently moved to Detroit and was looking
for clients. A private investigator.''

"That was a bit of a coincidence, wasn't it?"

"That's exactly what Mr. Spiro said. We were both
amazed at the coincidence.''

"Yes," Allie murmured. "It sounds almost too good to
be true.''

Yolanda stood to leave. "I'll get Ruth to bring you some
tea, shall I?"

"Tea would be wonderful, but I'll get it myself. Is Maria
with Aunt Effie?"

"No. Maria's in her room. Too upset to stay on duty,
she said. No one minds. The woman's been working for
Mr. Spiro forever, I reckon.''

"What about my aunt, then?"

"I was going to check on her right after popping in to
see you.''

"I should do that," Allie said. "Why don't you go
home, Yolanda? Get away from this place for a few
hours.''

"I might just do that, after I talk with the coroner.''

Allie got up and walked her to the door. "Thanks for
everything, Yolanda. Especially for being a friendly face
when I needed one most." Impulsively she hugged her.
"And thank you for being such a wonderful nurse to my

grandfather. I know he loved you—in his own special way.''

Yolanda chuckled, dabbing at her eyes at the same time. ''That's a good way to put it, Miss Allie. *His own special way.* Too right.''

After she left, Allie retreated into her en suite bathroom to wash her face. She'd had a light lunch and a nap after her workout and Joel's abrupt departure. Now, feeling ready to tackle the business of dealing with Spiro's death, she headed for Effie's room.

She tapped on the door, opening it slightly and calling, ''Aunt Effie?'' There was a muffled response that Allie took as an invitation to enter.

Effie was sitting in an armchair, her legs propped up on a large ottoman and covered with a lacy cotton throw. She put down the needlework she'd been doing.

''How are you doing, dear? I've been meaning to visit, but I've been so tired—emotional exhaustion, I think. Come and sit down.'' She gestured to the chair beside hers in the alcove of the large bay window.

Allie took in the dark circles beneath Effie's eyes and the pallor of her cheeks. The woman was obviously not very healthy, though Allie couldn't help thinking fresh air and exercise might accomplish more than Effie's daily intake of pills and vitamins. ''I'm okay, Aunt Effie. I came to see if there was anything I can do for you today. Any friends to call or arrangements to make.''

Effie gave a slight smile. ''Thank you, dear, but Christo has already called my friends, and I believe George has advised Spiro's friends and former business associates.''

''Well, can I get you something to eat or drink? Tea? Coffee?''

''We have staff to do that, dear.''

''I thought I'd save them the trouble.''

"I've been waiting for Maria to return for my lunch tray," Effie said, nodding her head toward a small table near the bed.

"Yolanda told me that Maria's in her room and doesn't want to be disturbed."

"That's not like Maria, though I'm sure Spiro's death has hit her a bit harder than the rest of us."

"Since she's been here so long?"

Effie looked down at the needlework in her lap. "Oh, that and...other things."

"Other things?"

A small shrug. Effie looked across at Allie. "I think Maria's been more than merely a housekeeper here," she said.

The penny didn't drop for Allie until Effie explained, "After Vangelia died, Spiro was a very lonely man." She paused. "Need I say more, dear? You can fill in the gaps, I'm sure."

Indeed, Allie could. But her curiosity was aroused. Why had Effie felt compelled to pass on this tidbit of gossip, which surely must be old news? To discredit Spiro?

"I've been wondering why you and your sons have continued to live with my grandfather, given your, uh—" she hesitated "—apparently negative feelings for him."

The needlework fell to the floor as Effie shifted in her chair. "That insinuation offends me, Allie. You make us sound like freeloaders."

"I didn't intend that, Aunt Effie. I just thought you'd have preferred your privacy as a family, you and George and Christo, living somewhere on your own terms."

Her explanation didn't appease Effie. "For one thing, we *are* part of Spiro's family. And family is...was very important to Spiro. Especially after the tragic business with…'' She hesitated, glancing at Allie as if testing the waters, then plunged on, ''Your parents.''

''What about my parents?''

Effie gave a delicate shrug. ''Katrina was an alcoholic and your father was a kidnapper, as well as a thief.''

Allie leaped to her feet. She wouldn't listen to another lie. ''My father was nothing of the kind. Yes, he took me away from an impossible situation. I'm not defending that behavior, although I believe he acted out of the deepest love for me. But he was no thief and his only betrayal of Spiro was taking me away from my mother.''

''You don't know anything, dear. Believe what you need to believe about your father, but rest assured that when he ran away that night, he took not only you but money entrusted to him by *my husband, Tony.* And that is why—'' her reedy voice was pitched in anger ''—Spiro has shared his home with us all these years. Because he owed us that. To make up not only for the money your father stole, but also to compensate me and my boys for the loss of their father.''

Speechless, Allie turned and made for the door. But Effie wasn't finished.

''If your father hadn't run off with that money, Tony would never have disappeared.''

Allie stopped in the doorway. ''I haven't the faintest idea what you're talking about. My father had to scrimp and save his whole life for everything. He had no money, except for what he earned. If your husband disappeared the same night his money did, then obviously he took it with him.'' All she heard as she stormed out of the room was Effie's indignant wail.

CHAPTER THIRTEEN

BY THE TIME Allie reached the kitchen, her heart rate had slowed to normal. She was greeted at the kitchen door by Ruth. "Oh, Miss Allie, I want to tell you how sorry I am about your grandfather. None of us could believe it when we found out this morning."

"Thanks, Ruth. It's been a shock for all of us."

"And he was in such fine spirits last night, too. When I took him his hot milk, he was even joking with me."

"Oh? When was that?"

"Just after Marko put him to bed. He said Mr. Spiro wanted some milk and he didn't want to disturb Maria."

Allie looked over Ruth's shoulder into the kitchen. "Where is Maria, by the way? I thought I'd take her some tea."

"What a nice idea. I'll go put the kettle on for you."

Allie followed Ruth into the kitchen. She perched on a stool at the counter while Ruth fussed with a tea tray. "I meant to do that myself, Ruth, rather than give you more work."

"It's nothing, Miss Allie. I'm happy to have something to do—keeps my mind off things." When the kettle whistled, she poured the boiling water into a small teapot and handed the tray to Allie. "I assumed you'd be having tea with Maria," Ruth said. "She'll be glad to have the company. I think the impact of Mr. Spiro's death has just hit her."

Allie thought back to Effie's revelation. "Yes, I'm sure. Thanks, Ruth. Where exactly is her room?"

"Down the hall toward the end of this wing. Just above the pool area. Oh, Miss, about dinner. Mr. George told everyone to take the night off. He said he'd order something in. Or if you want, you can browse through the freezer."

"That's fine, Ruth. I'm a freezer-microwave kind of girl myself," Allie said, returning Ruth's smile, and left the room.

Allie knocked on Maria's door, then waited. She had to knock twice more, before the door was cracked open.

Half of Maria's face appeared. One eye stared at Allie.

"Uh, I've brought you some tea, Maria."

The eye narrowed, as if in suspicion. Then Maria opened the door, turning her back on Allie immediately as she walked to a pair of chairs flanking a small coffee table.

Already regretting her impulse, Allie hesitated before following Maria to a chair. She set the tray down on the coffee table and began to pour the tea.

"Milk and sugar?" she asked.

Maria shifted her gaze from tea tray to Allie. She shook her head, saying only, "Clear."

When Allie handed her a cup and saucer, she wasn't sure whose hand was trembling more—hers or Maria's. She prepared her own tea before sitting in the other chair.

"Ruth told me that the staff have been given the night off," Allie said. "George will order in or we can fend for ourselves. If you like, I can bring you something from the freezer. I'm an expert at the microwave."

There wasn't a flicker of a smile in the older woman's face.

Allie blew gently on her tea and sipped. Maria's own cup remained on the table. Allie tried again. "Ruth wasn't sure if you'd eaten lunch—that's why she sent the muffins.''

"I'm not hungry," the woman finally said.

"You should eat something, Maria. Spiro would want you to."

The housekeeper peered down at her hands, folded in her lap. "You don't have the faintest idea what Spiro would want," she murmured.

The comment stung. "I suppose you're right. I wouldn't know what he'd want, but I like to think that I learned something about him in the short time I got to know him."

Maria said nothing, folding and unfolding her hands.

Allie watched her, tempted to reach out and still the hands. She picked up her tea and swallowed the rest of it in one go. "I'll take the tray back, then, if you're not hungry. Do let me know if you want me to fix you some dinner later."

The ploy worked. Maria raised her head, focusing her gaze on Allie first, then on the tray. She reached for her cup. "It should be cool enough now," she said.

Allie suppressed a smile. She started to leave, but Maria stopped her.

"Has there been any word yet? On the autopsy?"

"I doubt it's even been done yet. They took him away just before lunch."

"And the boys? What are they doing?"

"I've no idea. I haven't seen either of them since early this morning. Effie's resting in her room."

"Of course she is." Maria sighed. "That woman's been resting for years."

Allie would have laughed if the circumstances had been different. Besides, she doubted Maria meant the observation to be ironic.

"Thank you for the tea," Maria went on to say. "I didn't mean to be rude but…" Her voice faded.

"It's okay, Maria. You've good reason to be upset."

"I've spent most of my life here in this house," she said, her voice low and faraway. "Seen a lot of things. Learned as much about this family as anyone." She paused. "But was never really a part of it at all. Even after all this time. Still only the housekeeper."

Allie felt a rush of sympathy. "Whatever happens, Maria, I'm sure Spiro has taken care of you. I mean," she quickly explained at the sudden flare in Maria's eyes, "in his will. I'm sure he's left you a pension."

"The money isn't what I was talking about," Maria protested. "None of this is about the money."

Allie frowned. "What do you mean? None of what?"

Maria averted her face. "What I'm feeling."

"Of course it isn't! You cared for Spiro and he cared for you."

"Once maybe," Maria whispered. "Long ago."

"He did," Allie insisted. "He told me so, just the other day when we were at lunch."

Maria's gaze cut back to Allie. "He did?"

This time Allie averted her face, afraid Maria would see she was fabricating. "He told me he'd be eternally grateful to you."

"Grateful!" Maria snorted. "For being the good servant that I was."

Regretting the lie, Allie said, "I should go. Grandfather told me I could have the photo albums, and I want to collect the rest of them now."

"Take a good look at some of those pictures."

"What do you mean?"

"You'll figure it out. Anyway, I guess you won't be needed anymore now that the transplant is off."

Allie ducked her head, refusing to let Maria see how her words had hurt. "No," she said, turning for the door.

"Then maybe you'd best go back home. Leave the family to deal with things."

"I will go home soon," Allie said, "but as part of the family, I'll stay a bit longer to deal with things, as you put it." She marched out of the room and didn't slow down until she'd passed the kitchen and stumbled into the library, closing the door behind her.

There, she sagged into Spiro's favorite chair and burst into tears.

JOEL SET THE EARPHONES down. He couldn't listen another second. If he did, he'd be racing for his car and roaring off to the house to sweep Allie up in his arms and carry her away with him.

He'd decided to run the tape again in spite of what Steve had instructed. He needed to be certain Allie was all right. Still, he couldn't justify the time spent, even to himself. Other than picking up the morning conversation from Spiro's bedroom after his body had been discovered and the discussion between the doctor and the coroner, listening for another couple of hours had been a waste of time.

Until Allie had gone into the library and burst into tears. God. He swore at himself for not guessing how much she hid from the world. He ought to have picked up on that, instead of assuming that she was blithely handling all the emotion around the reunion with Spiro and then his death.

He dug into his shirt pocket for a stick of gum, wishing he could transform it into a cigarette. The chewing calmed him, giving him a few seconds to gather his thoughts. He needed to formulate a plan. He doubted he could keep the van up and running for another day. Mike would go along with it, but Joel knew Pat would give him a hard time. He might even report him to Steve. Pat was on an upward career curve and wouldn't be persuaded from it for a second, much less a day.

If he could keep Pat away for another few hours, he just might get something. Enough perhaps to convince Steve to give the job another shot. Joel thought for a moment, then rummaged through his backpack for his cell phone and punched in Mike's home number.

ALLIE GAVE HERSELF a few more minutes before collecting the rest of the photograph albums to take up to her room. She'd taken three with her last night and knew there were at least three left. Spiro had indicated the ones that contained photos of Tony and his family, and Allie left those on the shelf.

She was passing through the foyer to the staircase when Christo walked in the front door.

His face tightened. "What do you think you're doing?"

"Spiro told me I could have these albums," she explained, feeling like a teenager caught shoplifting.

"I don't think you should remove anything from this house," he said.

"I'm not *removing* them, Christo. I'm going to look through them. If you want me to leave them behind when I go, I will."

"When *are* you going?"

Allie sighed. After Spiro's death, that seemed to be the topic of the day. "I don't know, Christo. As soon as possible, I guess. That's what everyone appears to want."

His face softened. "Look, I didn't mean that the way it came out. It's just that George and I've been a bit tense lately. With everything. I don't know when the will is going to be probated, but of course you're welcome to stay until then."

The will. Allie remembered that Spiro had been going to sign the amended will that day. She supposed the old will would still be in effect and wondered why Christo hadn't thought of that. Or maybe he had; hence his magnanimous gesture.

"Thank you for that," she said, not bothering to hide her sarcasm.

"George and I promised Uncle Spiro to take care of you," he said.

Allie's face colored. His remark was eerily reminiscent of what she'd said to Maria. *Now that the shoe's on the other foot, you can see how patronizing it sounds.* And like Maria, she said, "I don't need taking care of, Christo. I've been managing quite well on my own." She continued up the stairs, aware that he was watching her the whole way.

Safely in her room, she heaved the albums onto the bed. The last thing she wanted to do now was to delve into the past. She was restless, eager to get out. Eager to leave. She reached for her cell phone, but tossed it on the bed, too. Calling Susan would merely make both of them feel bad. There was nothing to do but tough things out until she could leave. Which could well be tomorrow. Reassured by the thought, Allie went to the window and gazed out across the lawn and at the St. Clair River at the edge of the property.

Apart from the grandeur of the house, the scenery alone was magnificent enough to persuade anyone to stay. She could understand how Effie, a young widow, was tempted to seek refuge here. Even if it meant living with someone as strong-willed as Spiro must have been in those days. That thought led to another, more disturbing one.

How might she herself have turned out if her father hadn't taken her away with him? Would she have bent to

Spiro's will? Or been driven to seek pleasure or solace elsewhere, as her mother had? Allie shivered and wrapped her arms around herself.

The room seemed to close in on her. She couldn't stay inside a second longer. She changed into track pants and a long-sleeve T-shirt, then crawled under her bed in search of her running shoes. Moments later she crept down the staircase, slipped quietly out the front door, executed a couple of sloppy warm-up movements and started to jog down the drive. When she reached the main road, she decided to take the backstreets, away from the river.

She'd just turned onto the first side street down from the estate when her foot struck a rock, sending her into an awkward prolonged stumble. Allie bent at the waist, catching her breath. When she straightened, she caught sight of something that almost made her lose her breath again. A gray van, parked at the end of a driveway across the road. It had to be the same van, she thought, walking slowly toward it.

The windshield was blanketed by a cardboard cutout of large sunglasses to keep out sun and prying eyes. The windows were so darkly tinted, it was impossible to see through them. Allie rounded the van to the rear. The doors were locked, but she thought she could hear the low rumble of voices inside. She leaned against the doors, pressing one side of her head against them.

"Hey! What do you think you're doing?"

Allie jumped away from the door. A man was leaping from a car nearby and running her way. Patrick. And he looked angry. Allie spun around and sprinted toward Lakeshore Drive.

FOR SOME REASON, the words spewing from Pat's mouth didn't register with Joel with the same impact as the man's smarmy grin. That was when Joel drew back his right arm, formed a fist and would have followed through on the punch if Mike hadn't grabbed hold of him.

"That's all we need, Joel." Mike's voice cut through the haze of anger, thick inside the van.

"Where'd she go?"

"Back to the house," Pat said. "Jeez. She had her ear glued to the door. I told you I didn't realize it was her until after I yelled."

Joel pushed him out of the way and charged out the door, heedless of Mike calling him to come back. He dashed for his car, parked around the corner. She might have seen it, he thought, if she'd come that way.

Once behind the wheel, he turned on the ignition, jamming his foot to the floor, revving the engine to a cranking roar. Then he threw the car into drive, made a squealing U-turn and headed for Lakeshore and the Kostakis estate. When he reached the main gate, he didn't see her anywhere. Unless she was hidden by the curve ahead.

He slowed down, his fingers dancing on the steering wheel, itching to clamp on, while his foot, hovering nervously over the accelerator, urged him to gun the engine. But he didn't. He forced himself to drive at a reasonable speed, knowing she might be in the center of the drive, just around the bend.

But she wasn't. His eyes darted left and right. No sign of her. Maybe Pat had really spooked her and she'd run for help. *Nah.* She wasn't the type to automatically turn a problem over to someone else. No doubt she'd recognized Pat, had been frightened by his shouting and decided to buzz off. She would have turned onto Lakeshore and, perhaps thinking he might come after her, cut across the field adjacent to the estate grounds. It would have been rougher going, but not as obvious a route as the road and driveway.

Then he shifted his gaze right and sure enough, there she was, slogging through the plowed furrows of the field that bordered that side of the estate. He eased up on the accelerator and the station wagon groaned down into first gear. He really needed a new car, he was thinking, as he tried to come up with a plausible reason for being there. *The report I told her I had to write. Yeah. That might work.*

He swerved onto the grass, switched off the ignition and jumped out of the car. She didn't seem to notice him until he was directly in front of her. Then she uttered a small gasp that tore at him. He reached for her, grasping her to him, then held on. She clung to him a few seconds longer before pulling free.

"What's wrong?" she asked breathlessly. "What's happened?"

He realized how silly he looked. She didn't know he knew. Didn't know he'd been in the van, too. "I…uh, I've missed you, dammit. That's what's wrong. I've been worried as hell about you, wondering how you were managing."

She gave him a skeptical look, unconvinced.

"And what were you doing walking through that farmer's field?" he asked. "Look at your feet—they're caked in mud."

She stared down at her shoes. "I was out for a run and I saw that van again. You know—the gray one. I went to see if anyone was inside and I think there was. I heard voices. Then this guy came charging at me out of nowhere and I'm sure it was Patrick."

Joel worked his face into puzzled mode.

"The gardener's helper," she prompted.

"Yeah? Jeez, what was he doing? Where was this, anyway?"

As she gave a detailed description of the area, he

wrapped an arm around her shoulders and walked her to the car. "Get in," he said. "I'll drive you up to the house."

"What about my feet?"

"Huh? Oh, don't worry about the car."

She scraped her shoes on the lawn and climbed in the passenger side as he held the door. "Do you *live* in this car?" she asked after he got in and closed the door.

He peered around, seeing the interior with her eyes. It *was* a dump. "More or less," he admitted. He caught her grin and smiled. "Pretty bad, isn't it? Anyway, you're not here for the scenery. Tell me what happened."

He watched her face while she talked, noting the high color and pitch in her voice when she got to the part about Pat. He *had* frightened her, the jerk, though Joel suspected she wouldn't have reacted so strongly had she not had such a stressful day.

"What do you think he was doing there? He must be involved in something. Should I call the police?"

"No!" Joel said a tad too sharply. "I've got a suspicion, uh, that Patrick might be an undercover cop."

Her amber flecked eyes widened. "Really? What makes you say that?"

He shrugged. "Just a few odd things that have been happening. We saw him once before in that van, remember? And his explanation about that, if I recall, was pretty damn vague."

Allie was staring out through the windshield. Something was definitely on her mind.

"You okay?" he asked, daring to run his index finger down her cheek. She opened her mouth as if to blurt out whatever was bugging her, then suddenly clammed up. She turned away, but not before he saw a tear in the corner of her eye.

"Come here," he whispered, extending his arm to pull her closer. She didn't resist, and he knew at once she'd been waiting for him to do exactly that. Her face ducked into the crook of his shoulder and chest, almost at his armpit. As if she wanted to crawl inside him and hide. He shifted, angling himself so that his other arm could comfortably swing around, embracing her fully.

She reclined against him and her warmth pulsed through him. He felt a stirring of desire and pressed his hand on her back, pushing the softness of her breasts against him. He bit back a groan of pleasure, sensing she was seeking comfort, not sex. Lowering his face to the top of her head, he inhaled the unique scent that was her—Allie Newman. A sensation surged through him that he couldn't immediately identify. Until he realized it was familiarity—belonging.

He could have spent the night like that, the door fixtures digging into the small of his back and the steering wheel jabbing his rib cage. And Allie, half-lying, half-sitting on top of him. He felt as though he were floating on a cloud.

Until she yanked him back to earth. "So what are *you* doing here?"

"I was, uh, just bringing that report I had to write up. For Spiro. But I guess I'll be giving it to George now."

She raised herself off him, returning to the center of the seat. "Is it that important? To bring it back tonight?"

"I have to get moving on to Detroit, so no time like the present, I guess. I'll just drop it off and be on my way."

"Do you want me to give it to him?"

"Uh, no. I have to see him about some…unsettled business, anyway."

She craned her neck toward the back seat. "Where is it?"

He frowned. She was a suspicious one. "Way in the back."

"I don't see it."

"Well, how could you with all of that junk on top of it?" he said.

She laughed. Then she stared at him so long and so thoughtfully he doubted he'd be able to drive the car the short distance to the house without pulling her to him again and... She blinked, turned bright red and averted her eyes. *Reading my mind?* he wondered.

"I should get back," she murmured.

And without an excuse to put off the inevitable, Joel switched on the ignition and drove to the front door. When they got there, she thought of something else.

"If Pat's an undercover cop, who's he investigating and why?"

Okay, Kennedy, answer that one. "I heard a rumor that Christo has a lot of gambling debts. Maybe he's been involved in other things."

"Such as?"

Joel shrugged. "Remember I told you that there'd been rumors over the years that Spiro's importing-exporting business had been connected to less-legal activities?"

"*Less legal?* What kind of jargon is that?"

"Business that falls in a fuzzy gray zone. Not blatantly illegal, but kind of on the fence, so to speak."

He watched her mull this over, examining the logic of it. Or the lack of logic in it, he guessed. She'd pinned her hair back with some type of plastic clip that was now off-kilter, hanging loosely at the nape of her neck. Strands of rich, chocolate-brown hair dangled limply around her face. Not once since she'd been in the car had she attempted to repair the damage. He admired that in her—she had a focus that refused to be sidetracked by less important details.

When she turned her head his way again, it was clear she realized he'd been staring. But instead of being embarrassed, she met his gaze, running her tongue along her lower lip in concentration. Joel bit the inside of his lower lip, forcing himself to stay on task.

"I don't think Grandfather would have gotten mixed up in anything illegal. He had too much to lose. His reputation, for one thing." She frowned. "I don't believe what you're suggesting. It doesn't fit with the picture I have of him."

She frequently referred to Spiro as "Grandfather" now, not his first name. Was she imprinting her brain with his memory? Or fashioning an entirely new image of the man? Whatever the answer, Joel knew he'd have to tread carefully. She'd found and lost a grandfather in a mere few days.

"You may be right," he acknowledged. "Perhaps things were happening that he wasn't aware of. I know that George has more or less been running the business— with some help from Christo—for more than a year. Since Spiro's treatments began."

"How do you know that?"

"I pick up a lot of gossip, rumors and stuff through my various contacts. Part of my job."

"I thought you just moved to this area."

Joel bit his lower lip again. Jeez. What was there about Allie Newman that made him totally forget all sense of focus and procedure? "Yeah, well, I meet a lot of people from all over. It doesn't take long to gather information on someone."

"Did you have to gather a lot of information on me? I mean, there wasn't a lot to go on in that *People* magazine article."

Joel cranked open the window. "Stuffy in here," he

said. "Sure, but what I got came from Spiro. I told you that. Besides, once I was in Kingston, almost everyone I met on the street could point you out."

"True." She sighed and turned to gaze out her side window. "I'm thinking of leaving soon," she said. "There's no reason for me to stay here any longer."

He'd been expecting that, but now that the possibility loomed right in front of him, he didn't want to see it. She had to go home and he had to return to Detroit, and from there, who knew? Another case in another city?

"What about the rest of the family here?"

"Right," she said, bitterness highlighting the word. "My *family*—Susan—is in Kingston. The people here are related to me, but they're not what I'd call family."

The comment gave him insight into what she'd been feeling the past week.

She reached out and placed a hand on his arm. "But I don't blame you for anything, Joel. Please understand that. You were just doing your job when you came looking for me. It wasn't your fault that…well, that my family didn't exactly measure up to my dreams." She flushed, her eyes filling up again.

And with that, she opened the car door and climbed out.

Joel scrambled out his side. "Wait!"

Allie paused on the lower step.

"Call me before you leave, okay? Maybe we can…I don't know, get together for lunch or dinner. Or whatever."

She cracked a wobbly grin. "As in, a *date?*"

"Sure, why not? My job here's finished. No conflict of interest anymore."

Her smile grew confident. "Okay. See you later, then." She skipped up the rest of the steps and into the house.

Joel stood watching the front door, mesmerized as much

by his lie as the urge to dash in after her and confess everything. But years of training compelled him to withdraw, moving slowly and inexorably to the car and away from Grosse Pointe Farms.

And Allie Newman.

CHAPTER FOURTEEN

THE HOUSE WAS DARK and quiet when Allie ran inside, but for once, the emptiness didn't bother her. She locked the front door behind her, knowing the staff wouldn't be around that night and, carrying her muddy shoes, bounded up the stairs as if being pursued. It wasn't fear, however, that propelled her upward, but a surge in her spirit. The feeling of being in charge again. And it was Joel, she realized as she showered and changed into her nightie, who'd done that for her.

Merely being in his presence made her feel good—safe and capable of anything. Why this was so eluded her, but she didn't question the sensation. She simply wanted to revel in it. Along with the memory of his body against hers. Hard and demanding, yet gentle and inviting at the same time. He was a blend of contrasts, she thought. Distant and aloof, at times perplexing. But boyish, too. Like the way he'd gotten around to asking her out. Almost making it sound like a business meeting until she'd insisted on clarification. Then his blush at being forced to admit, yes, he was asking her out on a date.

And she thought, *finally,* the fact that they were attracted to one another was at last out in the open. No more game playing. Her awful day was ending with some promise. Allie wandered to the window to check out the last of the sunset.

The exterior house lights, set by timers, blinked on as

she stood there, watching the grounds and the river beyond fade into an inky-black void. Now that Spiro was gone, the estate seemed lonelier and more isolated than ever. He'd been at the hub of this little world, Allie realized. George, Effie, Christo, even the staff, were now like planets without orbits.

She wondered where her cousins were and if Effie had received any dinner. And Maria? The idea of facing either woman that day was unthinkable. No doubt George and Christo had taken care of their mother. As for Maria, hadn't she insisted earlier that she wouldn't want anything?

Allie returned to her bathroom for a robe. Perhaps she'd wander downstairs and find something to eat. As she rounded the bed, she noticed the photograph albums lying where she'd tossed them before her run. Except that now, two of the three were open. She frowned. They could have fallen open when she'd thrown them, although she didn't think they had. The possibility that someone had been in her room chilled her.

There was no one in the house except for her aunt, her cousins and Maria. And she couldn't think of a logical reason for any of them to look through the albums. For one, the things had probably been sitting on Spiro's library shelf for years, available to all. It didn't make sense, and because it didn't, Allie decided she must be mistaken. They'd obviously tumbled open when they'd landed on the bed and she simply hadn't noticed. Reassured, she headed downstairs to the kitchen and heated a frozen dinner.

While she ate, she replayed the scene in the car with Joel. She sensed that this particular scene would be buzzing through her mind all night long. Allie smiled at herself. Perhaps she'd been too long without a man. *No perhaps about it, Newman.*

The last time had been more than a year ago. She'd been involved with one of the teaching assistants in her department, but the superficiality of the relationship wasn't evident until her father died. There'd been no high drama around ending the affair. Just a series of broken dates and promised phone calls that had never materialized. The sad part of it was, Allie mused, she hadn't really cared.

Allie cleaned up after herself, turned out the lights and headed back to her room. As she approached Spiro's study, she noticed light from beneath the closed door. She hesitated briefly before opening it.

George and Christo were leaning over Spiro's desk, reading some papers. Startled, they raised their heads in unison.

"What are *you* doing here?" Christo asked.

Allie prickled. "I guess I could ask you the same question."

George moved away from the desk, his palms up in a placating gesture. "For heaven's sake, what's with you two? Christo and I are going through Uncle Spiro's papers, Allie, as you can see. We've been looking for his will."

"Won't his lawyer have a copy of the old will? The new one won't be valid now, anyway, if he didn't sign it."

"You're right," said George. "But we were curious to see it."

They stood together in an uneasy tableau until Allie said, "Was anyone in my room earlier this evening?"

The two men looked at each other, both shaking their heads.

"Why?" George asked.

"Nothing. My imagination, I guess." She started to leave. "Will you be making plans tomorrow for the funeral?"

Again, the exchanged glances. *Good grief, can't one answer a question without consulting the other?*

"We haven't thought that far ahead," George admitted. "It hasn't even been twenty-four hours since he died."

But your thoughts got round to the will quickly enough. Allie pursed her lips.

"I suppose you'll be going back to Kingston after the funeral," Christo said.

Allie blew out a mouthful of sour air. "Oh, yes," she said. "Good night, then."

She felt their eyes on her back all the way to the door and wondered, as she went through it, why that gave her the creeps. In spite of their lack of sensitivity, they had a legitimate right to be interested in Spiro's will. By the time she reached her room, she realized that the scene had felt weird not because they were rummaging through Spiro's papers, but because they'd seemed so furtive about it.

She removed the albums from the bed and set them on a dresser. Tomorrow she'd browse through them. Tonight she wanted simply to indulge in yet another game of what-if. *What if I'd extended a finger, from my lips to his? What if I'd raised my face from his shoulder to his cheek? Or managed to accidentally brush a hand against that obvious hard swelling beneath me?*

Allie flicked off the bedside lamp. No more games. She'd have to take a shower, instead. A cold one. She smiled, wriggling under the bedcovers. Maybe he'd call tomorrow. Or she could call him. *Yes,* she thought, *I will.* And just before dropping off to sleep, she had another more insistent thought. She forced herself from the bed and across the room to the door, turning the latch in the knob.

That last act was revisited later that night when Allie awoke suddenly to a shuffling noise outside her door. She sat up, but didn't turn on the lamp. The hall night-light cast enough of a glow beneath the door for her to see what looked like the tips of a pair of men's shoes. Then a soft click as the doorknob was turned. Once, twice. Allie's heart immediately shot into overdrive. When the adrenaline rush had subsided enough for her to find a voice, she called out, "Who's there?"

Silence. The feet disappeared from view, followed by the muffled sound of footsteps receding into the night.

JOEL TOSSED the earphones onto the pile of wires and auxiliary cables stacked on the cabinet inside the van. He switched off the tapes and sat for a moment, going over what he'd just heard. It wasn't a lot, but it was enough for him to know something was up. Then he put the headset back on and flicked the switch again. He had to get the whole thing straight. Who knew if he'd get another chance to hear any of it again?

Running the tapes one last time had been an act of impulse. He'd driven back to the van after dropping off Allie. Pat had already hightailed it out of there, no doubt anxious to tell Steve how Joel had disobeyed orders. As if any of it mattered now.

Mike had given Joel a worried but friendly shrug. "The kid's a browner," he muttered. "Forget about it."

Joel figured he already had. He'd promised to pack up the van and meet Mike the next day at the office. With the tapes. "So they can go back into the cold-case file," Joel cracked.

Mike's grin had broadened and he'd waved a hearty goodbye. Obviously relieved, Joel thought, that his partner wasn't going to screw up anymore. Then Joel had checked the time. Almost nine. And had thought, what the heck?

Why not? He could take another night in the car—or even the van—if necessary.

Which was when he'd picked up the boys, rifling through Spiro's study. At least, Joel presumed it was the study, because he'd heard the noise of desk drawers opening and closing. Looking for the will, he'd also gathered, from their frequent use of the word *it*. And not having much success, it seemed.

Then Allie's bursting in and the stunned brief silence. Her game comeback to Christo's question—*What are you doing here?* But as soon as she'd left, George had muttered, *We'll have to keep an eye on her. She knows more than she's letting on.*

Yeah? from Christo. *I don't get that at all. You're imagining things. Come on, let's go. It's not here. Besides, what does it matter now, anyway? Allie was right about that. And we already know what's in the old one.*

George: *Okay okay. Just one more thing to go through. I always wondered why the old guy kept that cigar box in his safe.*

Christo: *Is this really necessary George? I mean, there's no money stashed away. Haven't you figured that out yet?*

George: *Never say it's over till it's over.*

Christo: *Well,* that's *original.*

George: *Here it is. God, what a crappy old box. Well,* hello. *What have we here?*

Christo: *What is it? Let me see.*

George: *May be something, may be nothing. You put the rest of the stuff away, will ya? I want to have a look at this upstairs. Just in case our dear cuz decides to come back and check on us.*

Joel turned off the tape. So. The boys had found something. Not the will, from what he'd heard. But something important. What struck him most about the conversation was the reference to money. Was it an innocent remark? Joel wondered. Or did they know more than he'd thought?

He took off the headset and stretched, yawning loudly in the empty van. There were decisions to be made that night. Time to get a bite to eat and a large coffee. He'd come back later to pack up. Just before he left, he palmed the night's tape and shoved it into his jacket pocket.

ALLIE DIDN'T GET back to sleep until daybreak, so when someone knocked briskly on the door, she stumbled toward it, fumbling at the latch twice before she managed to fling it open.

"Yolanda!" she croaked.

"Heavens, what happened to you? You look terrible."

Allie struggled back to the bed and climbed under the covers. The nurse followed her inside and perched cautiously on the side of the bed.

"Were you out partying last night?"

"Ha. I wish."

"So what's all this about? Take one of your grand-daddy's vintage bottles of wine to bed with you?"

"Another I wish. I wouldn't even know where to look for one. No, I just couldn't get to sleep until dawn." Allie pushed herself up to half-recline, half-lean against the pillows. "What time is it now?"

"Promise not to shout at me?"

Allie managed a weak smile. "Promise."

"About eight."

Allie groaned. "I've only been asleep about two hours."

"Surely you got some sleep in the night."

"Not much."

"Thinking about your grandfather?" Yolanda asked softly.

"A bit. And also about other things. Plus—" Allie

broke off, deciding against telling the nurse about the person who'd tried to come into the room. What could Yolanda do about it?

"Plus?"

"Nothing, just missing people back home."

Yolanda nodded. "Of course. Never you mind. You'll be back home in no time. Anyway, I've come to say goodbye for now."

Allie pushed herself all the way up. "Goodbye?"

"My job here's finished. Mr. George gave me a very generous severance package this morning."

He doesn't waste any time, does he. Allie's sense of isolation doubled. "What about the rest of the staff?"

"Liz is here already, cooking up breakfast for everyone. Want me to tell her to send some up?"

"No, I'll go down. They're all busy enough."

Yolanda smiled. "I'm sure going to miss you. Even though we've just met, I don't know...I feel like I've known you forever."

"Me, too. You've been the only friendly face around here, Yolanda. I can't tell you how much I've appreciated that."

Yolanda stood up and crossed to Allie to hug her. "You take care now. Don't let those boys run the show, if you get my drift. Here's my home phone number," she said, handing Allie a folded piece of paper. "Please let me know when the funeral is so I can come."

"Of course."

The nurse paused in the door. "I know you didn't get to know Mr. Spiro well and that he wasn't really a grandfather to you in the true sense of the word, but I also know he cared for you very much." Her eyes got misty. "He was so excited about your coming here. The very day he found out he started writing a record of the family history for you. Said he'd been meaning to do it for ages and you were just the motivation he needed.''

"A family history? He never showed it to me."

"Likely he never finished it. Still, I saw him poring over it a lot in the last week. No doubt it'll turn up when you and the family go through his things."

"Mmm," Allie murmured, thinking of George and Christo.

"Bye, then," Yolanda said.

Allie watched her leave, threw back the covers and marched to the bathroom to wash her face. *A family history.*

Once dressed, she went in search of George. He was in the study, sitting at Spiro's desk and talking on the telephone. He waved a hand for her to sit down.

She thought back to her first morning at the house, talking to Spiro in this room. That meeting hadn't gone well, she recalled. They'd both been defensive and rather wary. A natural reaction, considering the history.

When George hung up, the first thing she broached was that. "Yolanda told me that Spiro was writing a family history for me. Have you or Christo found it?"

"No. Just old business correspondence, stuff like that. Nothing personal."

"If you do come across something like that, could you let me know?"

"Of course, Allie. By the way, I've some news for you." He wiped a hand across his face. He looked exhausted, Allie thought, wondering if he, too, had had a sleepless night. "I got a call this morning from the local police. The autopsy ordered by the coroner shows that Uncle Spiro didn't die of natural causes as we thought."

Allie leaned forward in her chair. The early-warning signs of alarm prickled at the back of her neck.

"He died of asphyxiation. Appears he was murdered."

Allie could hardly breathe, much less talk.

"They'll be here any moment to search the house and question everyone. I've been told not to let anyone leave." George stood up to usher her out the door. "Someone will come get you when it's your turn. I wouldn't worry if I were you. Especially since Uncle Spiro didn't manage to change his will, after all."

Allie shot him a questioning look.

"So you can't be a suspect, right?" He uttered a short, harsh laugh.

Allie jerked her elbow loose from his hand and left quickly before she said something she'd regret. But his parting gibe would come back to haunt her.

JOEL MASSAGED the back of his neck, stiff from another sleepless night in the station wagon. Still, he had more than aches and pains on his mind. There was Pat Sullivan, looming large. As was Allie, in a totally different context. He would get to Pat soon enough, leaving Allie as his number-one priority that balmy May morning. Saturday. The day Spiro would have had his transplant, if everything had gone as planned. If the old guy hadn't died.

When Joel had returned with his Chinese takeout last night, he'd been more than a little surprised to find the van gone. *Vanished.* He'd smirked at his grim joke, then reached for his cell phone. Mike confirmed that Pat, checking on the van, had called to say he was packing it up and would drive it to the office.

"I was just picking up some dinner, for God's sake," Joel had complained. "I said I'd do it. Jeez."

Mike's sigh was full of frustration. "Whatever. Look at it this way, he saved you the trouble. What's the big deal?"

"Well, for one thing, I had to spend another night in the station wagon."

A chuckle. "Cripes. That old wreck. Why don't you get an apartment like the rest of us poor slobs?"

"Yeah, yeah. Listen, what'd Pat do with the tape? The one from Thursday night?"

"I guess Pat told Steve about it. He gave it to the cops. It's in their hands now."

The tape in Joel's pocket seemed to burn. He was about to say something to Mike, then thought better of it. He still hadn't decided what to do with it. Or even if it had any significance. For now, he'd hold on to it. He told Mike he'd get back to him and decided to drive by the Kostakis place to see what was happening.

He pulled up to the main gate right behind a convoy of cruisers and unmarked police cars. Too late to see Allie now, he thought. He let the station wagon idle as the vehicles filed through. There was no way he wanted to get involved in a police investigation. What bothered him, as he reluctantly coasted past the estate, was the sobering thought that if Spiro had been murdered, then his killer was likely still in the house. *Along with Allie.*

CHAPTER FIFTEEN

THE SUMMONS came sooner than Allie had anticipated. She'd been pacing back and forth in the library since the police had arrived half an hour ago. She was desperate to talk to someone, but didn't want to worry Susan, who wouldn't be able to help, anyway. Calling Joel was an option, but she thought she'd wait until after the interview when she might have some solid information.

A uniformed officer came for Allie midmorning. The interview began on a genial note, with two detectives asking questions and another uniformed officer taping the conversation. Patiently Allie twice went through her story of how and why she came to Grosse Pointe Farms.

"And the name of this private investigator?" asked the older detective after introducing himself as Wayne Grady.

"Joel Kennedy."

"Do you know how we can get in touch with him?"

"I've got his cell phone number on a card up in my room."

"Can you give that to us at the end of our interview?"

Allie nodded. The other detective, whose name was Solarski, asked her to run through the events of Thursday night. When she told them of Spiro's announcement to her about his will change, both detectives leaned forward.

"Did he say that he *had* changed his will, or that he *intended* to?"

"He said he *had* changed it."

"And did he reveal that to the rest of the family, too?"

"I...I don't know if he did. I'm almost sure he didn't, but I can't say what he might have told anyone after we spoke. George and Christo were meeting with him after dinner."

"Yes, they told us about that meeting. So, let me get this straight. You knew your grandfather had changed his will to include you, but you don't know if he told the others."

"That's right."

"Then after dinner?"

"I helped Grandfather to his study, took some photograph albums he said I could have and went to my room."

"Did you stay in your room the rest of the night?"

"Of course. Where else would I go?"

Detective Grady and his partner exchanged a meaningful glance that wasn't lost on Allie. "So you never left your room at all after...what time would that have been?"

"I don't know. I think after eight-thirty."

"And did you hear anything at all during the night? Anyone moving around the halls?"

"I heard nothing until Yolanda woke me in the morning—about seven or so—to tell me he...he was dead." She faltered then, as if hearing the news for the first time.

The detectives waited a moment before continuing. "Tell us what you noticed when you went into the bedroom. You were with Yolanda, the nurse, and with your cousins." Grady looked up from the notebook he held.

"Yes, but only George was there. Christo came with his mother a few seconds later."

"Notice anything out of place in the room?"

"No. I'd only been in there once before. I doubt I'd notice if something was missing or broken."

"Did you happen to see a small tray with an empty coffee mug on it?"

Allie shook her head. "No, but I may have without remembering. Nothing like that is registering, though."

"How long, exactly, have you been here again, Miss Newman?"

Allie bit down on her lower lip. Hadn't she gone over this already? "I got here a week ago today."

"And a lot has happened in that week, hasn't it?"

That question gave her pause. Yes, a lot had happened. But she wasn't sure if any of it was relevant to this issue. Or was it? "I suppose," she finally said.

"You had a blood test to see if you were a match for your grandfather and it came out positive, is that correct?"

"Yes."

"And you were reunited with a family you'd never met before."

"Yes."

"And less than a week after your arrival, your grandfather changed his will to include you. Is that right?"

Allie shifted in her chair. All she needed to feel more uncomfortable was a bright spotlight aimed right at her face. "Yes, but..."

"But?"

"Well, I didn't ask him to do that. He just did it. I didn't know anything about it until Thursday night."

"Yet he didn't tell the original beneficiaries—George, Christo and their mother?"

"They must have guessed. They were dropping all kinds of messages and hints."

"Oh, yes? What kind of messages?"

She couldn't think straight. How to explain the innuendo, the raised eyebrows and veiled comments? "I can't say for certain. It was more of an impression I got, that's all.'' Her voice had dropped to a mumble.

"So when you left your grandfather for the night to go up to your room, it was clear in your mind that he had already changed his will to include you as a beneficiary?'' Grady asked.

Is this one of those trick questions? The kind that damns me either way?

"Do you want me to repeat the question, Miss Newman?''

"Uh, no...but I'm not sure what you want me to say.''

A knowing smile passed between the detectives. The thin one—Solarski?—said, "We want you to tell the truth, Miss Newman, that's all.''

"Then yes, it was clear in my mind. But that's not what I was thinking when I left him.'' She concentrated, trying to recall everything. "I remember thinking that...well, that I was feeling real affection for him.''

"For your grandfather?''

The subtext of his question seemed to be, *Why wouldn't you?* Allie tried to get the phrases right in her head, before uttering them. "Until very recently I didn't even know I had a grandfather. As I said, I've only known him a week.''

"So you did. What else were you thinking?''

"We'd been talking about the bone-marrow transplant. He told me not to worry, that it wouldn't be life-threatening for me.''

"For you. Implying that it might be for him.''

"I suppose so. There was a chance that it wouldn't work. His nurse told me that he might develop an infection that could become serious because his immune system was already so weak.''

"On the other hand, it could be successful and he could well have survived another five or ten years?"

"I don't know the exact prognosis, but obviously he would live a longer life."

Grady nodded, moving his lips wordlessly. Then he said, "I've made some inquiries about your financial situation, Miss Newman. Just general ones," he hastened to add. "There's no need to worry. But it seems that you do owe a substantial amount of money."

Blood rushed to her face. "I've still got some student debt from working on my doctorate."

"I see. Should we address you as *Dr.* Newman, then?"

Sensing he was mocking her, she shook her head, not trusting herself to answer.

"No?" He smirked. "Then can I say that your grandfather's decision to include you in his will was one that could have had a major impact on your debt?"

Alarms were ringing in her head. "It might have, except that I understand he didn't get around to signing the amended version, after all."

"But on Thursday night, the night Mr. Kostakis was murdered, you still believed that the will change had already occurred?" After a moment he said, "For the record, the interviewee remains silent."

The detectives seemed to reach a nonverbal decision through raised eyebrows, then Solarski said, "You can go now, Miss Newman."

She was almost at the door when he asked, "Is there anyone who can vouch for your statement that you were in your room all night after leaving your grandfather?"

The sudden lump in her throat made talking difficult, but Allie managed to whisper, "No...not really."

He nodded his head, as if she'd just confirmed something he'd already suspected. "We may have to talk to you again, Miss Newman. Please be sure to make yourself available.''

The tiny voice in Allie's head urged her to slam the door behind her, but she didn't. She had a feeling she was already in enough trouble. She was in her room scarcely five minutes when the uniformed officer arrived to take Joel's business card. As soon as he'd left with it, Allie realized she'd neglected to copy Joel's cell phone number. Knowing she couldn't telephone him, after all, she felt more isolated than ever.

She lay down on the bed and decided to browse through some of the photograph albums, picking up one that contained pictures of her mother as a child. She leafed through them quickly, sensing a journey into the past at that particular moment would be more than she could handle. Reaching for another, she opened it to a framed copy of a wedding invitation. Her parents'.

There was a touchingly ingenuous quality to the photos, she thought. A blend of simplicity and sophistication. The family grouping reinforced the disparate economic realities of both families, with her father's parents looking ill at ease in clothes that failed to match the expensive finery of Katrina, Spiro and Vangelia, his wife. She turned the page and drew in a sharp breath.

Someone had circled a portion of one photograph with a black marker. The picture featured her parents with Tony and Effie, and the circle highlighted the almost intimate placement of Tony's hand on Katrina's waist. Allie suddenly recalled the picture she'd seen of Effie and Tony at their own wedding, and the way Tony had seemed to be staring at Katrina, rather than at his own bride. A chill rode up her spine. She rummaged through the albums until she found the one with Effie's wedding and quickly flipped through it until she found the photograph. Again, someone had circled Tony's hand with a marker.

Allie thought she knew who that someone might be. She scooped the albums under her arm and went to find Maria. The housekeeper was finally roused after several insistent knocks on her locked door.

Allie was shocked at her disheveled and haggard appearance. The lack of surprise in Maria's face indicated she'd been expecting Allie. She opened the door just wide enough for Allie to squeeze through, and the first thing that struck Allie when she entered the room was a stale, sour odor. Maria wore the same housecoat she'd been wearing the day before, and Allie doubted that she'd been out of it since then.

Maria moved listlessly to a chair, leaving Allie to decide whether or not to sit. Allie suspected the housekeeper was seriously depressed and thought she'd better inform George as soon as she left.

She also reconsidered confronting Maria about the albums, but the woman noticed them immediately.

"You found the pictures," she said.

"Obviously. Was that you who came into my room yesterday? Was that when you marked them up?"

Maria fixed baleful eyes on Allie, her expression impassive and indifferent. Finally she said, "I wasn't sure you'd notice."

"How could I miss them? You've ruined them with marker."

"No. Noticed what I was trying to tell you. About Tony and your mother."

The pounding in Allie's ears increased. "Are you suggesting they were...that they..." She couldn't finish the horrible thought.

"Not suggesting. Telling. They'd been having an affair for years—long before she met your father."

Allie's legs wobbled. She used her free hand to clutch the back of the chair she stood beside. "Why are you telling me all this, Maria? What's the point? I never knew my mother, anyway. It's not as if you're tarnishing some image of her."

"Because I thought you'd want to know why your daddy left that night. Why he ran off with you."

"I do want to know, yes."

Maria heaved a loud sigh, as if the effort of talking was too much. "Eddie was supposed to be out on an errand that night. In those days you lived with your folks in the guest house. Tony came by, as he sometimes did when your mother was alone. Except he didn't know I was still there, in the kitchen. Eddie and Spiro had arranged to have me stay with Katrina when she was alone, to look after you. They couldn't trust her with you. They'd hired a nanny for the day, but the nights were risky, since your father was away a lot. As I said, Tony came over and the two were cozying up together on the couch when Eddie came back early. I could tell from the look in his face that he'd already guessed what was going on."

She paused, staring off into space until Allie asked, "Had they been having an affair the whole time my parents were married?"

"No. I know they were up to something when Katrina was in her senior year in high school, but after she met your father, she broke it off. Then Tony took up with Effie and—" she lifted her shoulders "—you know the rest. I think it all started up again not long before that night. Katrina suffered terrible depression after you were born. Baby blues, we called it. Spiro wouldn't hear of sending her to someone—said she should just shape up." She shook her head sadly. "Poor girl. That was just *one* of the mistakes that man made in his lifetime."

The bitterness in her voice chilled Allie. "So what happened after my father found them together?"

"He went crazy. Throwing things. Yelling. Attacking Tony. Your mother tried to stop them, but she was drunk. I came out of the kitchen, but they really only quit when you woke up and started to wail from your room. That stopped your father dead in his tracks. He told Tony to leave, that they'd settle things later. Said he had to do a favor for Mr. Spiro. Some job."

Allie sagged against the chair. "They had a fight and then what?" she prompted, hoping to encourage Maria to speed things up.

"Just when Tony was leaving, he said something strange to Eddie. I think that's what made him run off later that night."

Allie waited, gritting her teeth. "Go on."

"Tony said to meet him after the job was finished. He'd be waiting in the garage apartment. Told Eddie to bring the money there. Eddie said he didn't know what Tony was talking about. He was picking up a shipment for Spiro. Then Tony laughed and said something like, 'Trust me, if you deliver the money safely, you'll get a cut. But if anything goes wrong, there'll be hell to pay.' Then Tony left."

Money. Effie had accused her father of stealing money from Tony. "Then what?"

"That's it. Eddie left and your mother kept on drinking. She passed out and I put her to bed. Then I went to sleep, too. I didn't even hear your father come home later, but I know he did. Because the next morning you were gone and so was he."

The circulation in Allie's legs had chugged to a halt ages ago, it seemed, for she could hardly move them. But she did, ordering them to carry her to the door and through it. Along the still corridor of the ground floor, past the closed door of the study and across the foyer to the stairs. Up each one automatically to her room, registering that other bedroom doors were open now, as if ready for new occupancy. Her door was open, too, the bed inside freshly made. She hovered over it, then fell face forward onto the crisp bedcovers.

CHAPTER SIXTEEN

DAY AND NIGHT merged into a blur. When Allie awoke from her nap, it was dinnertime. She knew Susan would be home and called her. She carefully avoided mentioning the horrible interview with the police, though she did tell Susan about Spiro's murder and the subsequent investigation.

"How awful for you, dear. Would you like me to come? I can get a flight to Detroit and take a bus from there."

"No. I'll be fine. It's just such…a shock. I was expecting to go through the procedure today and now…"

"How's the family taking it?"

Trust Susan to consider the family. In stride, Allie was tempted to quip. But all that could wait. She steered the talk to another matter.

"Susan, do you know if Dad ever mentioned having another bank account anywhere?"

There was a low chuckle from the other end. "You mean, like a numbered account on some Caribbean island?"

"No, something like an emergency savings account that he used for special things."

"Do you need money, Allie? Is that what this is about?"

"Heavens no. Just that there's been some talk here about Spiro's will, and it got me thinking about Dad. Remember when you guys renovated the store? Did he get a loan for that or something?"

"*I* did. Come on, Allie, what's all this about?"

"Nothing really, Susan. I'll explain later. I'm not sure when I'll be home, but I'll call and let you know when I've made the arrangements."

"All right, dear. I'm so very sorry about your grandfather, but I can honestly say I'm looking forward to having you home."

Tears pricked Allie's eyes. Home was exactly where she wanted to be, too. She said goodbye, but before she rang off, her stepmother blurted out, "You know, something did happen several months before your father died. The interest payment on the loan was overdue—business had been slow and we'd overextended our inventory, stuff like that. It was pretty serious, though—the bank threatened to foreclose."

"What happened?"

"We sweated for about two weeks, then your dad came home one day and said he made the payment. Seems an old customer of his who'd owed him money for ages finally came through with it."

Allie spoke with Susan a bit longer before hanging up, then sat by the phone, mulling over what Susan had told her. The explanation was credible, Allie thought, recalling how poor her father had been at collecting from some people. Still, she wondered about the coincidence of it all. A check of the time showed that it was almost seven. Allie's room faced the rear of the estate, so she didn't know if the police were still around. Another encounter with the two detectives was the last thing she wanted that day. She decided not to risk going downstairs to get something to eat.

Instead, she curled up in her armchair with a book, unable to tackle any more of the photo albums after Maria's revelation. When Ruth came by half an hour later with a dinner tray, Allie was both surprised and grateful.

"You're quite welcome, Miss."

"How long have you been working here, Ruth?"

"About five years now."

"So you knew my grandfather before he got sick."

"Oh, yes. He was a much bigger man physically. And in spirit, too." She shook her head. "Sad how an illness can totally change you. I think Mr. Spiro hated passing over the business to George, but eventually he had no choice. It's hard to run a big company like that and go for chemo, along with all the specialist appointments and so on."

"Do you think he felt confident that George could run the business?"

Ruth hesitated. It was an unfair question, Allie knew, but she was curious.

"Like I said, I got the impression he didn't want to hand things over. There seemed to be a lot of meetings with Mr. Spiro and the two boys. Then Effie got involved, too. Finally he gave in. I think he just didn't have the energy to argue anymore. By then, he was at the peak of his illness. That was the first round. When he went into remission about a year ago, he tried to get involved in the business again. Even went to the office with the boys for a few months." Ruth frowned, remembering. "They had one big fight around that time. I know it had something to do with money, because I overheard part of the conversation." She smiled at Allie. "You'd be surprised how much people say in front of their hired help. Mr. Spiro was ranting at Christo about another gambling debt."

"Thanks for the information, Ruth. It may be helpful in the days ahead."

"Oh? Well, I'd better go and see if Miss Effie wants anything else."

"Have you taken anything to Maria? I'm worried about her."

"So am I. She's taken Mr. Spiro's death very hard. Probably because she's been here longer than any of us— except for the family, of course."

Family. "Where are the others, do you know? George and Christo?"

"I think Mr. George is working, either in the library or the study. I don't know where Mr. Christo is."

"Are the police still here?"

"The detectives are gone, but they've left some uniformed officers to stay the night," the young woman replied. "I'm glad, too, considering..."

"Considering?"

Ruth shivered. "That someone in this house must have killed Mr. Spiro."

Allie could only nod in sober agreement. There weren't a lot of people in the household to begin with. Unless... She thought of the gray van and Pat, whom Joel suspected was an undercover cop. *What if he isn't?* She hadn't mentioned the van to the detectives, because the interview had derailed her sense of calm.

"Did the detectives say when they'd be back?"

"First thing in the morning." Ruth made for the door, then stopped. "Have you by any chance seen a coffee mug around? It was the one Mr. Spiro always used. Tall and narrow with sailing boats on it. Know the one I mean?"

"I vaguely remember seeing him use it, but can't say I've seen it anywhere. Why?"

"I'm not supposed to say, but I don't see the harm in it, frankly. I took some hot milk in it to Mr. Spiro the night he died, and the mug seems to have disappeared."

"Strange. Maybe it fell on the floor and rolled under his bed or something."

Ruth shook her head. "They've searched the whole room and his bathroom. I don't know why they care. I mean, it's not as if he was poisoned or anything. And if he had been, then I would be the main suspect, wouldn't I." She gave a nervous giggle.

"Fortunately for you you're off the hook."

Ruth's face clouded. "Actually I'm not. Because I may have been the last one to see Mr. Spiro alive. Right?"

"No, Ruth," Allie said. "The person who killed him was."

"Right. Thanks for the vote of confidence. Fortunately they didn't seem too interested in me. Though they were very interested in the will part."

"The will part?" Allie, fork in hand, froze.

"Mr. Spiro asked me to sign some papers as a witness." She lowered her voice. "I don't know how legal it was because I didn't read more than a word or two. Aren't witnesses supposed to know what they're signing?"

"I guess so. How do you know it was a will?"

"Because he told me. And I saw the first page before he flipped through to the end. Last Will and Testament of Spiro Alexander Kostakis. I'd better go now. Miss Effie's waiting. And I'll pop in to see Maria, too."

Allie watched her leave, but her mind leaped to George and Christo, searching Spiro's study. She wondered if they'd found the will, after all. Or had the police beat them to it?

She pecked at the rest of her dinner and decided to return the tray to the kitchen herself, since Ruth seemed to be the only domestic staff left on duty. The house seemed empty, though Allie passed one uniformed officer sitting in the great hall, thumbing through a magazine.

On her way back to her room, she noticed Spiro's study door ajar and stuck her head in to see George, sitting at the desk and poring over what looked like a leather-bound book. His head shot up at her greeting and he instantly rested his elbows across whatever he'd been reading as if he didn't want her to see it. Allie found the gesture annoying. They just didn't comprehend that she wasn't interested in Spiro's money or his business.

"Allie, can I help you with anything?"

"No. I just noticed the open door and wondered who was in here." She took a step into the room. "Have you heard anything more about Spiro's death? About how he was killed?"

"The police think he might have been suffocated by one of his own pillows."

"As he slept? God, that's horrible." Allie fought back the painful vision of her grandfather fighting for his life.

"I agree," George murmured. "I admit we had our differences, but the old man was good to us over the years."

"Any idea when the funeral can be held?"

"None at all. They're not going to release the body until they know for sure they won't need to do any more tests. This homicide investigation has tied up everything. Including the probation of the will."

How inconvenient for you. In spite of the genuine sorrow in his voice, Allie didn't feel sorry for him. She figured he and his brother had had a great deal going for them over the years. "Well, I've been thinking that as soon as I can, I may go home. Of course I'd come back for the funeral," she added quickly at his expression.

"You can't go anywhere! That's what the police said."

He was emphatic, but she refused to be cowed. "I'm sure they meant until they had a chance to question everyone."

"My uncle's murderer is likely someone in this house." George stared hard at Allie.

Was he waiting for her to break down and confess, she wondered? The gray van suddenly materialized in her mind's eye. "You know, that private investigator—Joel Kennedy—told me he thought Patrick might be working undercover for the police. But what if he wasn't?"

"You've lost me. I don't have the faintest idea what you're talking about."

Allie moved closer to the center of the study. "You know Patrick? He's Sam's assistant. I kept seeing this gray van parked along Lakeshore Drive. The day Joel took me to the clinic, I saw the van and Pat was driving it."

George leaned forward, his chest hovering over the desktop. "Go on," he said, his face serious.

"I mentioned it to Joel and he said maybe Pat was an undercover policeman watching the house."

George sat still for so long that Allie wasn't certain if he'd heard her. She was about to repeat herself when he murmured, "What for?"

"Joel implied that maybe the police were investigating Grandfather's business dealings."

"As in a wiretap? Electronic eavesdropping?" His voice hit another octave.

"I guess. But…it's just conjecture," she said, backpedaling.

"Where's Kennedy now?"

"I…I don't know," she said.

"Do you know how to reach him?"

"No, but that detective has the business card Joel gave me."

George drew his hand across his face. He had a faraway look in his eyes. "If you hear from him—for whatever reason—let me know, okay?" He narrowed his eyes and studied her for a long moment. Then he added, "It's important, Allie. *To the family.*"

It was a test of her loyalty. Anger flared in her at the knowledge that this appeal to family trust came only now, in fear of some hypothetical police inquiry. "I doubt I'll be seeing Joel Kennedy again," she said, and eager to leave, backed out of the door.

She sprinted through the hall and up the stairs, slamming her bedroom door behind her. Spiro Kostakis had deserved better relatives, she fumed. All three of them had shown more emotion over the possibility of a will change than over Spiro's murder. Pacing to calm down, Allie almost missed the peal of the cell phone, buried between the pillows on her bed. She pounced on it.

"Susan?"

"Uh, no. It's Joel."

Allie sagged onto the bed. "Joel, thank God you called. The police took your business card and I've been desperate to talk to someone about what's going on here. It's all so confusing I hardly know where to start, but I don't think I can stand it much longer. Staying in this house, I mean."

"Whoa! I'm losing my own breath just listening. First of all, are you all right?"

She swiped at her eyes with her free hand. "Physically, yes. Emotionally, I'm a bit shaky." She laughed, but the sound that came out was more like a nervous bray.

"Do you feel safe there?"

Was it only last night that someone had tried to open her locked bedroom door? "Uh...yeah."

"You don't sound very certain."

"Last night someone tried to come into my room, but the door was locked."

He swore. "That doesn't sound safe to me. Look, I'm staying at this motel just a few miles along Lakeshore toward Grosse Pointe. It's called the Riverview. Original, eh?"

She smiled, guessing he was trying to calm her jittery nerves.

"I don't want to come up to the house. Is there any way you could meet me?"

She had a vision of the police, reading or maybe even dozing, downstairs. "I think so."

"Okay. I'll park south of the main gate, got it? I'll leave my parking lights on. When can you be there?"

"Ten minutes." She paused a beat. "Where are we going?"

"Someplace safe to talk and make some decisions," was all he said before he hung up.

Allie rushed to throw some things in her backpack—a change of clothes, her wallet, a few toiletries. And the phone. The rest could wait. It was dusk by the time she crept downstairs and slipped out the front door. She hadn't met a single person on her way.

Outside she stopped to take in a huge breath of fresh night air. She'd made this run several times in the past week, and now, even with her pack, it was an effortless course. By the time she reached Lakeshore Drive, she hadn't even broken a sweat. She picked up speed, glancing back twice to see if any car headlights were behind her. But there were no lights, no alarm bells.

When she figured she'd passed the fifty-yard mark, she had a mini panic attack debating what to do if Joel wasn't there. But rounding a curve, she saw the outline of a parked car ahead and the dim yellow of its low beams. Someone stepped in front of the lights and she ran toward him, slowing only at the last second, just before she threw her arms around him.

"Thank God!" she cried.

"That's not what I'd call a cautious approach," Joel

said, laughing softly. His arms tightened around her until she had to push him away to catch her breath.

"Come on, let's get out of here." He took her backpack and tossed it into the back seat, then held the passenger door for her.

When he switched on the ignition, she asked, "Where are we going?"

"My motel. We can figure out our next course from there. You have any dinner?"

"Yes."

"Good. We don't have to make any stops on the way." He pushed his foot to the floor and the car spun off the gravel shoulder, fishtailed twice and roared off down the road.

"Well, that should raise the alarm," Allie said.

Joel glanced at her and grinned. "Keep that sense of humor."

If only that was all I needed to get through this. She stared into the night and wondered if her life could possibly get any more bizarre. When they pulled into the parking lot of the Riverview Motel some ten minutes later, Allie thought to ask, "Why are you staying here, Joel?"

He braked and the car chugged to a stop. "I couldn't leave without knowing you were okay. I guess I was worried about how you'd react to your grandfather's death, and when I heard that he'd been murdered..."

"How did you find out? I only heard this morning."

"It was on the news—'Police investigating probable homicide.'"

She followed Joel into his room, which was directly in front of the parked car. When he flicked on the overhead light, she saw that the room bore a marked similarity to the inside of his car. An open pizza box with a single wilted slice remaining sitting on an unmade bed, newspapers strewn on the floor and on the only chair, crumpled pop cans here and there.

"Home sweet home," she murmured.

"Camping out too long," he said sheepishly.

"I'm glad you didn't say you needed a woman, or something like that," she said, then regretted the quip when she saw his face redden.

He didn't reply, just dropped her backpack on the floor and began to clear up the papers, empty food containers and pop cans. "Sit here," he said, shifting the chair closer to the side of the double bed. He switched on the bedside lamp and clicked off the overhead. The room suddenly grew cozy.

"Now," he said, perching on the edge of the bed in front of her chair. "I want you to tell me everything that's been happening. Don't leave anything out."

Allie talked for half an hour. When she finished, her mouth was dry and her eyes wet. Without a word Joel went into the bathroom and came out with a glass of water and a handful of tissues. He sat down across from her, his knees touching hers, and after she blew her nose, he reached for her hand and clasped it in his. "Do you mind if I ask a few questions?"

She shook her head. His eyes, dark as night, locked with hers. It occurred to her that, except for a single disastrous rendezvous years ago, she'd never been in a motel room with a man. The thought brought a rush of heat to her face.

Something flickered in his eyes. A question? she wondered. His thumb began to trace a circular pattern across the top of the hand he held. He opened his mouth as if to ask the first question, but then closed it again. Tightening his grip on her hand and tugging gently, he pulled her from the chair onto his lap.

Allie recognized then what she'd seen in his eyes. When

he brushed the hair off her forehead, she raised her face to his and closed her eyes. His mouth found hers, separating her lips with the tip of his tongue. Allie raised her hands to his head, holding it gently to hers. As if he might let go and break the lock of mouth on mouth.

Heat blasted through her as his tongue played with hers. He moved his lips to her throat, then to her neck and the hollow at its base, and Allie gasped. She shifted, turning into him, as his tongue flicked below the ribbed neckline of her T-shirt. She knew where he wanted to go and to help him get there, she reached down and pulled off her top.

"Are you sure?" His face was flushed, his voice husky.

Her answer was to cup his face in her hands and lower it to hers. Lips on hers, Joel's hands moved swiftly down her back, unhooked her bra and tossed it aside. Allie's breath caught in her throat. She arched back, offering her breasts to his hands, his mouth, his tongue. Pleasure rippled up from the tips of her toes to the hard nubs he sucked on, first one, then the other.

Her fingers dug into the hair on his head, clutching him to her breasts until every nerve in her body begged, *Now, now.* But then she tenderly pushed him away, unfolding herself from his lap in a single fluid movement that left him gasping.

"Allie?" His eyes pleaded.

She placed a finger on his lips and smiled. "Wait," she whispered, her hands fumbling to unzip her jeans until Joel's hands joined hers, pulling them down. She stepped out of them. "Now you," she whispered.

When he stood up, she saw at once that he was aroused. He yanked his shirt up over his head and quickly unfastened the belt to his jeans. "My turn," she said, her hands working the zipper.

He kicked his jeans aside and pulled Allie with him back onto the bed. She lay alongside him, moving her hands over his hard, lightly furred chest, stroking his taut nipples until he cried, "Oh, Allie!"

She found the band of his boxer shorts and tugged. Joel raised himself on one elbow, enough to yank the shorts down, kicking them out of the way. He rolled her onto her back and eased her panties down over her hips to her ankles, then sat back on his heels, his eyes traveling the length of her.

"You're so beautiful," he whispered.

"And you," she said, reaching to bring him down.

MUCH LATER, her back tucked against him, his hand cupping her breasts and his mouth at the nape of her neck, Allie uttered a long sigh, drunk with satisfaction.

"What're you thinking?" he murmured, lips nibbling, his fingertips lazily caressing her nipples.

"That I'm glad we didn't have to do that in the station wagon."

His laugh vibrated through her. "Allie, I—"

"What?"

He buried his face into the back of her neck, pushing more closely against her. "Nothing," he finally whispered. And after a long, disquieting moment, he added, "I wish we could stay here forever."

A wish that reminded Allie tomorrow was only a few hours away.

CHAPTER SEVENTEEN

ALLIE STIRRED against him, murmuring softly in her sleep. Joel waited to see if she was awake, and when he saw she wasn't, he inched back, gently settling her arms and legs back into place without disturbing her. He rolled over to face the window, catching a glimpse of daylight through the curtains.

It was time to move. But he lay a moment longer, still savoring the memory of last night. He looked over his shoulder at Allie. The covers had slipped, exposing the smooth V of her back and the sloping curve of her buttocks that had pressed so perfectly into him minutes ago. His hands recalled from memory every part of her and ached to explore one last time those sweet contours. He stifled a groan. *You're done for, Kennedy. You've crossed the line but good and there's no going back. She's not just another woman in your bed.*

But what a woman, he was thinking, her pleasure and appetite matched only by his. Had they made love twice, or was it three times? The night had been a dizzying carousel of sensations and now the sobering dawn. He shifted to the edge of the bed and slipped his legs out from under the sheet. Sitting up, he rubbed his palm across his face, wondering why he felt so achy. That is, until he thought of a good reason. He smiled, preferring last night's workout to the company gym. Maybe he could convince Allie that bed sport could also be a kind of training. Then he sighed.

The night was over. Now the hard light of day ruled. *Getting philosophical in your old age, Kennedy? Or realistic, the cold voice of reason suggested.* He knew only that he'd missed his chance to confess. But blurting the whole ugly truth right after he'd made love with the woman he'd dreamed about forever hadn't seemed wise.

"Joel?"

He twisted around. She'd partially turned over and the sheet had fallen, revealing a crescent of breast and the darker aureole. Joel smiled. "Sleep well?"

"Mmm."

Her smile was sultry, her eyes inviting.

"What time is it?"

"I don't know. Early."

Allie's tongue ran along her lower lip. "Then we still have time?"

He didn't get it at first, not until she raised an eyebrow and grinned. He eagerly swung his legs back onto the bed.

"NOW WHAT?" she asked. Allie's tongue flicked out of her mouth and scooped up the maple syrup trickling off her lower lip.

Joel handed her a napkin. "Time to go. More coffee?"

Allie set her fork down. "That's it for me. Go where?"

He signaled the waitress and motioned for the bill.

"Why do I get the feeling you're ignoring me?" she asked.

"You're damn hard to ignore," he said.

Judging from the leer in his face, he was thinking of a few places they could go together. "Try to stay focused Joel," Allie joked.

He leaned forward, speaking in a dramatic whisper. "Around you, that's not going to be easy." And winked.

Her laughter bubbled up. A few heads in the diner turned, but Allie paid no heed. She felt light and delirious, almost giddy. She stared at the grinning face across from her and thought she could explore those features all day long. Run her fingers up and down the knobby ridge of nose, the planes of taut cheek and firm, determined chin. Tease a line around the mouth that aroused every nerve in every part of her body. Crook a finger at those knowing eyes. A whole day, just on the face.

"What's that sigh about?" he asked after the waitress left with the payment.

The question brought her back. "Thinking about today."

"Right." He crumpled the receipt and tossed it onto the table. "Let's talk about today. I've got an idea."

"Yes?"

"Remember Maria's hinting about some money your father had taken?"

"Effie was the one who did that." Allie thought for a moment, then added, "But Maria mentioned an argument between Dad and Tony about money. Why?"

"We could go back to Kingston and check around. You know. See if there *is* any money."

"But there isn't any. Susan was very clear about that."

"Maybe your father had some papers tucked away."

"Susan's looked everywhere!"

He reached across the table and stroked her arm. "Allie, I know these questions are frustrating. But my years of investigation have taught me there's almost *always* someplace people forget about."

Allie bit down on her lower lip. "The only place I can

imagine something might be hidden is Dad's work shed. Susan may not have looked there.''

''There you go,'' he said, casting her a smile that left her inexplicably uneasy.

As she followed him out to the car, the brilliantly sunny May morning failed to dispel the feeling that a replay of last night and the early morning wasn't going to happen anytime soon.

THEY'D BEEN on the road for an hour and Allie had slept the whole time. She stretched, yawning awake, and looked over at Joel, intent on the road ahead. ''Did we go through the border point without any problems?'' she asked.

He looked at her and grinned. ''Yep. I told the officer we were returning from our honeymoon. He took one look at you and waved us through.''

''Sure.'' She grinned back, giddiness overwhelming her all over again.

''Seriously,'' he said, brow furrowing. ''What did you expect? An alert for you at all border crossings?''

''No, but—''

''Don't worry, Allie. As soon as we've checked things out at the house and you've had a visit with Susan, we'll call the cops in Grosse Pointe and offer to return. So don't worry, okay?'' His hand slipped off the wheel to squeeze hers.

''Okay,'' she said. Still, she couldn't help wondering why this was so important to him. His explanation that he didn't want her to have a negative picture of her father hanging over her for the rest of her life didn't quite satisfy her. She knew what kind of man and father Rob Newman had been. That was all that really mattered in the end. But there was a niggle of doubt deep inside her about the tale

Maria had told. A what-if that kept creeping into her consciousness demanding an answer.

Like, what if he hadn't come home early that night and caught Tony and her mother together? Worse, what if he *had* taken money that didn't belong to him? That was the one that rankled. Who did the money belong to and why did he take it?

"Another sigh?"

"I was just wondering if I'd ever know the answers to all the questions about my parents."

He reached out a hand for her again. "Move over here," he said, patting the center of the bench seat. "There's a seat belt tucked down in the groove somewhere."

When she was settled against him, her head nestled against the side of his chest and his right hand resting lightly on her thigh, he murmured, "Mmm, that's better. Too bad this isn't Spiro's Caddie. I could put it on cruise control and— Hey!"

Allie laughed. She placed his hand on the steering wheel and threatened, "I'll give you another poke in the ribs if you don't focus on your driving." She closed her eyes and, basking in the warmth and reassurance of Joel, drifted off to sleep once more.

JOEL PUNCHED in Mike's cell phone number, glancing at the convenience store, next to the gas pumps, where Allie had gone. Fortunately Mike answered immediately.

"Jeez," he cried. "Where the hell are you? You're in deep doo-doo, fella."

Joel closed his eyes. "Look, spare me the scolding. I've got a lead on the money and I'm going with it. If I find it, I just may get myself out of the doo-doo."

"I don't know, Kennedy. Steve is really ticked off and Pat's playing right into it." He paused to chuckle. "One thing, though. I'm not sure how this happened, but Pat was returning the van to the garage about six this morning and, get this, he was picked up by the cops. Seems there was an APB out on the van. They took him in for questioning, the whole bit. To top it off, he didn't have his ID with him and couldn't raise anyone on the phone to vouch for him." Mike laughed heartily. "He just got out about half an hour ago and he's madder 'n hell. Even thinks you had something to do with it, but I told him he was paranoid." Another pause. "You didn't plan a little fun with him, did you?"

"No, but I'd shake the hand of anyone who did. Pat deserves whatever he gets, far as I'm concerned. But forget about him for now. I want you to do me a favor. Make up some kind of excuse for me with Steve. I don't care what. This may be all over in forty-eight hours."

"I don't know, Kennedy. It's not the first time I've bailed you out."

"Yeah, but it'll be the last."

"Right. I've heard that before."

"Seriously. I…I've been doing some hard thinking the last twenty-four hours."

There was a brief silence. Mike whistled. "Uh-oh. This doesn't have anything to do with the Newman chick, does it?"

"No way. And she's not a chick."

"Omigod, it *is* her." Static sparked from the phone, and when it cleared, Mike was saying, "…with you now?"

"Of course she's with me. How else would I be able to search Eddie Hughes's farm in Kingston?"

"I hope you haven't done anything to compromise the case if it does get reopened. You haven't, have you?" He groaned.

Joel ignored him. "Mike, talk to Steve, okay? Give me

forty-eight hours. If you don't hear from me by then, you can call in the Mounties, for all I care."

Mike swore, more expressively this time. "You've got two days, buddy, then I'm haulin' your butt down here. Got that?"

"Yeah, yeah. Thanks pal." Joel clicked off the phone and shoved it into his windbreaker pocket just as Allie walked his way.

"Everything okay?" she asked.

"Yup." He started to climb into the car.

"You've got a strange look on your face, one that tells me you're not being totally honest."

Joel ducked behind the wheel. She was too observant. When she closed the door behind her, he sensed her staring at him and knew she wouldn't let it go. "I was just checking in with a friend of mine. Someone I work with once in a while. We may have this case and, uh, I had to tell him I'd be out of town for a couple of days."

She nodded. "I phoned Susan, too."

"You *did?*" Why hadn't he thought of that? If George or Christo got hold of the Kingston phone number, and it was likely in Spiro's records, they might call themselves. God only knew what they'd tell Susan.

"Is there a problem with that?"

"No, just that…you know, she might worry if we don't show up at a certain time. What did you tell her?"

"She wasn't even home. I left a message on her machine and said I was on my way."

He turned on the ignition. "That's okay, then, because, you know, anything can happen," he said, not wanting to alarm her about the possibility of George and Christo contacting Susan.

Allie frowned. "What do you mean by that?"

He shrugged. "We might get delayed for some reason. This way, she won't be expecting us at a fixed time."

The look she cast him was doubtful, but she seemed to accept his explanation and leaned back in the seat. Relieved that she'd bought his story about the phone call, not that it was so far off base, Joel drove out of the service center and headed east to Kingston. After a brief washroom stop two hours out of Toronto, his comment to Allie about being delayed came back to haunt him.

The first sign of trouble was a slowdown of vehicles on the highway. As soon as Joel realized the traffic jam ahead extended for more than a couple of miles, he crawled along in the right-hand lane, waiting for an exit ramp.

"Must be an accident," he muttered.

"Either that or construction. There's always a fair bit of that along this part of Highway 401. Does it matter when we get there?"

Forty-eight hours kept rolling over in his head. "Kind of," he said. "I've got that case—it can't be put off much longer."

"Oh," Allie murmured.

Something in her tone caught his attention. He glanced at her. She was sitting next to the window now, staring out at the stretch of field beside the highway.

"You okay?" he asked.

"Sure." But she didn't look his way.

"No regrets, I hope, about…"

That turned her head. "None at all," she said.

Joel couldn't read what she was thinking, but he knew something was troubling her. "Then what?" He reached for her hand and clasped it.

"I guess what you said—about having to go back for that case in forty-eight hours—made me realize you'd be leaving.'' She turned to the window again, cranking it down now that the car had slowed.

So that was it. She was looking for a sign from him. A promise, maybe, some sort of commitment. His mouth was dry. The next forty-eight hours was already jammed with problems. He doubted he could squeeze in even five minutes of thought about a future with Allie Newman. But he knew, deep down, that was what he wanted. He just wasn't sure that she'd still want the same thing after she found out the truth.

He released her hand and stroked the side of her cheek. ''We both have some unfinished business—you, with the police investigation and Spiro's funeral, and I've got the case. But soon all that stuff will be taken care of, okay? Then we can be free to talk and make some decisions.''

She flashed a wan smile, dipping her cheek into the palm of his hand. They sat like that, the station wagon creeping along the highway, until Joel spied an exit ramp ahead.

''I'm getting off here,'' he said, returning his hand to the wheel.

''That'll take you south to Highway 2,'' Allie said. ''It's a bit slower, because it's only a two-lane highway, but it goes right to Kingston.''

''Great.'' When they reached the exit lane, he swerved right and stepped on the gas. He wasn't the only driver to make the same move, so the going was still slow, but at least they weren't trapped on the main highway. They traveled south for almost forty-five minutes and then Joel spotted the sheen of water.

''That Lake Ontario?'' he asked.

''Yes. We must be near the first town. There's the sign straight ahead. Deseronto.''

''How far from there to Kingston?''

"Not sure. Maybe about half an hour's drive."

"Good. Then we can head right to the farm and start searching."

Her head shot from the window to him. "I'll need to find Susan first. She may be at the store. What's the rush?"

He saw the glint of suspicion in her eyes. *There I go again.* "No rush, just...you know—"

"Forty-eight hours," she replied.

"Yeah." He got the feeling she was already tired of hearing that excuse.

"So we can have a late lunch and then find Susan? Because I wouldn't feel right searching the place without her knowing."

"Yeah sure," he said quickly, wanting to ease her mind. That was when the station wagon emitted a crescendo of alarming groans, rattles and metallic clunks. It shuddered as Joel swiftly wheeled onto the gravel shoulder, and then chugged to a steamy, wheezing halt.

Joel slammed the steering wheel with his palm and swore.

"What is it?"

"No idea," he muttered, releasing the hood and jumping from the car. He stared at the engine, but it yielded no clues. When Allie was standing beside him, he asked, "Do you know anything about cars?"

Her eyes widened. "Not me. Don't you?"

"I can change a flat tire—that's about it."

She raised her face and squinted into the sun. "Deseronto can't be more than five or ten miles down the road. Maybe we can get a tow truck."

Joel slammed the hood down and sagged against it. He closed his eyes and counted to ten. Now wasn't the time to lose his cool. When he opened them, Allie was standing in front of him, a worried look on her face.

"It's okay," he said, and drew her to him. God, she felt great in his arms. He dipped his head into her hair, inhaling the flowery scent so familiar to him now. She wrapped her arms around his waist, pressing against him, and desire for her rushed through him, hot and urgent. His lips found the delicate lobes of her ears and he nibbled, drawing a shivery gasp from her, which excited him even more. She strained against him, her strong, slender legs enveloping one of his.

He moaned, pulling away. Their eyes met and they both giggled, faces flushed with desire. "Allie, don't do this to me."

"You started it."

Her face belied the teasing remark. Knowing that she wanted him every bit as much as he wanted her was exhilarating and frightening at the same time. *Time. Running out.* Now this. He swung away from the car and her, striding to the edge of the gravel shoulder.

"What are you doing?" she asked, sounding slightly put out.

"Hitching a ride into Deseronto."

"You're not leaving me behind!"

The plaintive cry tugged at him. Why was he taking out his frustration on her? "Of course not. C'mere." She did, and he wrapped an arm around her, hugging her close, straining to see against the glare of sun on asphalt, waiting for the first car to come along.

Fortunately they didn't have to wait long. Another motorist escaping the holdup on Highway 401 stopped. Allie grabbed her pack from the back seat, but Joel decided to leave his gear in the car, hidden under a blanket. He locked up the station wagon and hopped into the car with Allie. Twenty minutes later he arranged for a tow to the only garage in town. Okay, he told himself. Not doing too badly here.

Allie noticed a café across the road from the garage. "I'll go order something to eat."

Joel finished giving his directions to the tow driver and loped after her. It was a typical small-town diner and almost empty.

"You beat the early bird rush by a few hours," quipped the waitress, a fifty-something woman with tired, but friendly, eyes. "And just missed the noon crowd. Must be your lucky day."

Allie laughed. Joel smiled fondly at her while she gave her order and scarcely heard the waitress ask for his.

"Got it bad," the waitress said as an aside, moving away to get their coffees.

Allie reached out and clasped his hand in hers, and when the waitress returned with two cups of coffee, she asked, "You two newlyweds?"

They both laughed, though Joel saw Allie drop her gaze to her coffee almost at once. For a wild, crazy second he wondered if the town had a motel and if they'd have time…

Forty-eight hours. Less now.

He withdrew his hand from hers to pick up his coffee mug. The tow truck dragging the station wagon coasted by the window while they were eating. Joel didn't rush, knowing the mechanic had yet to examine the car. If the trouble was serious, maybe he could rent a car. He peered out the window, looking left and right.

"What is it?" Allie asked.

"Looking to see if there's a car rental place in town."

"Oh," she said a bit breathlessly, as if she hadn't considered the possibility of the station wagon being a goner.

He swallowed the last bite and stood up. "Don't rush," he said. "I'm going over to the garage for the bad news. Not that I'm hoping for any, but the car's never died on me like that.'' He tipped her chin with his finger. ''Don't worry, okay?''

She shook her head, beaming at him. She was still aglow, he realized, from the morning's start at the motel. If there hadn't been a crucial time issue, he thought again, they could check out the town. Look for a place to stay overnight. He tapped her chin lightly and whispered, ''I'll be back soon. When all of this is over, we can....'' He didn't need to finish. The look she gave him said the rest.

ALLIE ORDERED another coffee while she waited for Joel. When the waitress brought it, she said, ''Your hubby's dropped his jacket,'' and bent down to pick it up.

When she laid it on the table, something fell out of a pocket. ''Here,'' the waitress said, and handed Allie a plastic identity card on a nylon cord.

Allie stared down at the card in her hand. She didn't hear the waitress walk away. She couldn't hear anything but the blood pounding in her ears. Joel's face was imprinted beneath the logo of the Alcohol, Tobacco and Firearms Department of the United States government. *Joel Kennedy. Federal agent.*

She turned sharply to the window and the garage across the street. Joel was nowhere in sight. Beckoning to the waitress for the bill, Allie stood up and asked her, ''Is there a car rental place in town?''

''Nope,'' the waitress said. ''You okay? You look like you're gonna be sick.''

''I'm fine. Just a bit woozy.''

''Uh-oh,'' the waitress said, grinning.

''What about a taxi?''

''There's a guy just retired from that. He lives down the

road, first street on the left. Name's John Calvin. He's still got his cab and sometimes drives people into Kingston.''

Allie handed her the money Joel had left. ''Thanks. Keep the change.'' She picked up her backpack and headed for the door.

CHAPTER EIGHTEEN

ALLIE DIDN'T DARE look back, knowing if she did—if she saw him—she'd rush to confront him. But at that moment, all she wanted to do was get away from him. Because now she knew it had all been a lie. He wasn't a private investigator, but an agent of the U.S. government. And if he'd lied about that, she reasoned, then possibly he'd lied about everything else.

She rounded the corner of the first street on her left, and spotting a cab parked in front of a modest bungalow, sprinted for it, her pack flapping against her back. She managed to persuade John Calvin to leave at once, citing car breakdown and a family emergency. Allie didn't dare let herself relax until the cab breezed past the last stop sign in town.

"You sure you're all right?" He glanced at her in his rearview mirror.

"I'm fine now that we're on the way."

Sensing she didn't want to make small talk, he fell silent. She chewed on her lip, fighting back tears, and stared zombielike at the passing scenery.

If only he hadn't dropped his damn jacket and the card hadn't fallen out. *Then what? Would you rather continue on to Kingston ignorant of his deception? Perhaps even make love with him again?*

A wave of nausea rolled up from her stomach. She

opened the window and sucked in a mouthful of warm, fresh air.

"Want the air-conditioning on?"

"No, thanks. This is enough."

She closed her eyes. In spite of her desire to put Joel out of her mind, she couldn't focus on anything else. She saw again the expression in his face as he came inside her last night. *That wasn't a lie.* Her certainty about that was unshakable. So how much, she asked herself, had been false?

Had her grandfather or cousins known? Somehow she doubted it. They'd let him go, paid him off. And what was the story about Pat and the gray van? Were he and Joel working together? She remembered the scene she'd witnessed after Pat had almost run into her with Christo's car. Joel's face had been red with anger, his words threatening.

Eventually, as the cab reached the outskirts of Kingston, her thoughts came around to the why. Well, the money was a part of it, she felt certain; Joel's reasons for wanting to look for the money had been vague from the start. But her desire to get away from Grosse Pointe, to be home with Susan, had overridden her doubts. She hadn't really wondered about why he was so insistent, choosing to assume he wanted to help her clear her father's name.

More like *incriminate* him, she thought bitterly.

"Where to, miss?"

Allie's mind raced. Good question. Facing Susan right now would be a disaster. Allie knew she'd break down, burst into sobs, and then Susan would insist on hearing the whole sordid tale. All of which would take time.

Enough time for Joel to reach Kingston. For she knew he'd be heading here. Impulsively she gave the driver directions to the farm. As soon as the cab pulled into the lane leading to the house, Allie saw that Susan wasn't home. Tiggy barked furiously from the dog run. The dog's penchant for chewing inappropriate objects meant that Susan often left her outside in fair weather.

John Calvin couldn't change Allie's American money, but was more than content with receiving another twenty. She let herself into the quiet house and made for the kitchen, where Susan usually left any messages.

There it was, propped against the microwave.

Dear Allie,
So happy to hear you're on your way. I had a hair appointment in town and then will be going to the chiropractor. Likely won't be home until after six, as I promised to help close up the store. Beth's off today. There's a casserole in the freezer, or if you'd prefer, we can order in. See you soon, darling. Love, Susan

Allie blinked back tears, holding the note against her as if its cheery and loving contents could make the pain disappear. She checked the time. Just past four. She dropped the note onto the counter and headed for the kitchen door, which opened onto the backyard where the shed was. The one place Susan had told Allie she couldn't bring herself to search thoroughly.

JOEL CLENCHED his fist. He'd raced back to the garage immediately after finding Allie gone, his jacket and ID card lying on the table. In spite of his insistence that this was a dire emergency, the mechanic seemed to purposely take his time. He'd offered to phone a friend to find out if Joel could hire the guy to take him to Kingston, but kept stopping to speak to the other men working there. Finally Joel pulled out his card. The mechanic's eyes popped.

"Hey! Is that, like, the FBI?"

"Damn right," Joel muttered.

The arrangements were made in less than two minutes, and the mechanic's friend squealed up to the garage in another five. Joel hopped in, shouting to the mechanic that he'd call him about the station wagon. Fortunately the friend wasn't into small talk. Joel needed every second of the drive to put together a plan.

Such as, what would he tell Allie? *The truth, idiot. No more evasion.* He dug into his duffel bag for his cell phone and called Mike again. The guy must've been waiting for his call.

"Yep," Mike said.

"It's me."

"You've got...what? Forty-two hours or so?"

"I figure. So, how'd it go with Steve?"

"Guess."

"Did I get my time or not?"

"Oh, yeah, you did. But it'll cost you, buddy."

"No doubt. Listen, something's come up here."

"Not another problem, I hope, 'cause I don't reckon you've got time for any more of those."

Joel ignored that. "Have you heard anything about what's happening at the Kostakis place? About the murder investigation and so on?" Joel held his breath, praying he wouldn't hear there was an APB out on Allie.

"Yeah. Things are hoppin' there. My pal in the local detachment told me they've got someone for the murder."

"Who?" His heart thrummed against his chest wall.

"Someone who works there. The housekeeper. Someone saw a piece of evidence in her room—a coffee mug, I think—and she broke down and confessed early this morning. Then the two boys zoomed outta there as if the hounds of hell were chasin' them."

"Wait, slow down. Let me get this straight. The house-keeper—that would be Maria. She give a reason?"

"I didn't get it all. Complicated history. Some mental instability lately, too. Thought the old guy was cutting her out of his will after she'd given him the best years of her life. Yadda yadda."

"Okay. Get to the boys. How'd you know about them taking off?"

"Like I said, a friend of mine was one of the uniforms at the scene. Apparently shortly after they took Maria away, the boys piled into a car and vamoosed. Didn't say where they were going, and no one had the right to ask anymore." Joel's gut told him where they were headed and why. And the two-hour stop in Deseronto meant they were that much closer.

Before he switched off, Mike warned, "You'd better come up with something to justify all this, Kennedy."

Joel shoved the phone into the same inner pocket of his windbreaker where he'd foolishly left his ID card. Then he looked across at the man driving the car and asked, "Want to earn an extra fifty bucks? American?"

"Sure," the guy said.

"Then floor the bloody thing, will ya?"

TIGGY YELPED EXCITEDLY when Allie ran across the yard.

"Hi, girl!" Allie called. "Be with you soon." She pulled open the shed door. She hadn't been inside since she and Susan had tidied up a few months after her father's death. Susan had made a cursory search of the shed after Allie's phone call, but there was no obvious place to store papers, much less money, in the shed.

Allie scanned the interior from left to right, floor to ceiling. Dust motes caught by the sunbeams tornadoed in from the windows on each side of the small structure. The pungent scent of cedar and other assorted wood shavings assailed Allie. She covered her face, turning away to the open door.

But she knew it wasn't fresh air she sought. The shed was full of the tools of Rob Newman's carpentry trade. There were partially completed projects and discarded rejects. The canoe they used to take down to the lake every Sunday hung from huge hooks in the ceiling. The collection of childhood furniture he'd made for Allie that couldn't be stored in the house gathered dust in a corner. Allie's breath caught in her throat. Her father was everywhere.

She stuck her head out the door and inhaled deeply. The job had to be done. Joel would be arriving soon, and she knew she'd have the edge if she found the money first. Assuming, she reminded herself, there was even money here. She still couldn't believe that her father might have been mixed up in anything illegal. Or that he'd stolen money. Resolved, she stepped back inside.

The car trip from Michigan had given her a chance to delve into the past. After she'd told Joel about the time the bank almost foreclosed on the store, she'd realized how conveniently her father had come up with the money. At the time, she and Susan had accepted his explanation about collecting money owed to him, because Rob Newman had been notoriously forgiving of people who couldn't pay their bills right away. But at some point during the ride, she'd realized that what both Effie and Maria had told her about the money must have been true. For some reason, and she wasn't certain she wanted to know what it was, her father had run off not only with her but with Tony Kostakis's money.

And stepping back into her father's shed for the first time in almost a year, she was beginning to envision where it might be hidden. She paced the width of the shed, eyes darting about the walls, floor and ceiling. The section behind the canoe was empty. Likely Rob found it a nuisance to duck under the canoe each time he needed a planer or plumb line and chose to suspend the tools above his workbench.

She frowned, remembering something. The canoe hadn't always hung there. Years ago it was propped upside down on a stand in the garage. When Susan moved in, the second garage space was needed for her car. For a few days the canoe lay in the yard until Rob found a place for it.

Allie's movements quickened. A picture was forming in her mind. She was ten and thrilled at Susan's moving in. One day she ran out to the shed to tell her father something and burst inside. He was kneeling, hammering a baseboard into the rear wall. When she flung open the door, he cried out, startled, and dropped the hammer. He angrily told her that if a door was closed—even the shed door—she ought to knock before entering. Later that night, he tried to explain. By then of course, Allie had forgotten her hurt and scarcely listened.

Now she moved toward the canoe, ducked under it and stared at the baseboard. She squatted on her haunches, running her fingertips along its bottom edge. It wasn't loose, but it soon could be. Stooping, she headed back to the workbench, eyeing the row of screwdrivers until she found one that was broad and flat enough to pry off the board. She got down on her knees to work, inserting the tip of the screwdriver between the wall and board along the join. Rob had been a fastidious worker and the board was snugly in place. As she moved down the wall, she heard another explosion of barking from Tiggy. She paused. Was Susan back already? Worse still, had Joel arrived?

Allie crept toward the shed door and peered outside.

Tiggy was tearing back and forth in her dog run. The retriever had strong territorial instincts and had always been good for sounding the alarm when strangers visited the farm. Tiggy was the reason Susan didn't mind staying there by herself. So, Allie figured, there must be someone here. And that someone was likely Joel.

She dropped the screwdriver and marched across the yard to the kitchen door. As soon as she stepped inside, closing the door firmly behind her, she knew there was another person in the house. She could hear a faint scuffling.

"Joel?" Allie called. She moved through the kitchen into the hall, catching a glimpse of a darting shadow as she did. Allie froze. If Joel had come to the door and no one answered, he'd probably walk in. But he wouldn't be sneaky about it. The thought held her there, waiting and watching until she couldn't wait any longer.

"Joel? Susan is going to be here any second, so we'd better get this over with." She strode down the hall toward the living room.

George and Christo stood there, smiling sheepishly. Allie's jaw dropped.

"We knocked," Christo explained, "but since there was no answer and the door was unlocked—"

"What are you doing here?"

"That's our Allie," George murmured, casting a peculiar smile her way.

"I'm not *your* Allie. What's this about?"

"We've come to get something that belongs to us."

"I don't know what you mean." But she did.

"I've got a feeling you do," George said.

"Well, fine, then, have a seat, and when Susan and Joel get here, we can discuss this together." Allie gestured to the couch.

"Is Kennedy here?"

"How else do you think I got here?" she snapped. "Bus? Train?"

"We thought maybe you'd rented a car or something," Christo answered. "We could probably settle this right now, George, before he gets here."

"Shut up, Christo. I'm thinking."

Had the power dynamics shifted, Allie wondered, or had she misread the brothers' roles from the beginning? "Look, why don't you two head into town and find a hotel. Then come back here about eight or so. We'll air the problem then."

George flashed a smile. "You're not getting it, are you, cuz? We drove all the way here because we need that money *right now*."

"You don't have to shout. I told you before, George, there is no money. So if you're going to behave like that, you can damn well leave. Or do I have to call the police?" She turned her back on them and left the room. By the time she reached the phone in the kitchen, no doubt they'd realize she'd called their bluff and one of them, likely Christo, would capitulate.

Allie picked up the receiver as her cousins hustled down the hall after her. She grimaced, pretending to punch in 911, until a massive hand clamped down on hers, squeezing it in an iron grip.

She spun on her heel, butting headfirst into Marko's bulky chest. He laughed. George and Christo raced into the kitchen.

"Find anything outside?" George asked Marko, who was still holding on to Allie.

"Some crazy dog, but that's all. She was in the shed, though."

"Really? Let's go."

"There's nothing out there," Allie protested.

"Which means there is."

Marko led the way, pulling Allie with him. She caught Christo's eye on the way. "This doesn't have to happen, Christo. You could end up in trouble over this."

George laughed. "He's already in big trouble, Allie, and so am I. We both need the money, you see, or men much bigger than Marko will be coming after *us*."

"But what if there isn't any money?"

"There'd better be," George said softly.

Marko jerked her arm. "Come on," he growled. "Quit the yakkety-yak. Let's get this over with."

Get what over with? Allie wondered as they crossed the yard toward the shed. Tiggy went crazy. She sniffed trouble, Allie thought.

Marko swore at the dog before pushing Allie ahead of him through the shed door. She went sprawling against the workbench. That was the moment real fear seized hold of her. She sagged against the bench, pretending to catch her breath, while her mind raced to piece together some kind of a plan. Delay, she thought. Joel would be coming. *And please let him come before Susan.*

"Why are you so positive there's money?" she asked George directly.

"We found Uncle Spiro's journal. The one he started keeping when he knew you were alive. He wrote down the whole sordid tale, in case something happened to him before Kennedy could find you."

"Where is it?"

"In the car."

"Can I read it? There might be some clue in it."

"There's no clue in it about where the money's hidden. How could he have known? But he did specify how much and where it came from. He even knew why your father took it."

"I don't understand."

"It had to do with a job my father set up," Christo began.

"Shut up, little brother. Not now. There's no time. Didn't you hear her say that Kennedy was coming?" He turned to Allie. "I think you were in here because you remembered something—maybe from your childhood. Who knows? Maybe you've known about the money the whole time."

"I don't know where it is. Honest."

A silence more frightening than talk fell over them. Then George murmured, "Marko, help us out here."

Allie looked toward the doorway, where Marko's silhouette loomed. She waited, hardly daring to breathe.

"We could always find out how much she likes that dog out there," Marko said.

Fear clutched at Allie's throat. She forced down the panic that rose from her gorge. "She'll attack you. She knows you're threatening me."

"Yeah? Well, *she's* in a pen. And if I need it, I've got a gun in the car."

"No!"

"Up to you, cuz," George said. He wasn't smiling anymore.

"Okay, okay. I think it's over there, hidden in the wall behind the canoe."

"So lead the way," George ordered.

Allie ducked under the canoe and pointed to the baseboard. "In there, I think. I've already loosened the board. It shouldn't take much more prying to get it off."

"So get at it."

She hesitated. George motioned for Marko to move

closer to the canoe. "Get under that thing. Maybe your presence will make her work faster."

Marko chuckled and brushed past George. The idea came to Allie then. As Marko ducked his head, planning to crab-walk under the suspended canoe, she reached up and pulled the canoe back.

"Let me help," she said, and pushing with all her might, sent the canoe toward Marko.

It struck him hard on the shoulder. He fell backward and, stooping low, Allie dashed under the canoe as it swung back. She sprinted for the door.

JOEL TOSSED another fifty at Larry. He didn't have time to argue. Besides, it was his fault that the cop manning the radar trap on the outskirts of Kingston had flagged them down. By the time the ticket had been written out, he and the mechanic's pal were on a first-name basis. Larry had been pretty decent about it, too. Hadn't even dumped him out. Just muttered under his breath that the fine was definitely going to be added to the bill.

Larry waved a curt goodbye, made a squealing U-turn and roared back to the highway. But Joel's attention was already fixed on the farm. The dog's barking had grabbed his ear first. Then his gaze had shifted left and he saw the car. Spiro's Caddie. The boys were here.

He loped up the drive. The front door gaped open. A bad sign. He fought the impulse to call Allie's name. Surprise had to be on his side. He tiptoed inside and down the hall, softly opening each closed door he came to. Carefully peering round each corner. Wishing he'd brought his gun with him, but it was still in the duffel bag lying out on the drive. It was too late to go back. Instinct—and the silence in the house—led him to the kitchen. Spotting the open door, Joel hesitated in its frame.

There was a shed of some kind about fifty yards away. From where he stood, he could see the dog pacing nervously in its run. It kept looking at the shed. Every now and then it gave a frustrated yelp. *They're in there.*

Joel had no cover, so he would have to make a quick dash to hide behind the shed door. He counted. One, two, three...*go.* The unexpected movement startled the dog, and it was only a split second before it let loose a torrent of furious barking. Someone was bound to notice and come out to see what had set the dog off.

There was a burst of noise inside—shouting, the thud of footsteps. Joel made his move. He reached out his arms, grabbing at the person flying through the door. The momentum knocked them both off their feet, sending them sprawling to the ground. Joel got to his feet first, panting, wiping the dirt off his hands. He looked down at Allie and quipped, "We have this habit—"

She scrambled up, practically clawing at him. "George and Christo."

"I know," he whispered.

"Marko, too."

He swore under his breath. The picture had just been altered. Now he really wanted his gun. He grabbed hold of her arm. "Get round to the front. My duffel bag in the drive. My gun." Without a word she took off, disappearing behind the shed to take a longer back route to the house.

Marko came charging out the shed door and Joel lunged at him, grabbing the collar of his jacket and twisting. The jacket shot up around Marko's neck, choking him. The big man grunted in surprise. His massive hands reached back, trying to grab Joel's fists, but Joel kept pushing Marko toward the dog run. The dog grew frantic. Marko started weaving, trying to shake Joel loose. Knowing he couldn't hold on much longer, Joel gave one hard shove and sent Marko careering into the chicken wire.

The dog rushed at the fence, snapping at Marko through the mesh. Marko yelled out, rolling away and struggling to his feet. Joel sprinted for him, and as the large man got to his knees, landed a blow to the head that sent him tumbling backward. Marko now lay still in the dusty yard. Joel walked over, leaned down and felt for a pulse.

"Alive I hope?" George said.

He and Christo were standing in front of the shed. They were reluctant to dirty their hands to help out their partner, Joel guessed.

"He'll be fine. Out for a bit, though. Maybe until the police get here."

"He may still be here, but we won't." George slipped a hand into his jacket pocket and pulled out a revolver.

"George! You promised—no violence."

"What an innocent you are, little brother. Maybe you think it's all going to magically fall into place. The money. The inheritance. The business."

Christo shot him a look that said it all. George laughed. He motioned to Joel. "Get into the shed. If you don't give us any trouble, we'll just leave you helpless for a bit—like pathetic Marko over there."

"I'm not having anything to do with this, George," Christo whined. He crossed to the bench under a tree at the end of the dog run and sank onto it.

"Include pathetic Christo in that, as well," George muttered.

George was trying to be nonchalant, Joel figured, but he wasn't pulling it off. "It can end right now, Kostakis, and you'll be facing little more than a charge of uttering threats. Allie might even be persuaded to drop that."

"I lose either way," George went on, an almost undetectable quaver in his voice. "If I don't show up in Grosse Pointe with the money by noon tomorrow, the loan sharks get me. If I take the money and leave you, the cops'll be after me." He looked around him. "Where's Allie?"

Joel ignored the question, wanting to give Allie more time. He was afraid George would go looking for her. "So like you said, either way you lose. Wouldn't you rather be spending the next little while in a nice safe jail, instead of confronting the sharks?"

"Ha ha." George waved the gun at the shed. "Inside."

Joel sauntered toward the door. Allie should be showing up anytime. He hoped she'd slip him the gun and let him take care of the situation, rather than try any heroics. He was reaching for the door, with George about two feet behind, when a voice called out.

"Stop, George!"

Joel froze on the spot. *Please, Allie, no.* He didn't dare turn around in case the movement startled George, who might overreact. Which would frighten Allie, who also might overreact.

Every nerve in his body was coiled, ready to act. As long as the gun was aimed at him, George might not bother to spin around and aim at Allie. *He might just shoot me, instead.*

"Allie," Joel said, fighting to keep his voice calm, "put the gun down. George only wants the money and then he'll be on his merry way."

"It wouldn't be like that, Joel," she said from somewhere behind. "If he shoots both of us, no one but Marko and Christo will ever know he was here."

Joel closed his eyes. He wished she wasn't so damn

smart. Moreover, he wished she hadn't spelled it out so neatly for George, breathing heavily at his back.

"So don't make a move, George," she was saying now. "I was in cadets in high school. My father taught me how to shoot. I won a prize for marksmanship when I was an undergrad. And the gun is aimed right at the back of your head. An easy target, considering how big it is."

George emitted a nervous chuckle. As if he half believed her.

"Christo! You there?" George called out, his voice a tad thinner now than a moment ago.

"'Course I am."

Christo didn't sound well, Joel thought. God, he hoped the fool didn't do anything stupid, setting off both George and Allie.

"I want you to walk over to Marko and shake him awake," George ordered. "Either that or get the gun from Allie. I've a feeling she won't hurt you."

The hairs at the back of Joel's neck stood on end. He had a feeling she wouldn't, either. He heard Christo complain as he got up from the bench. Then the scraping of feet against the dirt in the yard and seconds later, Allie's "Don't, Christo."

Suddenly it was pandemonium. Joel heard ferocious barking and saw, out of the corner of his eye, a streak of gold. Turning around, he saw George lying on the ground while the dog, jacket lapel in mouth, snarled over him.

"Call him off!" Joel shouted.

Allie ran forward, gun still clenched in her hand. "Tiggy, come!" She had to repeat the command before the dog obeyed.

George, pale and shaken, staggered to his feet. Christo

ran to help him up, but George angrily shook him off. "You did that, didn't you."

Joel raised an eyebrow at Allie. "Did Christo let the dog loose?"

She nodded. "I tried to stop him because I was afraid George would shoot her. Thank God she was too fast for him." Her voice trembled.

Joel reached out for Allie's hand and gently pried the gun from her strong grip. "I can relate to that," he said. As he bent down to pick up George's gun, he heard Allie squeal and saw her take off. Whirling around, he saw a woman standing at the back door, her arms outstretched to receive Allie. He recognized her from the health-food store. Susan. The two women embraced, and then Susan disappeared into the house.

Joel watched Allie walk across the yard toward him, knowing confrontation time had arrived. Her stride was steady, but Joel saw the hurt in her eyes. He swallowed back the bitter taste of fear.

As she passed her cousins, her gaze flicked across them and the hurt in her eyes deepened. She came right up to him, her scent fluttering around him, the amber flecks of her eyes sparkling.

"Susan's calling the police," she said matter-of-factly.

Joel pocketed both guns in his windbreaker. "I owe you an explanation," he said.

She nodded, her face tight and pale.

"If you're willing to hear the condensed version now," he went on, "I promise to finish the rest of it later."

"I'm listening," she whispered.

He drew his hand across his face. His mind was slow and dull with fatigue, the aftereffects of an adrenaline surge. "In the beginning, it was just another undercover job. But all that changed the first day." He held up a hand at the disbelief in her face. "You've got to trust what I'm saying. I know that's hard to do, given what you've just found out. But since that moment in the park, when I knew what I had to tell you and...and what I *couldn't* tell you, I had enormous difficulty separating—"

"Business from pleasure?"

Joel saw the teasing in her eyes and smiled. God, he loved her. "It went much deeper than that. The moral dilemma...the fear...the *pain* of losing you and at the same time, being desperate to protect you—" He broke off, unable to continue.

She reached for his hand and clasped it in hers. Joel drew her to him, wrapping his arms around her, dipping his head to breathe in the soothing fragrance of Allie Newman.

GEORGE, CHRISTO and Marko were taken into custody after the police arrived and Christo admitted they'd threatened Allie and Joel. Allie filled Susan in with most of the story, while Joel accompanied the police to the station to make a statement there. Allie agreed to make hers in the morning.

Later, when Joel had returned and the last of the wine had been poured and the pizza devoured, Susan got up and made a pot of coffee.

"I've a feeling you two are going to need it," she said. "You probably have a lot to talk over."

Her intuition amazed Allie. On her way out of the kitchen, Susan kissed Allie on the cheek and, stopping next to Joel, said, "Allie will find some bedding for you. Feel free to bunk down wherever you like."

Once she'd left, Allie said, "Joel—" at the same time as he blurted her name.

"I think," he started again, "if we can still laugh together, things can't be all that bad." He moved along the couch until his thigh brushed against hers, then shifted to face her.

She could feel his warmth through the plush terry cloth of her robe.

"This afternoon I told you there was a long explanation, and if you can stay awake, I'll give it now."

"All right," she said, snuggling against him.

"Everything I said and did, everything I felt for you was the truth. You have to believe that, Allie, or there's no hope for us."

"I do believe it, but—"

His lips on hers silenced her. Wrapping his arms around her, Joel lifted her onto his lap. She curled up, tucking her knees against her chest and draping the robe over them. The steady drum of his heart beneath his sweatshirt echoed in her ear.

"Start talking," she murmured. "I'm getting sleepy."

"Okay. Feel free to interrupt anytime you like."

"Oh, don't worry, I will."

Joel chuckled. "All right, here goes. Let me take you back twenty-seven years. There was a power struggle going on in the Kostakis empire. Tony had expected to become heir apparent, but when Katrina married your father, Spiro invited him into the family business. There was a lot of competition between the two men."

Over more than simply business, Allie thought, recalling Maria's story. "Go on," she said.

"You've already heard that Tony was a gambling addict. He owed big money to some rough people. Spiro refused to bail him out again, so Tony made his own arrangements. He bought part of a hijacked shipment of alcohol from a mobster he knew. He planned to sell the liquor to a third party. He finalized all the details and enlisted some low-life buddy of his to drive the truck. The only hitch was, the third party he contacted was really an ATF undercover agent and Tony was about to become the victim of a sting operation. But it went very wrong."

"How?" Allie asked, dread growing inside her.

"The day of the job someone tipped off Tony, and so Tony persuaded Spiro to send your father in his place. I don't know what story he concocted, but I bet we'll find out in Spiro's journal."

"Where is the journal, by the way?"

"The police have it, but you'll get it back eventually. Anyway," Joel continued, "Tony and his buddy were supposed to deliver the booze and collect the money at a rendezvous at some park near the Detroit River."

"So neither my father nor Spiro knew anything about this sale?"

"Nope. Eddie took the money from the ATF agent and would have been arrested on the spot, but Tony's partner, the guy who delivered the truck of booze, panicked when the undercover agent identified himself. He ran the agent over as he tried to escape. The sting went all downhill from there. While the agents were chasing the truck, Eddie took off in his own car—with the money."

"He must have panicked, too."

"Either that or he thought he was still dealing with mobsters. I'm not sure what happened next, but in the early hours of the morning, the police found Eddie's car floating in the Detroit River."

Allie knew she could fill in some of the gaps. Eddie had found Tony with Katrina before going to pick up the money. That he still went was a testimony to his loyalty to Spiro, she decided. She tried to picture a younger, more impetuous Rob Newman having to deal with two such horrible events in a single night.

"How come the police didn't find my father?"

"They tried. Eventually they assumed he—and you—had been drowned, although no bodies were ever found. The case was filed but never actually closed. It wasn't reactivated until little more than a year ago. Some old marked American currency showed up at a bank in New York."

"The money Dad used to pay that loan!" Allie exclaimed. She fell silent then, thinking of her father's desperation.

Joel sensed the emotional toll on her and hesitated to continue.

"It's okay," she said. "I need to hear the rest, however painful it might be."

"Just stop me if you've heard enough." He stroked the tip of her chin. "Eventually," he went on, "the bills were traced to the payoff from the old sting operation. The case came out of storage and I ended up with it. I went to Detroit to set up a team. We already had wiretaps in place when Spiro learned about you. That was our big breakthrough. We figured you might lead us right to the money."

Allie gave that a long moment's thought.

Joel kissed her lightly on the forehead.

Wanting to distract me? she wondered. She pulled his head down to hers, forcing him to look at her. "Tell me again," she whispered. "How much was the truth?"

"I told you as much as I could at the time. Some of it I couldn't—stuff connected to the case." His eyes never left hers. "The rest—everything connected to me personally—was the truth."

She thought of her grandfather. "What about the murder investigation?"

Joel swore. "Sorry, I forgot in all the confusion. Maria confessed early this morning. That's when the boys left to come here. She also told police she'd tried to frighten you away—the pool incident."

"*She* left the note? Poor woman, she seemed so undone by everything. What about that night I heard someone following me?"

Joel's face was grim. "Marko. Apparently George mentioned something to him about wanting to get rid of you. He was the one who tried to get into your bedroom, too." He hugged her more tightly. "Allie, remember that everything your father did—running away, taking the money because he probably didn't know what else to do with it— he did because he was desperate to get you away from there. He'd had that quarrel with Spiro. He feared he'd lose you. Everything he did, he did for love of you."

"I know," she murmured, loving Joel for saying it, anyway.

He touched the end of her nose and smiled. "Can we continue this tomorrow? I'm getting tired. Aren't you?"

"*Are* we finished?" she asked, ignoring the hint.

"The money."

"I know where it is—in the shed."

"Can it keep until we hand it over to the local police tomorrow?"

"I guess so. I'll put Tiggy out in the dog run, just in case."

"Those guys aren't going anywhere for a while, Allie. Now, what did Susan say about sleeping wherever I wanted? Was that legit?"

Allie grinned. "Why? Did you have someplace in mind?"

Joel eased her off his lap and onto the couch, then stood up. "Yes, I do," he said, bending over to pick her up in his arms. "And a special person to take with me."

Allie wrapped her arms around his neck. "If you mean me, then I'm heading for the third floor and my childhood bed. Think you can make it?"

Joel smiled down at her. "I'll make it, my love. You can count on me."

EPILOGUE

SHE SPOTTED THEM beyond the yellow tape of the finishing line. Allie gathered a final reserve of energy and sprinted the remaining few yards. Then she slowed her pace and by the time they reached her, she was bent over at the waist, gasping for air.

Someone handed her a damp towel. A bottle of water appeared out of nowhere and she poured it over her head. When she straightened, flinging her wet hair like Tiggy shaking herself dry, they all laughed. Joel folded his arms around her, oblivious to the sweat coating her entire body. Susan gushed congratulations. And Ben, a miniature version of his father, simply smiled up at her.

Too breathless for speech, Allie let them lead her toward Confederation Park where the presentations would be made. When she sat down on the bench they'd been saving, Joel kissed her on the cheek. "You came in with the first twenty. Pretty damn impressive, out of a 150."

Allie merely nodded. It was a respectable placing. Her father would have been proud. She caught Susan's eye and winked. They both knew what she meant, and Susan's eyes filled.

When the presentations were over, Ben's cry of surprise caught their attention. "It's Jeb!"

"And what about Jeb's partner?" a deep voice called back. Ben had raced to the Seeing Eye dog and was crouched on the ground, his small arms hugging the Lab.

"What am I, then? Chopped liver, as the saying goes?" Harry McGuire's tone of dismay was belied by his broad smile.

"I'll hug you, Harry," Allie said, leaping from the bench and rushing to the old man.

"Well done, lass," he said, patting her back as she embraced him. "Someone told me you came in with the first bunch. That's just terrific."

"Thanks, Harry."

"So is the whole gang here, then? Your young man? Susan?"

"Yep." She turned to Joel. "Ben met Harry and Jeb when he was with me in the store yesterday. And Jeb, like Tiggy, was an instant hit."

"Fortunately Jeb lets me go everywhere with him," Harry said, "so I have almost as many friends as he does."

Joel laughed. "A real pleasure to meet you, Harry." He placed his hand in Harry's outstretched one.

Harry heartily pumped Joel's hand. "Likewise, though I understand you might be taking my guardian angel away from Kingston? Jeb and I are going to miss our dinners with Allie. I don't know if I want to let her go."

Allie decided to come to Joel's rescue. "Harry, when Joel and I have finalized our plans about where we'll be living, you and Jeb will be the first to know. Well—" she paused "—after Susan and Ben of course. And you'll be visiting."

"I certainly hope so!"

"Harry," Susan said, tucking her arm through his, "We thought we'd drive out to the farm for cold drinks and a snack before going on to dinner later at Chez Piggy. Will you join us?"

"With pleasure," Harry said. "Ben? Would you like to help Jeb walk me to the car?"

Ben patted Jeb, got to his feet and grasped the handle of Jeb's harness.

Allie watched them start off and felt her throat swell with love. This is my family, she thought. *My real family.* She felt Joel press closer to her. He bent his head down to hers.

"This is all that matters, isn't it?" he murmured in her ear.

Allie nodded, too overcome to speak. Joel wrapped his arms around her and held her to his chest. She knew this was where she really belonged—in Joel Kennedy's arms. He squeezed her. "I love you, Allie Newman."

"And I love you." She pulled back to gaze up at him.

Joel tapped the end of her nose with a finger. "So, have you also told Susan what we've planned for the rest of the summer?"

"Natch. Why wouldn't I?" She hesitated. "And Ben? Is he happy at the thought of another woman in his life?"

"For sure, but…"

"But?" she prompted.

"He wants to know if Tiggy can come with us."

Allie smiled. "I think Susan would be heartbroken if we did that."

"Exactly what I told him."

They continued walking, but Allie had something else to settle and she stopped. "Joel, after Spiro's funeral I promised the staff that they could stay on until the house was sold. Can we stop there on the way to Philadelphia and make sure everyone's all right?"

"Of course. Are you going to meet with Spiro's lawyer then, too?"

"He phoned last week to say that Effie had used part of her inheritance to buy a condo in Florida."

"Near her mother-in-law?"

"I doubt it. Apparently they've not spoken since shortly after Tony's disappearance." Once more the events of that long-ago night overwhelmed her. She thought of her grandfather's family history, now tucked away in her desk.

He'd written about that night with pain and remorse. When he'd discovered that Tony had lied to him, tricking him into sending Eddie into a trap, he'd banished Tony from the family. The check he'd written for his nephew and the threat that he'd hand Tony over to the ATF if he stepped foot in Michigan again were guarantees of Tony's silence. Years later Spiro learned that Tony had been killed in Las Vegas over a gambling debt, but had never told Effie, wanting to protect her from the truth.

"Thinking of Spiro?" Joel asked.

"How did you know?"

"You had that faraway look on your face."

His turn to stop this time, oblivious to Susan and Ben waiting ahead. Allie nestled into him, the refuge of his embrace working its magic as always.

"The lawyer also told me that George is contesting the will and Christo has made some kind of a deal with the prosecution."

Joel looked down at her. "He's damn lucky you dropped the uttering-threats charge against him. And I'm glad you listened to the police about George and Marko."

"Yes, those two were a lot scarier than Christo. Which is odd," she said, "because at first I thought he was the creepy one."

"Not that he's a Boy Scout," Joel pointed out.

"True enough." She shivered. "Unfortunately this will thing is going to keep George in our lives a bit longer."

"Only for the duration. I doubt you'll be having any family reunions to look forward to, though."

Allie sighed. "Poor Spiro. That's what he wanted all along."

Joel waited a moment before adding, "I'm afraid the events of twenty-seven years ago ruled out any hope of that."

He was right, Allie thought. Her grandfather had tried in his own way to make amends for that night, but too many lives had already been ruined. His will had left the house and its contents exclusively to her, with bequests to Effie and all the staff. Her cousins were to share the Kostakis business empire, unless one of them fell afoul of the law. In that case, it would revert to the other brother or, if both were indicted, to Allie. It was a peculiar codicil, Spiro's lawyer had declared, but the old man had feared one of them might turn out like Tony and destroy the business.

"Spiro's lawyer said that he thought Christo could manage the company with the help of the current vice president. Apparently he's made a complete turnaround in his attitude."

"So you're willing to give him another chance?"

"Shouldn't I?"

Joel drew her close again. "I'd expect nothing less of you, Allie." He kissed her softly on the lips. "That bed-and-breakfast you mentioned?"

"Hmm?"

"Think we could make some excuse and skip the dinner?"

Allie laughed. "No way, Kennedy." She glanced ahead, noticing that Susan, Harry, Jeb and Ben had reached the car.

"But," she murmured, turning back to Joel's eager face, "I'll more than make up for the time lost. Trust me." And her lips sealed the promise.

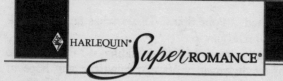

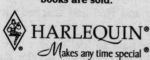

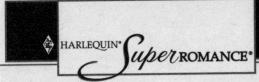

 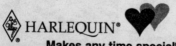

If you enjoyed what you just read,
then we've got an offer you can't resist!

Take 2 bestselling love stories FREE!

Plus get a FREE surprise gift!

Clip this page and mail it to Harlequin Reader Service®

IN U.S.A.	IN CANADA
3010 Walden Ave.	P.O. Box 609
P.O. Box 1867	Fort Erie, Ontario
Buffalo, N.Y. 14240-1867	L2A 5X3

YES! Please send me 2 free Harlequin Superromance® novels and my free surprise gift. After receiving them, if I don't wish to receive anymore, I can return the shipping statement marked cancel. If I don't cancel, I will receive 6 brand-new novels every month, before they're available in stores. In the U.S.A., bill me at the bargain price of $4.47 plus 25¢ shipping and handling per book and applicable sales tax, if any*. In Canada, bill me at the bargain price of $4.99 plus 25¢ shipping and handling per book and applicable taxes**. That's the complete price, and a savings of at least 10% off the cover prices—what a great deal! I understand that accepting the 2 free books and gift places me under no obligation ever to buy any books. I can always return a shipment and cancel at any time. Even if I never buy another book from Harlequin, the 2 free books and gift are mine to keep forever.

135 HDN DNT3
336 HDN DNT4

Name	(PLEASE PRINT)	
Address	Apt.#	
City	State/Prov.	Zip/Postal Code

* Terms and prices subject to change without notice. Sales tax applicable in N.Y.
** Canadian residents will be charged applicable provincial taxes and GST.
All orders subject to approval. Offer limited to one per household and not valid to current Harlequin Superromance® subscribers.
® is a registered trademark of Harlequin Enterprises Limited.

SUP02   ©1998 Harlequin Enterprises Limited

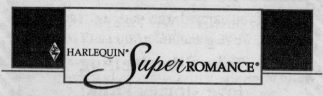

Princes...Princesses...
London Castles...New York Mansions...
To live the life of a royal!

**In 2002, Harlequin Books lets you escape to a
world of royalty with these royally themed titles:**

Temptation:
January 2002—*A Prince of a Guy* (#861)
February 2002—*A Noble Pursuit* (#865)

American Romance:
The Carradignes: American Royalty (Editorially linked series)
March 2002—*The Improperly Pregnant Princess* (#913)
April 2002—*The Unlawfully Wedded Princess* (#917)
May 2002—*The Simply Scandalous Princess* (#921)
November 2002—*The Inconveniently Engaged Prince* (#945)

Intrigue:
The Carradignes: A Royal Mystery (Editorially linked series)
June 2002—*The Duke's Covert Mission* (#666)

Chicago Confidential
September 2002—*Prince Under Cover* (#678)

The Crown Affair
October 2002—*Royal Target* (#682)
November 2002—*Royal Ransom* (#686)
December 2002—*Royal Pursuit* (#690)

Harlequin Romance:
June 2002—*His Majesty's Marriage* (#3703)
July 2002—*The Prince's Proposal* (#3709)

Harlequin Presents:
August 2002—*Society Weddings* (#2268)
September 2002—*The Prince's Pleasure* (#2274)

Duets:
September 2002—*Once Upon a Tiara/Henry Ever After* (#83)
October 2002—*Natalia's Story/Andrea's Story* (#85)

**Celebrate a year of royalty with
Harlequin Books!**

Available at your favorite retail outlet.

HARLEQUIN®
Makes any time special ®

Visit us at www.eHarlequin.com

HSROY02

Three masters of the romantic suspense
genre come together in this special
Collector's Edition!

Unveiled

NEW YORK TIMES BESTSELLING AUTHORS

TESS GERRITSEN
STELLA CAMERON

And Harlequin Intrigue® author

AMANDA STEVENS

Nail-biting mystery...heart-pounding sensuality...and
the temptation of the unknown come together in one
magnificent trade-size volume. These three talented
authors bring stories that will give you thrills *and*
chills like never before!

Coming to your favorite retail outlet in August 2002.